THE ALLINGHAM MINIBUS

THE ALLINGHAM MINIBUS

by Margery Allingham

William Morrow & Company, Inc.
New York   1973

Printed in the United States of America.
Library of Congress Catalog Card Number 73-9839

ISBN 0-688-00178-5

1 2 3 4 76 75 74 73

Contents

He Was Asking After You

DORNFORD killed Fellowes somewhere in Australia. Apart from the fact that it was a reprehensible sort of thing to do anyway, it was particularly unpleasant because they were friends and it was done for gain.

I knew them both. They and my brother George had been to a prep school together and had gone on to Layer in the same year.

Dornford was a little chap with protruding, pale-blue eyes and a greater capacity for terror than any man I ever knew. He took medicine finally and, although he did get his degrees, never practised because he was not capable of it.

His brief periods of locum work were histories of disaster. Fear was ingrained in him, including a passionate terror of poverty, which was unfortunate, because his private means were less than three hundred pounds a year.

Fellowes was his exact opposite. He was a great heavy person, dark-skinned and powerful, and he had a way of going out after the thing he wanted which was positively frightening because of its energy.

He had about fifteen hundred pounds a year of his own and leaned towards an adventurous career.

Why he put up with Dornford no one ever really knew. My own opinion is that Dornford was put in his care at school, and looking after the terrified little creature became a habit with him.

Anyway, after they left school, Dornford was always dragging along behind Fellowes, sponging on him a little but too indeterminate a personality to be a serious nuisance.

Finally Fellowes actually grew to like him, or at any rate to depend upon him for company. All the same, how they came to go into the Australian bush together is not altogether clear.

Fellowes suddenly developed an interest in primitive tribal

customs. He wanted to investigate them for himself, and he took Dornford with him, possibly because he happened to have had him staying with him at the time the expedition was planned, or perhaps he thought Dornford might conceivably be useful minding the medicine chest.

They set out from Adelaide one fine day and Fellowes never came back.

He died of snake-bite.

When he returned alone Dornford explained that he had not the necessary serum with him, and that, despite heroic efforts, his 'poor friend had passed away'.

There was a considerable scandal at the time, largely due to a truly horrible story which the bearers brought back with them. It described Fellowes calling to his friend in his agony and Dornford sitting with his hands over his ears and his eyes closed while the beads of sweat rolled down his face.

After this someone who ought to have known thought he remembered that Dornford did have the serum with him, and altogether there was so much talk that he was lucky to scuttle back home to England without an inquiry.

There was trouble over here, too, when it turned out that before starting on the expedition Fellowes and Dornford had solemnly made wills in each other's favour.

Dornford's story was that Fellowes had known it was going to be dangerous and had insisted on the precaution 'in case'. No one believed him, but no one wanted an open scandal, and Fellowes' relatives were wealthy people.

Nearly everyone cut Dornford, though. He did not seem to care. He netted his inheritance and came to live in the village next to ours, which was unnecessary of him since there are so many other villages.

We used to see him about in our market town and, it being ridiculous to quarrel with a neighbour, we kept up a reserved acquaintance with him.

The first letter came to him from Melbourne. Jenkinsone, who had been at university with the two of them and who had corresponded in a dilatory way with him for some years, wrote one of his rare letters. It was a straggling epistle of the 'do you remember . . .?' variety favoured by the lonely Englishman abroad.

One paragraph so rattled Dornford that he called on my brother to show it to him.

'*By the way, I met old Bucky Fellowes in the street here to-day. He said he was prospecting, whatever that may mean. He was asking after you.*'

Dornford was a bit green when he pointed to the final sentence and his pale eyes bulged horribly.

'Must have been some other chap, mustn't it?' he said. 'Jenkinsone was a muddle-minded ass, wasn't he?'

'Yes,' we said dubiously, remembering him. 'Yes, perhaps he was.'

Dornford went back to his old-world cottage reassured.

The second letter came from Colombo. Dornford did not show it to us for some days and when at last he did he was so nervous that he giggled hysterically all the time he talked.

'It's from Mrs Wentworth,' he said. 'The wife of a Colonel my father used to know.'

We read it in silence. The postscript was interesting. '*P.S. We met such an interesting man on board ship. He seems to be an old friend of yours—a Mr Buchanan Fellowes. He was asking after you.*'

'Odd co-coincidence, isn't it?' giggled Dornford. 'T-two people making a silly mistake like that? We buried Bucky, you know; buried him deep. It was under a great spreading tuberous plant. The branches were like snakes. I-I can see them now.'

He was rather beastly and George took him away and gave him a drink.

There was peace after this for nearly two months. Dornford had a small red car and we saw him about in it once or twice. He still looked a bit pallid, but then he was never a healthy type.

The third letter arrived one very hot June evening. We were having a party when Dornford rang asking my brother to go over immediately. George refused but promised to drop in later in the evening. Long before the appointed hour Dornford had arrived at our house. He hid in the study and George had to leave his guests and go in to him.

Because I was curious I wandered along myself some minutes later to find them both staring at a sheet of flimsy paper. Dornford looked as though he had been very sick and even George was disturbed.

The letter was from Dornford's uncle. He was on a cruise in the Mediterranean and had written from Port Said.

'How small the world is!

'Walking along a foreign street, surrounded by every sort of national-ity, caste and creed, who should I meet but a friend of yours. He recognised me from seeing me at a Speech Day at Layer more years ago than I care to remember.

'We exchanged cards-or rather I gave him mine. He was temporarily without, having been some time away from home. His name was Buchanan Fellowes. Wasn't that friend of yours who died in Australia a Fellowes too? I did not like to ask him if it was a relative. He was asking after you.'

We soothed Dornford as best we could, but it was not easy.

'Bucky must have had a brother,' said George without convic-tion.

Dornford looked at him with a lop-sided smile and eyes blank with fear.

'He was the only son of his mother, and his father was d-d-dead,' he said.

We let him go home.

Naturally we did not forget him. There had been a dreadful note of urgency common to each letter which left itself firmly fixed in one's mind.

George and I went over to the cottage the following morning, and spent an hour or so doing our clumsy best to cheer Dornford up.

'It's a hoax,' I said, trying to sound convincing. 'Someone's trying to scare you . . . someone you knew in Australia.'

My voice trailed away as the miserable little creature dropped his face into his hands. George grimaced at me angrily, and we stood helplessly together looking around the prim little room furnished with the fake antiques and the little bits of Birmingham brass. It was one of those cottages in which the front door leads directly into the main room, so that when the postman called the letter fell directly on to the mat at our feet.

Dornford, who had put down his hands at the sound of the knock, sat staring at the grey envelope on the floor without attempting to pick it up. He was shaking all over, and his small insignificant face was utterly without expression.

I found to my astonishment that I was a little afraid of the letter myself. It was George who retrieved it.

'I should read it,' he said, throwing it over to Dornford. 'You're getting jumpy and inclined to dramatise the thing. This may have nothing to do with the business at all.'

Dornford took the letter with fingers which curled.

'It's from–my–old nurse,' he said. 'She's a dear old–old–g-girl. I believe she's g-genuinely fond of me.'

He was tearing the envelope to ribbons in his efforts to get it open, but the sight of the old-fashioned spidery writing seemed to cheer him considerably.

'She-she lives at Southampton,' he remarked absently.

'Southampton?' I echoed sharply, and wished I had bitten my tongue out.

Dornford goggled at me. 'Southampton,' he whispered. 'Southampton. Oh my God, that's where he'd land. Read it, George. Read it aloud.'

It was an uncomfortable moment, and George took the sheets of paper and cleared his throat rather noisily before he began. I have never heard him read so badly.

It was a very ordinary affectionate note until halfway down the second page, when the passage we had all half expected occurred.

'I must tell you, Mr Johnny; who do you think I met in the street this morning but young Mr Bucky Fellowes. He seemed very pleased to see me, but would not come in, although of course I asked him to. I must say he did not look at all well, in fact I was surprised to see him up and about when he looked so queer. But he tells me it's not a healthy

part at all where he's been so I expect that's it. He was asking after you.'

Dornford tottered over to George's side and looked over his shoulder.

'Yesterday's date,' he said huskily. 'Yesterday in Southampton. To-day - where?'

We were terribly afraid he was going out of his mind. He barricaded himself in the cottage, and in spite of our protestations built a fire and crouched over it, although it was July. He was terribly cold, he said.

George did his best with him.

'Look here, Dornford,' he said at last in a determined effort to hang on to sanity at all costs, 'there must be a perfectly logical explanation for all this. I'll go down to Southampton tonight and see the old lady. Either she's made a mistake, or she's had the story put up to her. I say, why don't you come with me?'

Dornford was too terrified to set foot outside the house, however, and in the end George did not go either, for the fifth letter came by the evening post. It was from a girl we all knew, and there is no need to give her name. Only one paragraph mattered.

'I saw Bucky Fellowes in Bond Street this morning. It was marvellous to see the old man again after all these years. He has altered terribly, of course, but a stretch at home will put him right.

'I was so surprised to see him (some idiot told me he was dead) that I am afraid I may have been a little offhand with him. You know how one is when one's flustered. If you see him, give him all my love and tell him to look me up. I've never forgotten him. He was asking after you.'

Dornford had one more letter. It came while George was with him on the following day. It was a note from Andrews, landlord of The Feathers. It came by hand, and was to the point.

Dear Sir, There is a gentleman here asking for your address. His name is Mr B. Fellowes. Would you like me to send him up? Yours faithfully, B. Andrews, prop.'

Dornford began to gibber, and to soothe him, George went back to The Feathers with the bearer to interview the practical joker. He was not there. Andrews had left him in the parlour and could only suppose that he must have gone out. He was a grey sort of gentleman, he said.

We never saw Dornford again, at least not alive. He was lying on his face on his own hearthrug when George got back. Old Meadows, our local doctor who did the P.M., said his heart simply stopped.

We were all very shocked, of course, but not deeply grieved or brokenhearted. Dornford was not a lovable soul in life, and death did not make him any more attractive. He was buried in the village cemetery. A more quiet, unobtrusive ceremony was never performed. There was not even an announcement in the local paper, let alone the London ones.

There Dornford's story should have ended except for one little thing which was curious. Two days after the funeral I had a note from Maisie Fielding, my scatter-brained fashion-artist friend. She was over from her home in Paris for one of her brief London visits. After a well-nigh undecipherable letter about nothing at all she added a postscript:

'Coming down the Haymarket, my dear, who do you think I've just seen? – Clinging together as usual. Bucky was in front, striding along with his friend clutching his coat tails. It was no use trying to stop them. They seemed to be in a terrible hurry. Heaven knows where they were going.'

Publicity

'Benedick,' murmured Tadema, just loudly enough for the cadence of his fine voice to be audible all round the dressing room. The intonation did not quite satisfy his fastidious ear.

'Benedick,' he repeated, giving the word this time a sadness and a certain pride.

Then, with an assumption of carelessness which could have been only for his personal benefit, since he was entirely without other audience, he took up the copy of the illustrated weekly once more and studied afresh the full-page snapshot of himself and Chloe standing on the steps of her mother's house in Brook Street.

Her new make-up looked very well, he thought. She was youthful yet sophisticated and arresting without being actually vulgar. A dear girl.

Of himself he was not so sure. Photographs were notoriously unkind. Yet it was certainly like him and he peered affectionately at the gallant and romantic figure which the London public knew so well. He re-read the paragraph slowly:

'The surprise of the little season has been the engagement of Lady Chloe Staratt, beautiful daughter of the Earl of Scaresfield, to Sir Geoffrey Tadema the bachelor actor knight. Lady Chloe, besides being an acknowledged leader of her set, is thought by many people to be the smartest woman in town. Sir Geoffrey is the great lover of the stage, but until now he has proved himself impervious to Cupid's darts. Their many friends have been surprised and delighted by this romantic love match.'

Tadema threw down the paper and smiled. The Press had been magnificent. The dailies had been generous with space and there had been several long interviews in the cheaper Sundays. But the old *Telltale* had come up to scratch. They had done the thing with the right delicacy. Some of the dailies had mentioned the discrepancy in age, he had been sorry to see.

At fifty-one Tadema looked, from the stage at least, sixteen or seventeen years younger. His figure was as good, or nearly as good, as ever it had been, and he had changed hardly at all in the past ten years.

His astonishing success was all the more extraordinary in view of his limitations, histrionically speaking. In addition to his face, which had a propensity for expressing passionate emotion decently repressed, he had a natural charm of manner and two endearing mannerisms.

His nervous shake of the head when addressing the beloved kept his feminine gallery in ecstasy, and his sudden smile, so disarming in its warmth, moved the same body to audible quavers of delight.

Obviously it was not these alone which had kept the name of Tadema in foot-high letters on the board outside the Gresham for nearly fourteen years. He had other assets.

An excellent business man, he had a gift for finding the right sort of play and, of course, he had his instinct.

In what circumstances an instinct becomes genius and when genius is transmuted into art it is difficult to say, but with Tadema publicity was all these three. His public, who very properly believed what it inferred, read, or saw with its own eyes, knew that Sir Geoffrey Tadema was romance made carnate.

It also knew that his conquests were myriad and that his life was the constant pursuit of the one woman of the perfect heart, a vaguely defined lady, but easily identifiable by every woman in his audience.

Since in private life Sir Geoffrey was a normal bachelor of somewhat fixed habits this public façade of his was no mean achievement. Publicity was his hobby and he worked at it with diligence and delicacy.

Jealous colleagues spoke bitterly of vast sums spent in bribes, betraying that they knew nothing of the art and of newspapers less. Wishart, of the *Telegram*, once looked down from his eminence of forty years of journalism to observe that old Tadema got away with it by being so damned topical, but even he had only a germ of the truth.

Sir Geoffrey himself honestly believed that he represented the secret soul-mate of all unloved women in London, but he over-estimated himself, as he began to find out when TV became popular.

It was this discovery that was ultimately responsible for Chloe. On the 'box' Tadema's years were irritatingly apparent and his famous personality curiously artificial. On the stage he was still a force, but his last play had run only fourteen months instead of the customary eighteen and he felt himself slipping. It was not a landslide yet by any means but the sands were stirring beneath his feet.

He had been considering a happy and romantic marriage for some time as a new medium for the Personality when he first met Chloe, then on the crest of her first wave of public interest. She was the most photographed young woman of the season and he admired the way she worked at it.

The thought of marrying her did not then occur to him, but now, when he realised she was not out for money and titled obscurity but was preparing for a career as a public person, the beautiful idea had come to him. The hour was propitious. Chloe's adventure with masked bandits, who had chivalrously restored her possessions because of her charming face and endearing manner alone, had just come out.

Chloe had been too much of a sport to prefer a charge against the criminals and had only confessed the story to a newspaper man after pressure. This risky business had come off very well considering, although Tadema had felt it dangerously crude at the time. He felt instinctively that an engagement would be a sound move for both of them.

Chloe saw it, of course. Tadema warmed to her with real affection when he saw her grave eyes when he proposed. He was a little in love even. It was typical of him that he should have done the thing so thoroughly once the ulterior motive had been faced and shelved in the back of his mind.

He was hurt when she used the twenty-four hours which she demanded before giving him an answer to allow a pet paragraphist to get into print with the rumour, but he was mollified by the Press reception.

'Our great lover.' 'The man who understands women.' 'Real romance at last.'

The epithets were most gratifying.

'The old hound!' said Wishart, grunting through his ragged moustache when he saw the middle page headlines. 'He's done it again - right on the dot. It's second nature with him.'

At the moment Tadema was very pleased.

He was so happy, even, that when a total stranger walked in upon him – an unheard-of thing at any time and almost sacrilegious before a matinée – his smile did not fade.

The newcomer paused in the doorway and stared at him disconcertingly. No expression at all passed over his youthful and vaguely familiar face. After a moment or two of this stern scrutiny Tadema's good humour wavered. He rose to his feet and was about to make the obvious inquiry when he suddenly recognised this thick-featured boy. Quite apart from any little professional feeling which an old public favourite may experience when faced with a new, Tadema conceived an instant dislike of Gyp Rains, the young flier with the cold blue eyes who stood in his dressing room doorway and regarded him so uncompromisingly.

The aviator's first remark did not help to dispel his animosity.

'I've come to see you, sir, because I felt it was my duty,' he said.

The stereotyped but unexpected words were not aided by the curiously expressionless tone in which they were uttered and Tadema's irritation increased. He loathed young men who had the impudence to address him as 'sir' anyway. He fell back upon the particular brand of sarcasm of which he was master.

'How very nice of you,' he said. 'Perhaps you would sit down and be as decent and as dutiful as you can in the few moments which I have at my disposal.'

Had he said nothing at all he could hardly have made less impression upon Mr Rains's stolid and bony countenance. The young man advanced into the room, placed himself within a foot of its owner, and recited, still in the same monotone: 'Chloe did not want me to tell you, sir, but I realised that even a man of your age has his feelings and I thought it was the only right thing to do, so I've come to warn you. I always do what I think right,' he added with unexpected naïveté, and Tadema, who had the uncomfortable impression that he was back on the stage with the stock company of his early youth, caught a glimpse of something glazed in the blue eyes and realised that he was dealing with a man labouring under intense excitement.

But he had no time for any feelings Gyp Rains might have been imperfectly concealing. He had heard the name 'Chloe' and a great fear had descended upon him. He was about to subside stiffly into his chair, but subconsciously recognised it as the movement of an ageing man, and checked it hastily.

'Perhaps you'd better explain a little more fully,' he said easily. 'What's all this about?'

'It's a secret. Chloe and I are to be married. We've fallen in love and we're going to elope. I start on my big flight tomorrow night and she's coming with me. They'll find her in Athens, of course, and I don't suppose they'll let her go on but we're getting married late tomorrow.'

'Are you talking about Chloe Staratt?'

'Of course.' Mr Gyp Rains seemed to regard the question as surprisingly unnecessary.

'I see,' said Tadema with awful solemnity. 'I see. And what do you intend me to do about it?'

For the first time during the interview Gyp Rains's face changed. His eyebrows rose. His eyes became round and foolish.

'What *can* you do?' he said. 'I only came to tell you.'

It has been said that the chance answer of a half-wit can confound a brilliant counsel by its very simplicity and it was so in this case. Tadema's mouth opened but no sound came. Mr Rains continued: 'I've only told you,' he said gently, 'because I did not think it was the decent thing not to. You can't do anything. You see that, don't you?'

The final question was put gently.

'Look here, my boy–' Tadema was clutching wildly at straws, '–I don't want to appear offensive, but you don't think that something Lady Chloe may have said may have given you a wrong impression? I mean–'

'Oh no.' The shining countenance was blank as ever. 'I brought this along. She couldn't keep it very well, could she? She saw that as soon as I put it to her.'

And, advancing towards the dressing table, he set down amongst the grease paint the very large and expensive diamond-and-platinum ring which Sir Geoffrey had chosen only a few weeks before and had paid for but a few days previously.

There was a long and difficult pause. Gyp Rains braced himself for the final effort.

'Both Chloe and I rely upon your decency, sir. We know you won't give us away. Chloe's afraid of trouble with her father, you see, and so far you are the only person in the know. You won't let us down, will you? I know that.'

And, having dropped his bombshell, Mr Rains, latest darling of an air-minded British public, smiled kindly at Sir Geoffrey Tadema and walked stolidly out of the dressing room, a ridiculous, humourless and unconquerable figure.

Tadema acted the big scene silently by himself for perhaps two minutes. He paced the floor, he looked at the ring, he peered at himself in the mirror, he threw the ring away, picked it up again, put it in his pocket, shrugged his shoulders, wiped his eyes, and went through every pantomime which the most exacting producer could have desired.

And then, having reacted in this perfectly normal way, he pulled himself up abruptly and began to think. There were many words which fitly described Chloe, but he was not the man to fall to cursing. Behind his fury there was a quiet part of his mind which could almost admire her. As a piece of publicity it was superb–the discovery in Athens, the secret marriage and that stolid, love-besotted boy to back her up. *There* was a story to delight the most blasé of journalists!

It was while he was visualising this flux of newsprint that he suddenly saw his own name. A wave of hot blood rose up in his throat and passed over his head, so that his hairs tingled. He saw himself deflated, saw his carefully built up personality blown away in idle sheets down a dusty road. This would be the end of him. This would be disaster. The beautiful romantic figure drowned in tears of pity, if not derision.

He bounded to his feet again. Something had got to be done. Yes, by God, something had got to be done and how much time had he? When had the lunatic said he was flying? How much time?

The callboy knocked at his door.

'Five minutes, Sir Geoffrey. Curtain's up.'

There are times when the mind panics, moments when the imagination takes the bit between its teeth and carries a man headlong through vast avenues of nightmare much more vivid than actual experience can ever hope to be.

In the intervals of the worst performance of his life Tadema lived through the whole gamut of human humiliation. He heard himself pitied and derided, heard his age discussed and fixed at an erroneous sixty-five, saw his perennial youth withered and his beautiful façade torn down to reveal a travesty of himself, ten times more false than any illusion of the past.

Even in his saner moments, when he regarded the situation coldly, the prospect of being publicly jilted by Chloe for a younger, wider-known man was not inviting, to say the least of it.

To do him justice, he had very little thought of retaliation as such. His mind was completely taken up with self-protective projects.

Even so, his immediate plan of campaign was most difficult to decide, and there was the vital question of time. When had the insufferable young lout said they intended to elope? Tomorrow night? Tadema paused in the middle of the repudiation scene in the second act and stared glassily at Miss Miller, who played the girl. She gave him his cue and an apprehensive glance under her lashes. It was not like the old man to lunch unwisely. She hoped devoutly that he was not going to have a stroke.

By the middle of the third act Tadema had it all worked out. If Chloe was going to elope the following day she would be discovered in Athens the next morning and would make the evening papers of the same day. That gave him only until tomorrow to set up a counter-blast, only until tomorrow to get into print himself with a sensation which would make her effort an anti-climax.

His mind revolved feverishly. Today was Tuesday. Therefore it could be done. It was just possible if he acted promptly.

There was only one vital question to be settled: what on earth could he do? It is one thing to have an instinct, or even a genius, for getting oneself into the news in the right context but quite another to evolve a safe, yet sensational, stunt and carry it out in less than twelve hours. Tadema was desperate.

He dismissed his dresser and stood staring through the minute window of his dressing room at the roofs and spires of London, deep blue in the evening light.

At length he turned slowly away and switched on the light. A flood of hard white radiance disclosed a stocky, yet by no means graceless, figure. The adjective now was, perhaps, purposeful rather than romantic, but an attractive personality all the same: a gallant, middle-aged gentleman preparing to defend himself.

He had decided on the first step. Where it was going to lead him he had no idea, but, like all true artists, he trusted to his instincts and prepared for action.

The inspiration for the second move would come, he did not doubt. Necessity, the proverbial mother, should provide.

Having committed himself to the undertaking, he went about his preparations with artistry and dispatch. The nondescript grey suit taken down from the peg in the big store where no one recognised him, since no one expected him, fitted well enough to look comfortable.

The soft shirt was equally unarresting, as were the brown shoes, socks, tie and underwear–Tadema was justly famous in theatrical circles for his passion for detail – which he collected on his journey round the shop.

At a minute before the store closed he walked out with half a dozen or so packages stowed away in a new suitcase.

Fifteen minutes later the cloakroom of Tottenham Court Road tube station received the case, and Tadema taxied home to his Mayfair flat to bathe and dine before returning to the theatre for the evening performance. He was not exactly happy, but he experienced that curious sense of elation which comes to those about to take a desperate plunge.

The discovery that Sharper, his old-maidish and inappropriately named man, had let Lessington into the study to wait for him was an unexpected blow.

Lessington was a plump, bald, fortyish person whose early effeminacy had grown up into effeteness. If his plays had not been so competent Tadema could not have tolerated him. As it was, he fraternised with him but grudgingly.

Lessington was in form. Aperitif in hand, he posed before the fire, and just had to tell old Taddy the perfectly marvellous notion he had had for the new show. He launched into a tedious recital of a plot in which a middle-aged man falls in love with a young girl, undergoes the usual misgivings, and is at last convinced that his love is reciprocated and his duty is to marry.

'Of course I shall put it over,' said Lessington. He spoke with assurance, and Tadema reflected bitterly that he would. Lessington had a knack of serving up the coldest of cold mutton on a salver worthy of better things.

'It's just a weeny bit topical,' Lessington continued archly. 'You're not very grateful, Taddy.'

'Splendid, my dear fellow, splendid!' said Tadema with great heartiness, since a warning voice in the back of his mind bade him behave normally. If anyone should guess there was anything unusual afoot the whole strength of his project would be ruined.

He got rid of Lessington only when he was departing for the theatre. Conversation had been a great strain but he had weathered it. Lessington, he knew, would now be prepared to swear that dear old Taddy had been completely himself, and to report that they had spent a very happy hour discussing a new play.

Back at the theatre Tadema put on a very careful performance. The relieved Miss Miller found the Old Man in the best of humours. He accepted a supper invitation for midnight and agreed to give a magazine correspondent an interview after the show.

As the time wore on he was conscious of a growing nervousness, but he had made up his mind, and in the interval before the third act he wandered into De Lara's room and stood chatting for a minute or so.

Paul Ritchie, his own understudy, who shared the dressing room, was lounging disconsolately in his corner, he saw, but the young actor said afterwards that the Old Man never once looked in his direction after the first affable nod.

After leaving De Lara, Tadema, who was wearing the striking pin stripe suit in which he appeared in the third act, was seen by Lottie Queen on the staircase leading up to the roof. He smiled at her, graciously congratulated her on her performance, and passed on.

It went through that lady's mind that it was odd that he should be wandering about the theatre when time was getting on, but it was a habit of the company to go up to the flat roof when the weather was close, and she thought no more of the incident just then.

An electrician observed him higher up on the staircase immediately below the roof, but the man said no word passed, and that was all the evidence the united company could supply when the inquiry was instituted.

At the moment when Tadema stepped out upon the dark roof, the dizzy lights of the city below him, he was trembling with excitement, but he realised that he had very little time and moved swiftly, stepping daintily across the leads to the desolate collection of builders' debris which he had observed there earlier in the week and the recollection of which had given him his idea.

The Gresham Theatre was an old-fashioned building whose

rococo parapet was barely four feet away from its nearest neighbour, the Ever Safe Insurance Company's premises.

At one particular point a younger man might have sprung from one roof to the other, but Tadema preferred the plank. Pulling it out from beneath the folded sacks, he pushed it into position and prepared to climb across.

It was a risky proceeding for a man of his years and unathletic habits, and it is possible that had he seriously considered the physical side of the venture his nerve might have failed him. As it was, however, his thoughts were occupied only by the other aspect of the plan, the enormity of it, the courage, the complete ruthlessness.

It took his breath away. To walk out of the theatre in costume in the midst of the play! To go on to the roof and thence to—disappear!

Told of any man it would be a piquant story, like the beginning of a mystery yarn, but when the man was Tadema—oh the head-lines would be large and the wind would seep out of Chloe's sails! Would she start, even? Sir Geoffrey doubted it.

He stepped out on to the insurance company's leads and thrust the plank back sharply. It clattered on to the theatre roof so noisily that for a moment he was afraid. Discovery at this juncture would be disastrous. But there was no untoward sound from below and he went on.

The fire escape descended into a narrow alley behind the building. As Tadema went down the spidery stair a new cause for alarm confronted him. London is a crowded city and the ever-watchful police are suspicious of shadowy figures on the fire escapes of dark buildings. An arrest or even an inquiry would be too embarrassing even to contemplate.

Sir Geoffrey reached the pavement white with apprehension. He went unchallenged, however, and sped through the darker streets towards Tottenham Court Road.

For the next half hour his mind was taken up completely with technical details. It is a simple thing to plan to change all one's clothes, and with them one's personality, in the toilet room of a large and crowded station, but it is a surprisingly complicated project to carry through. Sir Geoffrey had completely over-looked the hampering qualities of a sense of guilt.

In spite of these unexpected difficulties, however, his meta-morphosis was remarkably successful. One does not dress up and pretend to be somebody else practically every night of one's professional life without becoming an adept at the art. At twenty minutes to eleven, when Paul Ritchie was ploughing through the last act at the Gresham, a mild looking provincial gentleman walked on to Liverpool Street station, a newish suitcase in his hand.

This stranger bore a superficial resemblance to the debonair Sir Geoffrey, it is true, but, since it is a curious fact that the actual face and figure of the normal man contribute but three points out of ten to his appearance, clothes, context and colouring making up the other seven, none of the weary passengers glanced at the grey-suited figure with any sort of recognition.

Tadema himself was gradually getting the feel of his part. As he became increasingly aware of his safety he experienced a new sensation. He felt free. He had ninety pounds in cash on him in an envelope, all he had dared to collect without leaving traces of flight. His watch, studs, wallet and a letter or two were still in the clothes he had worn on leaving the theatre, and which were now stowed away in the case in his hand. He felt light and irrespon-sible, almost as though he had really walked out of life as cleanly and as mysteriously as the world must soon believe.

He glanced at the station clock. His train, the Yarborough mail, left in thirty-five minutes. Why he had chosen Yarborough he did not know, save that it was at a fair distance from London and was on the coast.

He had no definite plan in his head as yet, but he relied upon the long, slow journey to bring counsel. The first and most impor-tant step had been taken, and Chloe had been passed at the post. That was the main thing, and the rest, he thought superbly, would come.

The suitcase, and/or its contents, must be disposed of to the best possible advantage. Obviousness dictated the coast. Hence Yarborough, since Brighton would have been ridiculous. But all that was yet to be arranged. Inspiration would arrive.

Tadema smiled and the man who had been watching him so intently for the past ten minutes from the other side of the platform moved a little nearer.

Duds Wallace walked round Tadema, eyeing him covertly. The height was okay, he decided. So were the shoulders. And there was about the same room round the waist. But, above all, the style was right and in Duds' opinion, style was what mattered.

With a certain section of the Railway police Duds Wallace was something of a pet and a curiosity. He was unique. His long criminal record, which comprised some sixteen convictions, related an odd history of misdemeanour and proved conclusively that whatever other qualities Mr Wallace might have possessed the gods had not made him versatile. His programme was always the same. Whenever his somewhat finicky taste dictated that he required a new outfit he stole a suitcase.

This in itself was sufficiently unenterprising but he carried his orthodoxy a step further. Invariably he stole a suitcase from a railway station and–invariably this was the hallmark of a Wallace activity–his victim was a man who closely resembled himself in build, colouring and a quiet, inexpensive taste.

The obvious disadvantages of his unoriginal methods never seemed to dawn on him, with the result that any slightly stocky complainant of medium height who reported the loss of a good-sized suitcase was instantly handed over to Sergeant Buller, who would grant his visitor one glance and reach for the telephone.

Two or three hours later Mr Wallace, in private life a comparatively respectable bookmaker's clerk, would be pulled in, always astonished and explanatory, but more often than not actually clad in his victim's missing garments.

It was typical of Duds' mentality that he complained bitterly in court that the police would pick on him.

Buller, who was a logical-minded man, had explained the

whole business to Duds over and over again, but Mr Wallace continued to be repetitive and remained astonished.

At the moment Mr Wallace, whose sartorial ambitions alone seemed to lead him into wrong-doing, was downright ashamed of his appearance.

He was dead shabby about the elbows and his suit had that skinny appearance which comes with age. It looked as if he and the garment had been immersed in water for some time and had dried without being separated.

His shirt was not good either. There was a long thin hole where the cuffs had frayed. Duds' sharp brown eyes rested on Tadema's portmanteau. There was a suit in that, he would bet on it; a suit, shirts, pyjamas and with luck a pair of shoes.

He glanced at the actor manager's feet and those decent brown shoes with the round toes swept away his last remnants of doubt.

Having made up his mind, Duds followed his routine closely. When the train came into the main platform Tadema selected an empty second class compartment, placed his bag on the corner seat to reserve it, and, as his watcher confidently expected, stepped out on the platform again and wandered off to look for a paper.

As soon as he was lost to sight Duds entered another empty second a little lower down the train. Instead of sitting down he passed on into the corridor and wandered up to Tadema's compartment. His casual manner was excellent. He gripped the suitcase with just the right familiarity and carried it out into the corridor.

As he passed on down the train he glanced into each carriage inquiringly as he went by. Tadema was nowhere to be seen. It was really very simple.

When Mr Wallace reached the end of the train, which had pulled into the shadow of the passenger bridge, he walked out of the last compartment, passed through the main booking hall and, turning up the dark hill, melted quietly into the street.

Tadema discovered his loss when it was too late to do anything about it. When he returned to his compartment the train was on the point of starting and, missing his case, he came to the conclusion that he was in the wrong carriage and walked out into the corridor to locate his property.

They had passed Ilford, at the beginning of a long non-stop run, before he was convinced that his bag was not on the train. Irritated and disconsolate, he threw himself down in a corner seat and glowered.

Apart from the normal sense of insult which invariably comes to one on discovering that the misfortunes which seem so natural in others should have overtaken oneself, Tadema felt he had a special grievance. Without his clothes there was really no point in him going to the coast at all, yet here he was, entrained for Yarborough of all places. The very foundation of the plan he had intended to evolve upon this journey was removed. Moreover, he could have no redress for the loss of his property. In the circumstances he could hardly go to the police. It was all very exasperating and augured, he could not help feeling, bad luck to the venture.

He reviewed his position gloomily. If things were not going to go right they were going to go very badly indeed. However, he comforted himself with the thought of the sensation in the morrow's papers and, after some moments of happy contemplation, some of his old confidence returned and he leant back, content to wait for inspiration to arrive. Something, no doubt, would turn up. He slept.

He woke with a start at one minute to four in the morning to find himself bundled out on to a dark and clammily cold railway station, without overcoat or luggage. His first thought was that he was by some monstrous injustice or mistake in hell, but afterwards, when the kaleidoscopic events of the previous afternoon and evening returned to him, he reconsidered his decision and concluded he was mad.

But in ten minutes or so his indomitable faith in himself had returned. He had been forced into a delicate situation, compelled to take an unconventional line. A regrettable but minor mishap had deprived him of his bag, but he was still the captain of his press, still the keeper of the personality.

He looked about him. No provincial town is at its best at four o'clock on an autumn morning. Tadema did not know the place and did not particularly want to. His best plan, he decided, was to leave Yarborough. He consulted a weary porter.

'First train, sir? Where for, sir?'

'Anywhere,' said Tadema recklessly. 'The first train to leave this station.'

The man looked at him curiously and replied that there was a slow branch line train leaving in an hour.

'Take you to Ebury, Lessing and Saffronden,' he concluded.

Saffronden. The name struck a familiar note in Tadema's memory. There was a theatre in Saffronden, or rather there had once been a theatre there; the Theatre Royal, a little dark house with a smell. Through the years that smell crept back and assailed again the nostrils of Tadema, a camphory, dampish odour with a bite in it, unique and unforgettable.

The old 'Hearts Afire' company under Benny Fancy had played there for a week way back in 19 . . . Tadema forgot the year.

Another memory returned to him. It was very vague but it conjured up a sensation of warmth and stuffiness and amusement. It was a joke, he fancied, and something to do with cocoa of all things; something excruciatingly funny. He brightened up.

'I'll go on to Saffronden,' he said, adding abruptly as he returned to the temporarily forgotten porter, 'There's a bookstall there, isn't there? What time do the morning papers arrive?'

Both bewildered replies having proved satisfactory, Tadema, the fugitive, entered the Saffronden train.

He was waiting on Saffronden station when the papers arrived and he pounced upon a copy of the *Trumpeter* and turned the pages over feverishly. At first he thought he was not mentioned at all and a feeling of bewilderment passed over him. It was not until the third time that he searched the paper that he found the small paragraph tucked away at the bottom of a page:

'Sir Geoffrey Tadema, the well-known actor manager, was forced by indisposition to retire from the cast of "Lovers' Meeting", now enjoying a successful run at the Gresham. Sir

Geoffrey's part in the third act was played by his understudy, Paul Ritchie. Sir Geoffrey is confidently expected to return to his role at this evening's performance.'

Tadema swore softly under his breath. What an idiot Wentworth was! As a business manager he was intelligent and economical, but in an emergency he always did the wrong thing. If only the fool knew it he was wasting precious time. Oh, well, he'd have to rely on the evening papers. The lunatic would be sure to do something by that time. Doubtless he had the wind up properly. Tadema could not repress a chuckle at the spectacle. 'Dashing about like a demented hen,' he said to himself as he walked down the winding hill from the station into the main road of the town, which had miraculously become much smaller and sleepier than he remembered it.

By the time he was breakfasting in the commercial room of the Red Lion his trepidation had returned. Time was so very short. By this time tomorrow Chloe would be well on her way to Athens and a short time later the wires would be buzzing.

He was beside himself with impatience and a growing sense of impotence in the matter. There was nothing he could possibly do to speed things up. A wire to Wentworth saying 'I've disappeared you fool' would be ludicrous and quite horribly disastrous if it fell into the wrong hands.

Moreover, this temporary setback was taking his attention from the plan he had to evolve. He had relied upon the morning newspapers to give him a lead. Whatever he did, it had got to be good. Tadema did not shut his eyes to the danger of the whole thing fizzling out into an incident that had to be explained away: 'Temporary amnesia', 'actor finds strain too great', 'betrothed's flight breaks up elderly fiancé'. That was the sort of thing which had to be avoided at all costs.

By the end of breakfast he had decided to wait. Nothing could be done at the moment, so much was painfully obvious.

By paying in advance and sending out for some pyjamas Tadema dispelled any doubts which the clerk at the Red Lion might have entertained concerning him and, having bathed and shaved, he retired to bed, leaving instructions that he was to be called with a cup of tea and an evening paper as soon as that sheet should have arrived.

He lay awake for some time, fuming at Wentworth and worrying over his predicament, but his night's journey had been long and uncomfortable and he dropped off into a fitful and uneasy sleep.

However, he was awake and pacing up and down the room in pyjamas and a bed quilt when the chambermaid arrived. The girl set down the tea, and would have spoken, but Tadema had pounced upon the folded paper and she went out again huffily.

For a moment Tadema's eyes refused to focus, and he was conscious of a thrill of pure apprehension as he shook out the paper. The next moment, however, he was staring, his pale eyes starting out of his head.

Right across the front page and surmounting a large photograph of himself were the words:

'TRAGIC DEATH OF FAMOUS ACTOR. Dies in Stage Clothes. Early this morning a man was knocked down and terribly mutilated in the Gray's Inn Road. From papers in his pocket the police discovered him to be the famous stage actor Sir Geoffrey Tadema. The actor manager had not been seen by any of his associates since the interval after the second act of "Lovers' Meeting" at the Gresham Theatre last night.

'When Sir Geoffrey's body was found it was clad in the clothes which he wore in the play. His friends can give no explanation for the tragedy.

'Mr Henry Sharper, Sir Geoffrey's valet, broke down at the mortuary when he identified the body, and has been taken home to relatives, suffering from shock.'

Tadema let the paper drop from his hand. His eyes were glazed and the expression upon his face was mainly pathetic.

'Well - I'm damned,' he said aloud, and added as a gleam of intelligence returned to his blue eyes, 'I am, too.'

'Tragic death'. Tadema sat on the edge of his bed in his new pyjamas and re-read the words until they became meaningless and afterwards horribly clear again. He was, of course, completely unaware of the existence, or rather the pre-existence, of Duds Wallace, that luckless seeker after sartorial correctness, who, clad in his new glory, had blundered blindly into a car when on his way to air his plumage.

But it was obvious that some such disaster must have occurred. Tadema read every word the paper had printed about himself and then, with disaster weighing numbingly upon him, he dressed carefully and went downstairs.

He collected the other papers and carried them off to his room. They had the same story, of course, but with a few added details.

There was only one mention of Chloe. *The Trumpeter* observed that Sir Geoffrey's fiancée, Lady Chloe Staratt, was out of London.

'Thinking of some way of cashing in on the story,' thought Tadema grimly. 'Or, more likely, trying to prevent the young lout from blethering his side of the affair.'

For the first time a faint smile passed over the actor's lips. Chloe was frustrated all right: temporarily rendered speechless, it seemed. His enjoyment in this aspect of the affair was short-lived as his own position became painfully apparent. As far as publicity was concerned, he had certainly scored heavily. His name and prowess filled all three papers, but what of the future? There was an ancient jest concerning the young man who, on being promised a legacy if he got his name in the news, cut his throat to achieve it. The similarity of his own story made Tadema squirm. What could he do? What on earth could he do? How could he return without providing the greatest anticlimax of all time?

He toyed with the idea of simply walking back into his part and meeting the subsequent inquiry with a more or less plausible story. That would be a sensational course in all conscience and would serve his purpose very well unless Chloe eloped. And she would; he knew it instinctively. Chloe would elope and people would draw the inevitable and unfortunately true conclusions.

The only way to prevent her going off and marrying someone else immediately was for him to remain dead. If he remained dead, how could he ever resurrect himself? How could he ever explain why he had allowed some unknown man to be buried in his stead?

Thinking of burial, Tadema returned to the newspapers. 'The funeral arrangements will be published later.' This was a dreadful side of the farce. In his mind's eye he saw old Wentworth flying about in a panic, poor Sharper prostrate in the house of inquisitive relations, the company, the wretched author, the flowers, the solemn ceremony and the grief of the few people who were fond of him; Ma Biggs, his housekeeper and old Wally Bell, the comedian.

No, it was horrible. It was dreadful. It had got to stop. But what could he do?

He wandered out into the town. Some of the passers-by glanced at the stranger in their midst with the mild interest of country folk and Tadema might have been alarmed for the safety of his incognito had he cared about it.

Fortunately, or unfortunately, he was perfectly safe. The carefully taken studio portraits reproduced in the newspapers showed a man twenty years younger, with darker eyes and deeper and more interesting shadows than this pale, worried-looking, middle-aged man who hurried along so fast and yet, had they known it, so aimlessly. As far as the man in the street was concerned Sir Geoffrey Tadema was dead.

The queue outside the pit impeded his progress and finally pulled him up. He stood staring at the shabby old theatre for a moment with the first interest he had shown in externals since the advent of the evening papers.

The Theatre Royal was on its last legs, or at least its plaster pillars were crumbling. Tadema was shocked. A genteel shabbiness it had always possessed, besides its characteristic smell, but in the old days it had never looked like this. The meanest cinema in the meanest street had not this dreadful decayed poverty. To Tadema the Theatre Royal Saffronden looked like some depraved and leering old harridan clad in filthy finery, all the more depressing because he had known her in her better days.

The Chasberg Stock Company was playing there, he gathered from the bills. The piece that week was 'Beggar's Choice'. Tadema took a box.

He remembered the play as soon as the curtain rose. It was an ancient melodrama about a racehorse, an impoverished lord and the inevitable Lady Mary. He had played in it himself many times in his old rep days.

He almost enjoyed it. The contemplation of the past at least took his mind off the horror of the present. Seated well back among the crimson curtains, the pungent camphory smell tingling in his nostrils, he looked down at the old stage and remembered with a hint of sadness something he had long forgotten, the excitement of those early days.

His job had kept him busy then. Plays had followed so fast upon one another in those days that no one was ever word perfect. The underpaid stage managers were always unreliable. No one knew if the props would turn up in their right places, or even if the curtain would descend at the end of the act. It would be nerve-racking and terrible now, but in those days it had been rather fun.

Tadema, already extremely sorry for himself, nearly wept when he remembered how long ago it all was.

He had been watching the Lady Mary for some minutes before he recognised her. It was a trick of her voice which finally caught his attention, and made him lean forward in the box and peer more closely at her face. She was older, of course—far too old for the part. Tadema could not remember her name but her voice was familiar and she had a way of smiling that came back to him.

He could not see his programme and relied upon his memory. What was the woman's name? Chrissie something, he was inclined to think, and they had travelled together. It must have been in the old rep days.

She had improved, he thought suddenly. That was it; in the old days she had been appalling. Appalling and rather sweet. His

mind, anxious to escape from the world of reality outside the
theatre, seized avidly on the problem within. Tadema closed his
eyes and delved back into the past. The voices on the stage helped
him considerably. He remembered whole sequences and there
was one scene on the steps of a hotel just off the racecourse which
returned so vividly to his mind that he sat up abruptly. That was
it! Her name was Chrissie and they must have played this part together.

It wasn't such a coincidence, if one thought of it. He had played
in the provinces for fifteen years and there must have been a great
many actresses who claimed to have played with Tadema. Some
of them Sir Geoffrey could remember much more clearly.

This woman was only a vague memory. But he knew her. Her
name was Chrissie something and she had been rather sweet. It
had been very long ago, he decided; in his early days. He didn't
think there had been a ghost of an affair. If there had he would
have remembered. He turned his attention to the stage. Whole
scenes, he realised, were modern interpolations. Much of the
bravura had been dropped. It was all very interesting.

When the lights of the first interval went up he looked at the
programme. 'Lady Mary . . . Miss Chrissie Dilling.' Chrissie
Dilling; that was the name. How could a woman have gone
through a lifetime of leading ladyship with a name like that?

He was debating whether to send his card round and had indeed
half decided to when he remembered his predicament with a
start and the whole dreadful business poured back into his mind.
He did not go out of the theatre, however, but sat there till the
curtain rose again. At least he was hidden and inspiration must
surely come in time.

Fortunately for him the second act opened with a scene in an
attic room which he remembered. It was a tragic parting in which
the impoverished lord refused for his honour's sake to accept the
overtures of the infatuated Lady Mary. The words came back to
him so clearly that he was irritated by the rather hopeless boy
playing the part when his inflections and interpretations were
unfamiliar.

Chrissie had improved. She was almost good in an old-fashioned way. Not West End standard, of course, but first class for the provinces. She held the audience, too. They loved her.

Something else returned to Tadema's memory. He seemed to hear Chrissie complaining that someone always struck a match in her big scenes and it put her off. Always at the most dramatic part that little pin point of light out in the dark audience would catch her eye, telling her that there was someone whose attention she was not holding.

Softly and feeling indescribably guilty, Tadema drew a box from his pocket. He waited for the right moment and struck the match. He was leaning forward and the flickering light caught his face, accentuating the hollows and darkening eyes.

Miss Dilling wavered, her glance rested on the box, and then, with a little shrill cry, she clasped her hand over her heart.

Tadema started back in his box. He did not see her gallant recovery, did not see her struggling on with the scene. The only thought in his mind was one of intense excitement, and, curiously enough, of relief. He was alive. The secret was out; whatever disaster might accompany the revelation he was alive again. Somebody knew it. He slipped out of the box and hurried round to the stage door.

He was sitting in the dressing room when she came in from the stage, still a little pale under her make-up. Tadema rose and gallantly held out his hands.

'Why, Chrissie!' he said.

The woman stared at him and for an uncomfortable moment he thought that she was going to faint. Stock company actresses are more or less inured to shock, however, and Miss Dilling revived. She came into the room, shutting the door carefully behind her.

'Well, Geoff,' she said, and added awkwardly after a pause, 'I was only thinking of you this evening.'

As soon as the words left her mouth she bit her lower lip sharply and regarded him apologetically with round eyes. Tadema remembered the trick. He remembered the eyes, too, and it must have been some sort of little romance here; nothing serious; just a boy and girl flirtation perhaps. She was several years younger than himself; ten, perhaps; he was not sure.

Miss Dilling continued to stare.

'Well, I don't know what to say, I'm sure,' she said at last. 'The papers are wrong, of course.'

The morning papers published a fresh Tadema sensation. Lady Chloe Staratt had been led by an apparently friendly *Trumpeter* reporter into an admission that her engagement to Sir Geoffrey had been broken off on the morning of his disappearance. Whereas the weeping, broken-hearted Chloe might have made a pretty enough picture to grace any suburban breakfast table, it was considerably marred by an independent statement by Mr Gyp Rains in the same paper to the effect that his own marriage to Lady Chloe had been fixed for the morrow, this announcement being backed up by the evidence of a special licence.

The Trumpeter, never famed for its delicacy, published the two stories one after the other and the report of the inquest in the next column. Since the coroner's jury brought in a verdict of 'death by misadventure' and vetoed absolutely any question of deliberation, the combined effect of the three stories was unfortunate as far as Chloe was concerned. Tadema, reading the paper over his breakfast in the hotel lounge, was almost sorry for her.

Most of his sympathy, however, he reserved for himself. The morning's news had brought him no respite. He was still a dead man and to revive with honour looked like proving an impossibility.

He was still faced with the problem of finding the means of returning to life without appearing either a petulant and jilted lover or the victim of a sudden fit of mental aberration, or, of course, both. For a time he let his mind dwell sadly on what might have been, but sighed and put the vain imaginings from him. It had happened. He was in the devil of a mess.

He had just decided to lie low for another forty-eight hours at least until opportunity, if not sheer necessity, drove him to action, when Miss Dilling arrived. Tadema was pleased to see her, but only mildly so. By morning light she looked most of her age and her clothes were painfully provincial. However, her smile was friendly and admiring.

She came out with her request immediately, her eyes meeting his anxiously. She hardly dared to suggest it, but Derek Fayre, her leading man, was really too ill to play and Mr Lewis was so worried. The incognito would be preserved, of course. No one knew. She had simply spoken of him as an actor friend and that had given Mr Lewis the idea. After all, they had done the show so many times in the past. It would be like old times. Would he? Would he? Dare she ask?

The idea appealed to Tadema from the moment it was presented to him. It is possible, of course, that he might have smelt a rat if anyone but Chrissie Dilling had put the thing up to him. But she was so patently without second motive, so obviously anxious only to play at old times again. All women were sentimental, Tadema thought privately; all except that hussy Chloe.

Over supper the previous evening he had asked Chrissie why she had never married. Her reply had been heart-breaking.

'Oh, you know how it is,' she had said, wrinkling her nose at him. 'First it's a career. Afterwards there's no one around the theatre quite good enough. And then—you just don't.'

Poor old Chrissie, her old-fashioned sophistication that was sophistication no more. She just hadn't.

Tadema smiled at her. She had a gift for making people feel pleasantly condescending.

'My dear girl, I'm too old,' he said.

'Geoff, don't be ridiculous.' Her sincerity did him good.

He went to rehearsal with her like a lamb. He had a glorious time. Every nervous criticism put in by the breathless Mr Katz for verisimilitude's sweet sake amused and delighted him. Things which would have rendered him speechless in his own theatre here struck him as being funny, and the old play came back easily. Right words, wrong words, delicious gags, they slipped to his tongue and he let himself go.

The irony of the situation as he knew it he found exquisite and all the more so since he had an appreciative audience in Miss Dilling. He made covert references to the truth, fooled about and behaved generally like an irresponsible child, while Chrissie Dilling played up to him, and the sparkle returned to her eyes.

Neither of them so much as thought of Mr Lewis, which was perhaps fortunate. Breathless, laughing, and twenty years younger, Sir Geoffrey knocked off for lunch. He and Miss Dilling ate sausages and drank beer at the Red Lion and reminisced. Tadema put the world of reality into the back of his mind. He felt reckless and somehow slightly truculent. If the world combined to mock and frustrate him, at least he was a fine old trouper still. Yes, by God he was! And secretly he longed for the show.

There was an electric atmosphere in the Theatre Royal that night. The whole company was in a state of whispering hysteria. The only two innocent participants in the comedy were frankly and engagingly happy. The first act went with a bang. Tadema was aware of a large and appreciative audience and gave his best. The personality revived in all its early splendour. Miss Dilling was carried away.

No curtain calls till the end of the show; that was the rule of the house and it was observed.

Tadema climbed happily out of mess jacket into hunting pink and from hunting pink to naval uniform without a dresser or a qualm. He romped and gagged and threw his weight about atrociously, while the provincial audience rejoiced with him. It was a glorious night.

When the final moment came on the steps of the castle and the lovers were reunited with the immortal line, 'Marry me, Mary. I'm a man again', Sir Geoffrey swung Miss Dilling into his arms and kissed her in the style of his predecessors with a sound that was heard at the back of the gallery.

The gallery rose and the grand, glorious sound of applause poured sweetly on his head. Tadema, gallantly leading Miss Dilling, took the curtain. Not once or twice, but again and again they came forward. At last Miss Dilling fled and Tadema took the final call alone.

As he stood before the curtain the light shot up in the theatre and he looked around. The crowd was still applauding and Tadema bowed. He was superbly happy.

As he raised his head again, however, he stiffened. Directly in front of him, in the middle of the first row, was a boiled shirt, and above that shirt sat the smug face of Evans of *The Trumpeter*.

Tadema, grown old again, glanced sharply down the line, his blood chilled. There they were, all of them: Richardson, Playfair, Jones – the whole gang.

He walked back through the curtains, his head held stiffly but his eyes unfocused, strode through the sniggering throng behind the scenes and entered the dressing room at the end of the corridor.

Miss Dilling paled before his expression. He told her what he thought coldly and all the more bitterly because of his great humiliation. Miss Dilling wept.

'I didn't – oh, Geoff, I didn't.'

'Nobody else knew,' said Tadema. 'Do you realise,' he went on with sudden heat, 'that to get a little publicity for your paltry little company you've sacrificed and made a fool of me? Publicity!'

He laughed rather theatrically and would have made his exit on that word but they were upon him like a pack of dogs. They all swarmed in through the door, jostling, laughing, eager and content that the chase was yielding a kill.

They were all there, the half-dozen that he had seen in the stalls and more that he had missed. Even Evans in his affected boiled shirt was condescending to hurry like a mere reporter, since duty and the story demanded it.

Tadema, obscuring the tragic Miss Dilling, faced them.

'Let's have the story, Sir Geoffrey – the whole story. It'll take a bit of explaining, you know.'

That was Richardson, grinning away like a Barbary ape.

'A remarkable performance, Tadema. I didn't think you had it in you.'

Sir Geoffrey had often wanted to kick Evans but never more than now.

'Come, Tadema, was it because of Lady Chloe? You've seen the papers, of course. What poor devil did you lend your clothes to?'

They were jostling him; hectoring him. His mind shuttered.

'We'll let you down lightly. It was the engagement, of course?'

'Gentlemen?' Tadema raised a protesting hand, '–just a moment. Just a moment, please.'

The sound of his own voice gave him confidence. It always did; it was so absolutely right.

'Since you've hunted me out–I almost said hounded me down–' the easy, rounded phrases slipped out softly, '–I suppose I must tell you the truth.'

'I should say so. I'm holding a line,' muttered someone and was instantly suppressed.

Tadema went smoothly on.

'Lady Chloe Staratt has said that our engagement was broken off the day before yesterday. Lady Chloe is a very sweet and charming girl but she is not quite accurate. Our engagement was broken off last Sunday–'

'Why? The whole story. We must have the whole story.'

Tadema shrugged his shoulders and threw out his hands. A faint smile which was not wholly assumed played round his lips.

'Even an actor has private affairs, gentlemen,' he murmured. 'And yet–well–since you've come for the truth–'

Turning swiftly like a conjurer he took Miss Dilling's quivering hand.

'This is Miss Chrissie Dilling,' he said simply. 'My first love and my last. This evening she has honoured me by accepting the proposal I made her when I first arrived in this town yesterday morning.'

He paused for the announcement to sink in and then, when he was sure he had all their attention, added superbly and with great dignity: 'Even at my age, gentlemen, romance is not wholly dead. There is always one woman–somewhere.'

He watched them scribbling and his smile widened. Inspiration had arrived.

Chrissie Dilling, that rare woman, did not speak.

Some days later Sir Geoffrey Tadema turned away from the contemplation of his wedding presents to glance at the proofs of an interview which his fiancée had granted to a woman's magazine. Chrissie had brought it to him and now stood at his side while he ran a pencil along the lines.

'Christiana Dilling glanced at me and I thought I saw something very charming in her wistful blue eyes. "Of course, I always hoped he'd come back," she confessed.' Tadema lifted the pencil.

'We'll take out that "hoped", my dear,' he said, 'and put "knew". It's better publicity.'

The Perfect Butler

KNOWLES was the perfect butler, and, since the word knows no qualification, he was only that; yet there were some who would have stretched the point and claimed that he was more than perfect, inasmuch as the very art of buttling achieved under his hand a flowering, a golden renascence it never before had known.

At the moment he was in his pantry at the back of a great Georgian house in Berkeley Square, considering the polish on the Georgian spoons. His son, young Harold, was attending to the spoons, his face pink and absorbed as he rubbed away with the leather.

Young Harold was his father's only anxiety. The boy came from an unbroken line of butlers as ancient as the family which they served.

When the present Knowles looked at young Harold and realised everything the lad had to live up to he trembled. The past can be a cruel master, especially when legend has strengthened its hand, and Knowles feared for Harold. Could Harold make the grade? There were times when his father lay awake wondering.

When they were alone, as now, in that blessed interval when tea is a thing of the past and dinner only a partly realised dream in the chef's mind, Knowles would talk to young Harold and impart the deeper secrets of his calling.

Since young Harold was only fifteen and still human, and Knowles was fifty-five and superhuman, the conversation was liable to have a one-sided quality, but there were rare occasions when the imperfectly subdued nature of the boy got out of hand. This was one of them.

'I saw Lady Susan this afternoon. She had been crying,' he observed, rashly.

Knowles set down a mellow spoon with great deliberation

and, taking a pair of small pince-nez from his waistcoat pocket, placed them carefully on the bridge of his nose.

'You *saw* Lady Susan?' he said. 'Where was she?'

'In the hall,' faltered the helpless Harold, observing only too late the abyss widening beneath his feet.

'And where were you?'

'At the top of the service stairs,' stuttered the boy.

'Where you had no right to be.'

There was a long and awful pause. Young Harold had been well grounded in the first rules of service, and 'Thou shalt not give back answers' was graven on his soul.

'The young servant,' said Knowles, giving the word its true dignity, 'has to learn to serve the family with his mind, his body and his affection, but without his human nature, Harold.'

'You must notice things and not notice them, if you take my meaning. That is to say, you must see everything, but only retain in your head those matters which may possibly concern you.

'I remember the case of the gentleman with kleptomania who dined with his late lordship,' he observed, unexpectedly. 'Now it was my duty to notice that he had a pair of very fine salt cellars in his hip pocket when he left the table, but it was not my duty to mention the fact to him or to any one else. I made a point of helping him on with his overcoat as he left, and then I ventured to suggest that the awkward bulge spoiled the set of his coat. I begged him to allow me to send a messenger round with the contents of his pocket the following morning. I was not rude, you understand, Harold; just respectfully solicitous and, of course, firm. He gave up the salt cellars rather grudgingly, I remember, and, of course, his lordship never knew.'

The deep voice ceased, and Knowles eyed his son.

'Quiet, impersonal, and firm; that's the line, my boy. It takes time to learn it, but it's worth it in the end. When you're a good butler, you know that you're more than a man. In your sphere you are infallible. Crises may arise, difficult situations may start up and face you, but with training you can look them in the eye and not see them, if you take me.

'Besides,' he went on with apparent irrelevance, 'there's nothing so vulgar as vulgar curiosity.'

Harold followed his father's train of thought perfectly and was silent, his mind busy fitting together the odd words he had gleaned among the whispers which had been agitating the servants' hall all day.

Knowles, too, pondered on the unfortunate situation which had arisen above stairs and on the disastrous paragraph in the morning's papers. However, decency and respect and even simulated ignorance he could and would enforce in his own domain below stairs, and in Knowles' opinion it would be as well if there were another equally competent person in charge of the world outside.

He was disturbed in his thoughts by the muffled buzzing of the front door bell. What instinct persuaded the old man to answer it himself he never rightly knew, but he strode out into the passage, swept Edward, the footman, out of the way, and mounted the service stairs with a brisk purposefulness quite unlike his usual pontifical stride.

As he entered the main hall, which in deference to her Ladyship's wishes was kept but softly lit, he was aware of a minor crisis. The front door was swinging wide and through it rushed the warm, rain-laden air of the city's evening.

Knowles had just mastered his first sense of outrage at this unheard-of indignity when he saw the visitor. Without his pince-nez Knowles was very near-sighted, and the man was standing in the darker part of the hall by the Doric columns. The old man had to go up to him before his features were clearly visible, yet Knowles had recognised him the moment the man had entered his blurred vision, and now, as the butler peered into those striking features, small beads of perspiration appeared upon the high forehead above the perfect face, and Knowles' plump hands were damp and clammy as the night wind from the square.

However the quality of perfection is not lightly cast down. Knowles stood his ground and looked the newcomer glassily in the eye.

Before that stare, as unnatural as his own, the visitor wavered and turned slightly, so that the old man saw his absence of collar and another very unpleasant thing about his chest and the shoulder of his coat.

Still Knowles stood his ground and waited, as was his custom, for the visitor to speak first.

'Take me up to Lady Susan, please Knowles.'

The butler stood perfectly still, his eyes, accustomed by long practice, focused upon those other eyes. The absence of collar and the other things Knowles no longer saw.

'Lady Susan, sir?' he said, with just the right intonation of surprise. 'Ah—surely you're under some misapprehension, sir, if I may venture to say so?'

'Don't be a fool, Knowles.' The newcomer was angry. 'You know perfectly well who I am—Captain Lester Phillips. You've admitted me a dozen times. Take me up to Lady Susan immediately, or must I go without you?'

He made a movement, but in spite of an icy chill of apprehension Knowles stood firm. He gave his celebrated little cough.

'I—ah —still think you've made a mistake, sir,' he said gently. 'Lady Susan no longer lives here.'

'No longer lives here?' The newcomer's eyes wavered for a moment. 'But I saw her here only two nights ago—only last Wednesday. You showed me up yourself.'

He paused, and Knowles, seizing the advantage, spoke again.

'Not last Wednesday, sir,' he said, calmly. 'That was—ah—if you'll forgive me saying so, some years ago, long before the family moved. I stayed with the house, sir. You'll hardly come up and see Mr Goldberger, sir?'

'Mr Goldberger?'

'My new employer, sir.'

'I see.'

A bewildered expression had crept over the visitor's pallid features. He looked lost, frightened. If it had not been for the absence of collar and those other things Knowles could have found it in his heart to sympathise with him. As it was, he ushered him gently towards the open door.

On the threshold the stranger paused.

'You don't know where's she living now?'

'No, sir. I couldn't say.' Knowles swallowed. 'After the family migrated to Australia I lost touch with them, sir.'

'Australia? Are you sure, Knowles?'

Knowles' eyes did not falter. 'Australia, sir.'

'How long have they been there?'

'It must be nearly ten years, sir.'

Just for a moment the visitor's wild eyes rested upon the perfect face.

'You don't look changed, Knowles.'

It was then, perhaps, that, in the face of the greatest danger, Knowles reached the highest peak of his perfection.

'I never change, sir,' he said magnificently.

'I see.'

Without further ado the tall figure flung itself down the stone steps and strode out into the square, where the blue London night swallowed it.

Knowles so far forgot himself as to watch until it disappeared. Then he closed the door and went slowly down to his pantry. Ignoring Harold's inquiring glance, he passed on down the narrow room to his private cupboard, which he unlocked.

The bottle of Napoleon brandy left to him by name in the will of his late lordship was brought forth. Knowles poured himself out a generous tot and swallowed most of it. Then he replaced the bottle, locked the cupboard, and, assuming his pince-nez, drew his own copy of the *Daily Trumpet* from its place among the silver-towels. The late news paragraph slipped in on the front page was not hard to find. Nearly every servant in the house had stolen a surreptitious glance at it at least once that day. Old Knowles read it through once more.

'Young Guardsman's Tragic Death.

'Early this morning the valet of Captain Geoffrey Lester Phillips, son of Major-General and Mrs Lester Phillips, of Horton, in Norfolk, found his employer sitting before his dressing table, dead. His throat had been cut and a non-safety razor lay by his side.

'It was announced in these columns only the day before yesterday that the marriage which had been arranged between Captain Lester Phillips and Lady Susan, younger daughter of Lord Tollesbury, would not take place.'

Knowles folded the paper and returned it to the drawer. For a while he sipped the remainder of his Napoleon with a connoisseur's relish. Then he glanced at Harold.

'And that's another thing, my lad,' he said. 'The perfect butler should be able to turn away anybody without giving offence—anybody or *anything*.'

The Barbarian

THE idea was born to her on her nineteenth birthday and she took to it eagerly and nursed it lovingly. It was a great idea and she recognised it for that and from that day dedicated her life to it. What happened therefore sprang from it and from no other source.

At the time she was already beautiful in a fine and unfashionable way. Five feet eleven, straight backed and deep bosomed, she had thick yellow hair hanging to her waist and a great clear-cut face with a wide smooth forehead, a long nose delicately moulded with the same clean mastery that one notices in petals of camellias, and eyes that looked proudly and yet simply out at one from under the clear narrow arches of her brows.

Louis Fyshe, the crookback poet, said 'A Northern Queen' when he first saw her. There was, as Fyshe said, something queenly about her even then, something aloof and regal, and there was the north there too. The little crookback had a genius for seeing things like that and putting a twisted forefinger down upon them. Oh, yes, the north was there; under the fairness there was the darkness, the dark barbaric god-likeness of the north; and the white-hot passion that is born rather of ice than of the warm languor of the sun.

She was a thing apart from the flimsy, witty crowd around her; she towered above them in every way. Just as her strong beautiful body was larger than theirs, so was her mind and the strange uncivilised soul of her. She had not their little brilliancies—the vivid sparklings of small jewels. The meshes of her brain were too wide to catch such gold fish. The elemental human was so strong in her that they could not but recognise it and be drawn.

One after another they all proposed to her. At one time it was said that there was not an eligible man of her acquaintance whom she had not refused. Yet no one blamed her, no one called her foolish. Everyone wondered, of course, but that was all.

It was Fyshe who discovered the reason. Fyshe who, in one of his brilliant flashes of insight, laid bare the great idea, or rather ideal, which she served so tenaciously.

'She's waiting for a match,' he said.

'So's her mother—anxiously,' said someone and giggled.

Fyshe turned on him scathingly.

'You misunderstand me,' he said, 'I was speaking English—I said a match. She's waiting for a match, a real match. A man who can fit her. That's her great idea.'

As soon as it was spoken people realized that they knew it. Elfrida was waiting for a lord and master. One could almost imagine her challenging her suitors to a hurling match or a bout with spears. Once it had been pointed out it was obvious.

Fyshe went on, his little bird's face wrinkling hideously as he talked and his dark eyes burning.

'Yes, she's waiting for a god. Poor Northern Queen, she's born too late. The world's too civilized, too fined down, too crowded for her now. I'm afraid she'll wait for ever, it's not likely there'll be another strayed Olympian born this age.'

'All the same, whatever you say about gods and matches, Fyshe, she's turned down half the best fellows in town,' said Meyer from his corner by the fireside.

'Yes, and half of them didn't come up to her shoulder,' said Fyshe quickly, 'and the other half couldn't for the life of them follow the big simple way she reasons. She has five times more physical courage than anyone among them and I don't believe there's one, save young Thynne, the fighter, who could knock her down.'

Meyer began to laugh.

'My dear, boy,' he said, 'this is London, England, in the twentieth century. It's not necessary for a husband to be able to knock his wife down nowadays.'

'But don't you see that Elfrida is not a product of nowadays?' Fyshe was growing angry and his jaw twisted in a peculiarly ugly way. 'Elfrida is born out of her time, she belongs to the age of gods and heroes, she doesn't fit in here, she's a barbarian—a gentle

barbarian who finds the world too small, too finicky for her. Just
as the gilt chairs in her mother's hideous drawing-room are too
small, too dainty, for her to sit upon comfortably, so the ideas,
the wit, the fashions, the cynicisms of the men who love her are
all too dainty, too exquisitely intricate for her to grasp. She's too
big for them, that's all.'

'It's a darn pity then,' said Meyers dryly, 'because she'll never
get a husband at the rate she's going.'

'I'd rather see her dead than married to a misfit.'

Fyshe spoke quietly and it was pretty obvious that the man was
more than half in love with her himself.

'I'd rather see her dead!' he repeated. 'It's her great idea. The
ideal she's set herself. She knows that could she find her match,
the man physically, mentally, spiritually her complement, then
nothing could stop them. They would be the perfect product of
the earth, the natural lords of it. She realizes that, I'm sure of it.
Quiet and honest with herself she simply sits waiting for her
complement, steadily turning away all comers who would make
her but three-quarters of a perfect whole.' He paused and added
bitterly, 'Some of us couldn't even make her that.'

Again there was something in his voice which made the rest
glance at him sharply. It was queer to see him blush, it made his
dark face more murky than ever, and his eyes grew almost red
and shone painfully. Presently he left, then they pulled his
arguments to pieces but he was right. Elfrida was waiting,
waiting for the man to match.

He came quite suddenly.

Eric Ponsonby, who was also in the Guards, took him along to
the Audley street house one day. Meyer saw the meeting. He
said he was sitting in the drawing-room facing the door and
forming part of the group round Elfrida, who sat in one of the
high-backed chairs by the window, when Eric and Vickers came
in.

Meyer admitted he was impressed himself by the man's
appearance. He was a most amazing-looking fellow. Tall as a

giant, sinewy as Cain, yet supple and fair-skinned. He looked clever, too, with a wide firm mouth and eyes that stared straight in at one's own when he spoke.

Eric brought him round to Elfrida, greeted her himself, and then introduced Vickers.

Meyer said he never would forget her face when she saw him. He swore she gasped audibly and stared. Most people thought they had met before but they had not, not on this earth anyway. Vickers seemed a little surprised at first, Meyer said, but in a moment or so he was as smitten as she was. She had swept him off his feet entirely. He sat down opposite her and they began to talk, neither of them taking the slightest notice of anyone else in the crowded room. There was something so simple and natural about the way it happened, they just fell in love under everybody's nose as blatantly as they do in operas. An engagement was announced a week later and Elfrida was overwhelmed with callers and congratulations.

Louis Fyshe was peculiarly apprehensive when he heard the news and moved heaven and earth to get himself introduced to Vickers immediately. When he saw him he seemed relieved but surprised–almost wondering. He exchanged one or two words with him, congratulated them both and then went off sighing and smiling to himself–a poet and a hunchback.

More than probably, Elfrida did not notice him.

She was in love. Her great shapely body seemed on fire with it; her mouth and eyes, always proud, were prouder still. She positively seemed to grow under its influence, finally to unfold her last petals and show herself the perfect flower in its full pride. All the time he stood at her side, wondering at her, glorying in her while lesser men, his one-time rivals, stood round them envying and admiring.

The chapel was crammed at the wedding. When they came down the aisle after the ceremony those tears which are born of the sudden sight of great beauty started to many eyes. A man and his wife, the perfect match.

It was a wonderful idea to dress her in a white medieval gown with her tightly braided hair wound about her sleek head, for as she strode along at his side, her head held very high and her eyes alight with an almost haughty joy, she seemed, as Fyshe had said, a Northern Queen, a queen beside her king.

In full uniform and without a trace of nervousness he dominated her all the time–not too much so that any of her dignity or beauty was lost but just enough to make one realize she was the captive, he the captor.

'God let it happen to restore man's faith in the world as a world,' said Fyshe.

When they came back from the honeymoon they took a house just off Portman Square. They seemed to fascinate Fyshe, perhaps because they were so different from himself. Anyway, he used to haunt the place and whenever one dropped in he was sure to be there, squatting in some corner, peering out at the two of them with his bright bird's eyes.

They had a wonderful place there. It suited them and that meant something. Great wide rooms with mighty fireplaces, oak walls and fine pictures. Several Brangwyns, a John and a great battle-piece by an unknown. The furniture was extraordinary, they must have had it made for them. Great heavy oak pieces beautifully carved but weird and barbaric. When you saw her sweeping down the room in one of those plain tight-fitting gowns she affected, you had a curious feeling that you were visiting a twelfth century Danish queen at home.

It was Meyer who first pointed out that something was wrong between the two although Fyshe must have noticed it long before and kept silent.

Meyer said she was not happy, and furthermore, he said that Vickers was to blame. How, he did not say, because he knew no more than anyone else. Fyshe told the truth of it long after. He knew because he loved her and he used to sit and watch her struggling with herself and every pang she felt was echoed in him.

The crookback should have been a woman, the intuition he had.

Fyshe said she found him out three months after the honeymoon but that she managed to blind herself to it for a year after that.

Vickers was weak–horribly weak.

He had no special vices. He drank little, did not gamble, took no great interest in women. Yet there was no special virtue in him on that score, none of these things amused him. There was no greatness, no friendliness, no strength in the man; no warmth, no mental or spiritual life. He was small, weak, pitifully blind and narrow.

His body was the one really noble thing about him and that was magnificent. It would almost seem that his mind had been sacrificed to produce that body with its beauty, its strength, its utter largeness and perfection. In that alone he fitted her. As far as the rest went she might have married almost anyone else and fared better.

It broke Fyshe's heart to see her for she loved her husband. Loved him with a love which matched the rest of her. A mighty love, a whirling torrential sea of love which she poured out upon him with all the eagerness and generosity of her great heart.

An ordinary man might at least have withstood the flood and remained himself even if he lost her by it, a barbarian like herself could have matched it with his own and they two might have been carried by the force of their mutual loving to the farthest shores of their ambitions; but Vickers, a weak nature, went down before it like a sandcastle. Mentally and spiritually he was drowned in it.

Fyshe said that she refused to admit it to herself. Refused to realise that she had made a mistake, that she had not accomplished her ideal, that after all she had married a small, misfitting man. She clung to her ideal of him even when Vickers proved over and over again that he was nothing but the shell of a giant, that his heart and mind and soul were practically non-existent, and she steeled herself not to look in at him, and cheated herself and held her head high.

This went on for some time. Fyshe said it was terrible to see her.

Time after time she gave him chances to prove himself a man – little chances, little chances which woman-wise she engineered to give him an opportunity to restore her faith in his greatness and his strength, and every time, of course, Vickers let her down. He could not help it. He had to, he was but what he was.

She was patient; pathetically patient, and eager to find a lord and master in him if only he would let her.

Fyshe saw it all. He said he watched her fighting against the inevitable realisation like a fanatic fighting for his creed. It seemed, he said, as if she would not allow it to beat her. As the great waves of fact, made by the myriad drops of little things, beat themselves against her one after another, she refused to be crushed by them. It was her barbarism, as the poet said, it was her Northern barbarism which kept her so steadfastly blind.

She refused to accept her defeat. Refused to acknowledge the trick the gods had played upon her. She had set herself to conquer fate, to conquer fact, to disprove that which existed.

As the months passed the fight became harder. It seemed as if she must become convinced in spite of herself, but she fought on. And every day, so Fyshe said, she grew more and more of a wild thing, more and more beautiful and more and more barbaric.

Then it happened.

Fyshe told the story once years afterwards. There were four of them in his dusty study and his husky drawl sounded strained and emotional in the warm, smoke-misted room.

'He died of pneumonia, you know,' he said, 'eighteen months after they were married and she mourned him faithfully and passionately. I came into the room at just that moment when he reached the crisis and gradually took the turn for the worse which killed him.'

He paused deliberately and relit his pipe but no one spoke and presently he went on again.

'He was very ill and I visited them so often that I used to go in and out as I pleased. I knew when I entered that day that Vickers had been practically at death's door, although I had heard the doctor say that so long as nothing untoward happened such as a draught catching him or the fire going out, he might be expected to recover. I had really gone along to congratulate her on this and I pushed open the door quietly, expecting to be met by a rush of warm, sick-room air. There were curtains hung across the corner where the door was so that no sudden draught could possibly reach the bed. These curtains were thick heavy things, weighted at the ends, yet as I came in they were swaying to and fro. I shut the door quickly, frightened for a moment that I had let in the draught and then I went forward and pulled aside the curtains.

'Vickers lay in the bed hardly breathing, the bedclothes thrown clear of his great chest and neck, while a current of cold rain-soaked air rushed in upon him from the open window. Elfrida was in the room. She stood with her back to me staring out across the square. Her straight back was stiff as a soldier's and her head was held high and defiant.'

His voice stopped and they sat round and stared at him. He backed farther into his chair and hugged his knee.

'You—you went out without speaking,' said someone, and his voice sounded strident and unnatural.

'Yes,' said Fyshe. 'Without speaking, without a sound. She never knew I came.'

There was another pause, then he said: 'The next time I saw her was at the funeral. I daresay you remember it, an extraordinary—a wonderful affair.'

His voice sank to a whisper as he remembered the majesty of it and he rocked backwards and forwards, a grotesque figure in the big chair.

'It was barbaric though,' he went on suddenly. 'It horrified some people. They called it vulgar—ostentatious—but it wasn't, it was magnificent. It was beautiful, sombre, terrible—the funeral of a god. The great house dismantled—the open coffin—the gorgeous pall—it was all majestic, Northern, and, as I said, barbaric. Some fools who didn't understand her blamed her for it—they said she made a show of Death. I could have killed them. If Elfrida made a show, she made it for the honour of the dead and from no petty, horrible thought of personal glorification. She would not understand such reasoning. She mourned him at the funeral, and she mourned him ever afterwards—her husband, the man she married. Her grief was terrible, freezing, petrifying grief and it was sincere —no woman loved more than Elfrida, no woman grieved more deeply.'

'I don't see how you make that out,' said Meyer, 'if as you say she—'

Fyshe interrupted him.

'Her grief is sincere,' he said, and his black eyes flashed, 'she mourns her husband, the man she married. If she had allowed herself to think clearly she would have mourned him a week after her marriage: as it was however, his body had to die before she could allow herself to see that he was dead.'

'Or that he never existed!'

Fyshe smiled curiously.

'Not exactly,' he said, 'for from the day she first saw him—he existed—for her. Oh, her grief was sincere, as sincere as her love was. When I went up to her that day, where she sat in the great dim room with the solemn preparations for that mighty funeral going on around us, she looked up at me and I saw in her face a depth of sorrow so deep, so majestic and awful that it struck me dumb, and made me feel I was a little soul incapable of feeling a tenth so much. I mumbled something about Vickers at last and her eyes darkened a little. Then she sighed and looked steadily and honestly into my eyes.

'"He was a king of men," she said, "my husband".' Fyshe finished speaking. There was a stir among his listeners and then Meyer spoke again. 'I don't see,' he said obstinately. 'She must have been a hypocrite, Fyshe, she killed him—'

'Killed him!' The hunchback poet crouched forward in his chair and stared at the other man in fierce exasperation. 'No, she didn't kill him, Meyer,' he said. 'Don't you understand—she gave him birth!'

Mr Campion's
Lucky Day

WHEN Mr Albert Campion arrived at the luxury flat,
Detective Inspector Stanislaus Oates had just reached the
unwelcome conclusion that Chippy Figg was not, after all,
guilty of the murder of the man in the sitting-room.

Chippy, who was fidgeting in the kitchenette, his peaky face
yellow with anxiety, had been saying so for some time.

'I was with me auntie all the evening,' he was protesting, as
Campion, an ineffable glow of well-being about him, appeared
in the doorway. 'She'll swear to it, auntie will.'

'I don't doubt it, my lad,' said Oates gloomily. He turned and
caught sight of the slender newcomer in the horn-rimmed spectacles. 'Oh hallo, Campion, glad to see you. Come over here, will
you? There's nothing to grin about, let me tell you.' Taking his
old friend by the elbow, he pushed him firmly across the wide
passage, now crowded with officials, to the sitting-room. As the
door of the brilliantly lit apartment closed behind them his
exasperation boiled over. 'Ten minutes ago I had a pretty little
open-and-shut case to show you, yet the moment you come
beaming into it it turns sour on me.'

The smile had vanished from Mr Campion's face as his eyes
took in the scene. He stood looking down at the heavy figure of a
middle-aged man, bald and running badly to fat, which sprawled
over the desk before the curtained window.

'Nothing exactly decorative about this,' he observed grimly.
'Shot?'

'Yes. From the doorway. Death instantaneous. He's the owner
of the flat and lived alone here.'

'I see. Our friend in the purple suit didn't do it.'

'Chippy. No. Couldn't have. That's the devil of it. Constable
Richards, who lives next door to Chippy's aunt and who over-

looks her lighted kitchen from his back door, gives him an alibi.'
He paused. 'Look Campion, consider this. It's now midnight.
Two hours ago we were called in by a doctor who lives in the
apartment above this one. He–'

Mr Campion coughed. 'Introduce me to the corpse.'

'Well–' Oates hesitated, '–his name was Fane and he wasn't
pleasant. He made money on the turf and more in ways less
orthodox.'

'Blacking merchant?'

'No evidence to date but considerable suspicion.'

'Dear me,' said Mr Campion mildly. 'Continue with the
doctor.'

'He phoned at ten and his story is quite straightforward. He
knew Fane slightly and came in here at a quarter to six to give
him a draught for a violent headache. Fane refused to go to bed
because he was expecting Figg. The doctor left in time to reach
a cocktail party some distance away at six.'

'Did the doctor know Figg?'

'Slightly. The whole block did. He's a colourful figure who
always called on Fane on Thursday nights. He does quite a lot of
bookmaking.'

'Any more on Figg?'

'A little. Last week the two quarrelled and were heard all over
the building. Tonight, while the doctor was at the Eclipse
Sporting Club, he received a mysterious message on the phone
in a cockney accent telling him to go to Fane quickly. He hurried
back to find this door on the latch and Fane lying as you see him,
still warm, the radio going full blast.'

Campion eyed the set. 'Powerful?' he inquired.

'Terrific. The couple below say it was roaring from ten minutes
to six until the doctor turned it off after he found Fane. No one
could have noticed the shot above the row.'

'Depressing neighbour. Anyone see anything?'

'No. The porter says he saw no visitors but he's been in and out
of the hall and might have missed anyone. It seemed certain that

Figg had slipped by him, but, as you heard, his alibi is perfect. He didn't arrive until after we did.'

'Lucky chap. Can I see the doctor?'

'Of course. He's still in his flat upstairs. I doubt if he can add to what he's said already.'

Campion said nothing and was still silent when the doctor came bustling in a few minutes later.

'I admit I did not know him well,' he said waving at the dead man, 'but it was a shock, you know, a considerable shock. Poor fellow, he was still warm when I found him, but there wasn't a hope.'

'No,' said Campion, 'not with a bullet through his heart. Tell me, doctor, have you a large practice here?'

'None at all. I've retired.' The man seemed put out. 'I thought I made that clear. No, a G.P.'s life is too arduous for me, I'm afraid. I gave up medicine six years ago. Did you get hold of Figg, Inspector?'

'Yes, but the man has an alibi.'

'An alibi? But I could have sworn I . . .' The doctor bit back the words but Oates seized on them.

'You were going to say you recognised his voice on the phone.'

'No, no, I can't be as explicit as that but I must admit that at the time it went through my mind that the voice resembled—Good Heavens, sir!'

The final exclamation was addressed to Campion, who had suddenly moved forward and, exerting all his strength, pulled the body up off the desk.

The sight was terrible. The entire corpse moved in one solid mass, the knees remaining bent, the head thrust out stiffly.

'Rigor very well advanced,' muttered Mr Campion, a little breathless from the exertion.

'Good lord, yes. Much more so than I had expected.' The doctor's eyes had widened. 'It does happen, of course I've known it to be instantaneous. Cadaveric spasm, we call it. In this case . . .'

He got no further. Campion had released his hold on the body allowing it to return to its original position. In his other hand was a sheet of paper torn from the scribbling pad which was covered with figures. It had lain hidden under the dead man's head. When he looked up his eyes were hard. 'How much did you owe him, doctor?' he inquired softly. 'He was putting on the pressure, I suppose? What did you do with the revolver? Leave it at the club?'

'This is a monstrous accusation, sir. My solicitor . . .'

'Really, Campion . . .' Oates began nervously.

Campion's voice silenced him. 'Fane has got you, doctor. You may have shot him but he'll convict you–with this.'

He held the paper out to Oates who snatched it. The doctor stared at it over his arm.

'It's only a list of his day's winnings,' he said angrily. 'There's no proof of anything here.'

Campion's thin forefinger pointed to a single item: 4.30 Iron Ore won 6–4 £133.6.8.

Oates raised worried eyes. 'I don't get it,' he said. 'What are you driving at?'

'Iron Ore didn't win,' said Mr Campion. 'It passed the post first, and was credited with a win in the stop press of the afternoon editions but there was a spot of bumping and an objection was sustained. This was announced on the sports news. If Fane was sitting here with the radio going at six o'clock he could hardly have missed it unless . . .'

'Unless?'

'Unless he was dead by then. The doctor says himself he saw him at ten minutes to six–quick, Oates!'

He sprang after the flying figure of the doctor who eluded him only to crash into a couple of constables in the vestibule.

In the excitement Mr Figg, ever an opportunist, quietly took his leave.

Later the Detective Inspector looked round for Mr Campion. He found him sleeping peacefully in the bedroom with such a beatific smile on his face that Oates took pleasure in waking him. 'How did you do that?' he demanded.

Campion yawned. 'Doctor's evidence,' he said. 'What man

with a headache sits by a blaring radio? Besides, a cadaveric spasm, as you know, is instantaneous. The doctor did not notice it when he found the body therefore it was ordinary rigor which takes some hours to develop.'

Oates laughed. 'Fair enough, but I still call it luck,' he said. 'You just happened to know the details of that race. It's your lucky day.'

Mr Campion's smile broadened. 'I couldn't agree with you more,' he murmured. 'I had a tenner on the second horse. That was how I knew.'

Oates grunted. 'Long odds?'

'Fifty to one.'

'Good lord, what's its name?'

'Amateur,' whispered Mr Campion. 'That was why I came to back it. I'm not a betting man.'

'Tis Not Hereafter

WHEN I was sent out to the small house on the marsh to look for the ghost there, I went stolidly and uncomplainingly, as is my nature.

I was an ugly, over-energetic little beast in my late teens, and had just begun to realize that my chosen profession of journalism was not the elegant mixture of the diplomatic service and theatrical criticism which my careers mistress had led me to suppose.

The general direction in which the house lay was pointed out by the postmaster of the most forlorn village ever to have graced the Essex coast. He stood leaning over a narrow counter with a surface like cracked toffee and shook his head at me warningly.

'That's no place for a young lady,' he said. 'That's a terrible funny place down there. You don't want to go there.'

It was encouraging to hear that the house on the marsh not only existed but that there was something definitely odd about it.

Our editor was a difficult man whose pet maxim was 'If you hear something, go and tear its guts out.'

His present story sounded unhappily vague. Someone, he said, had come to him at the Thatcher's Arms in the High-street and told him of a terrorised village which was in a state of near panic because of a ghastly white face, a woman's face, which had appeared at the window of a lonely house on the marsh. It was my duty to go and bring back the ghost or its story.

'It's great,' he said. 'Most important thing that's happened down here since the municipal election. Go and thrash it out. They'll all be on it.'

By 'all' he meant our rival, the *Weekly Gazette*, with offices a little lower down the town. I rather hoped they would. Bill Ferguson, their junior, was a friend of mine and I had looked out for him on the road. However, he had not appeared and I had been depressed at the prospect of unearthing yet another mare's nest when the postmaster had raised my hopes.

'I want to see the ghost,' I said cheerfully. 'Who's seen it so far?'

'There's a lot on 'em seen it,' he confessed unexpectedly. 'That's a proper vision.'

I got out my notebook.

'Who's seen it? Who can I talk to?'

'They'll be out at work now,' he said. 'Best wait till tea-time. They'll be home just after five.'

I looked out through the cluttered window at the sky. It was getting on for four o'clock and as grey and bitter as only a February day on the marsh can be.

'I'd better see the house now and get the stories when I come back,' I said. 'What's the tale about the house? Why should it be haunted?'

He eyed me thoughtfully.

'There was a shootin' down there years ago,' he said. 'Likely that's it.'

'Very likely,' I agreed blithely. 'Who was it?'

He was vague, however. At first it looked as though he was hiding something but at last it became obvious that he actually knew very little.

'There was a young couple took it from London,' he said. 'The lady she got herself drownded and the man 'e shot hisself. Now she's come back and sets peerin' out the window. You don't want to go down there, I keep tellin' you.'

'I do,' I said. 'Who were these people? When did it happen?'

The postmaster sighed.

'That I couldn't say. Afore my time. I ain't been here above twenty years. Ah, that's a dreadful tumble-down sort of a place!'

In the end he directed me. He was not actively against my going; merely passively disapproving.

I drove down that chill, windswept little street to the point where the road suddenly ceased to be a road and became a waterlogged cart-track, and where a decrepit gate barred my path. I left my car since it was impractical to take it farther, and set out over the saltings on foot.

The house came into view after about half a mile of cold and uncomfortable walking. It sat huddled up on a piece of high ground, a miserable wooden shack of a place with a brick chimney leaning crazily on one side. At the big spring tides it must have been surrounded and, having a simple gregarious nature, I felt I understood the young woman who had drowned herself rather than live in it.

It was still some considerable distance away, and I plodded on, hoping with cheerful idiocy to see something pretty grisly in the way of spectres for my trouble.

It is hard to say at what particular moment I suddenly became afraid. Alarm settled down on me like a mist, and I was aware of feeling cold and a little sick long before I realised what it was. I think I must have recognised fear at the instant that I came near enough to the house to see the details of those two upper windows which peered out at me like dreadful dead eyes under the rakish billycock hat of a roof.

I remember pulling myself together irritably and then staring round aghast at that wide, desolate world of cold grey sea and marsh and sky.

The sight of the man struggling along behind me restored my balance. The sober earth returned to me, and with it a rush of relief. I was not alone. The human race had not miraculously died out in half an hour. I stood hesitating.

It was not Bill. The newcomer was not a labourer nor a fisherman. I saw his short raincoat with satisfaction. Here, no doubt, was the rest of the Press.

I shouted at him, my voice sounding very small and shrill in the cold emptiness.

'Hullo!' I bellowed. 'You from the *Gazette*? Come to see the ghost?'

He shouted back but I did not catch the words. His voice, too, was caught up and dispersed in the void. I heard scraps of it, unrelated notes, before it was sucked upward and devoured in that hungry air.

As he came closer I saw that he was a pale, ineffectual young man, hatless and with fair hair. His coat was buttoned up to his chin and he was blue with cold.

'Well, there's the house,' I said as he came up.

He nodded and surveyed the decrepit cottage, which looked more shabby and less horrific now that I was not facing it alone.

I glanced at the sky.

'If we're going to burgle the place by daylight we'd better hurry,' I said. 'At first this whole thing sounded like a cock-and-bull story but down in the village they seem to have seen something.'

'Yes,' he said and regarded me with unhappy pale grey eyes. 'I've heard them talking. They've seen a woman in a sun-bonnet.'

'A sun-bonnet?' That was something new to me and I felt a momentary resentment against my friend the postmaster. 'I'm glad she needs it,' I said facetiously.

He did not smile.

'It's hot down here in the summer; just as hot as it's cold now. There's no shade anywhere.'

The thought seemed to depress him and we ploughed on towards the house. The nearer I came to the place the more scared I grew. It was not a blind, exciting terror; rather a cold suffocating sense of disaster and frustration and despair.

I glanced at my companion and thought he must have experienced much the same reaction, for he looked wretched, and his teeth chattered slightly. The sight of his alarm gave me courage and amused me. It was a natural feminine desire to show off. I struggled against my terror and became almost hearty.

'I'm glad it's a woman,' I said foolishly. 'She's more likely to be at home. There was a tragedy down here some years ago. You've heard all that, I suppose?'

'Oh yes,' he said. 'I know what happened. But I don't see why the woman should come back. It was the man who had hell down here.'

'Ah,' I said complacently, 'that's what you think because you're a man. It's the woman who always feels things most. She's come back to look for the boy friend, of course.'

'Do you think so?' he said and looked so soft and sentimental that I began to lose interest in him. The discovery that he was dopy made him seem less useful as an ally and the cold began to creep up and down my spine again.

We had reached the high ground by this time and we made our ascent to that horrible cottage in silence. There was no need to climb in through the windows. The door hung crazily on one hinge and when I pushed it it clattered back with a noise that sounded like an explosion in that damp, silent greyness.

My colleague hung back.

'I don't want to go in,' he said.

There was more than repugnance in his voice. It rose on to a note of pure terror and combined with my own unreasoning alarm to make me thoroughly irritable. I regarded him coldly.

'Do what you like,' I said, and added with unpardonable priggishness, 'if you want to do your job properly you'll search the house with me.'

I stood, half in, half out, of the little brick-floored hall.

There were two rooms downstairs, a kitchen and a parlour. A flight of stairs led up between them. From where I stood I could see the ground floor was deserted.

I looked at the rickety stairs, and then at the man.

'Coming?' I demanded.

He went to pieces rather horribly. His face began to work.

'I'm sorry,' he gasped. 'I can't. I can't. I don't want to see . . . anything.'

Leaving him I clattered up the stairs making as much noise as my shoes would let me.

The two little rooms under the roof were empty and I was glad of it. They were dry and airy, too, which was queer, and they had an odd lived-in feeling. Downstairs the place was like a tomb. Up here it was almost pleasant. I stood listening.

I thought I heard someone breathing. It was a beastly delusion and I was afraid again. There was a cupboard in one room, but I did not open it. I went back to the staircase.

Something on the top step caught my eye and I stooped to retrieve it. Then I fled.

He was waiting for me, his face pale and blue with cold and his hands deep in his pockets. Now that the ordeal was over I was inclined to swagger.

He stood staring at me with a forlorn weariness on his face.

'Nothing there?' he said, and he seemed disappointed. 'No beautiful girl in a sun-bonnet and leg-o'-mutton sleeves?'

'Nothing at all,' I insisted.

He did not seem to hear me. He was looking back at the cottage and his face was twisted and disappointed. He stared so fixedly that I turned myself and looked up.

Then I screamed.

The face at the upper window was surrounded by a faded lavender sun-bonnet, the crumpled streamers hanging limply beside that pale and sunken countenance. The woman looked straight at me. I saw her eyes.

'Come,' I said hoarsely. 'Come.' And I gripped the little thing I had picked up on the stairs.

It was a moment of panic, but I saw him hanging back, his face drawn and puckered like a child's, and I remember his idiotic remark, so completely foolish in the circumstances.

'She's old,' he said. 'Oh, my God, she's old!'

I left him. I dashed into the house, raced up the stairs, and jerked open the cupboard door in the second bedroom. An old woman crouched in the corner and remained quite still as if she were invisible.

I pulled her out violently.

'I knew you were real,' I spluttered. 'I knew it. I found a new hairpin on the stairs and I knew a real woman had been here. What are you doing? What are you doing, frightening people?'

She looked up at me and began to cry, and I was ashamed of

myself. She was so little and old and faded. She looked silly, too, in a rough tweed coat and skirt, with the ridiculous sun-bonnet perched on her sparse grey curls.

'I didn't mean to frighten anyone,' she said in a thin little voice. 'I'm so sorry. Oh, dear, I've been so silly, and now I shall be late for tea. Miss Fell does get so cross if we're late for tea.'

I pricked up my ears. I knew Miss Fell. She kept a guest house on the other side of the marsh and did a lot of entertaining in the summer.

'Are you staying at Fairview?' I demanded.

'I used to live here long ago,' she said. 'At least, I once came on a holiday here, and last month I suddenly made up my mind to come and see the old place again. I took rooms with Miss Fell and I've been walking up here in the afternoons. I'm so sorry if I've frightened people. I had to see the house again. I was happy here for a little while, and then–I wasn't.'

I looked down at her. She was very small and had once been pretty in a fluffy, unintelligent way. It was then that I had one of my rare flashes of insight.

'So you weren't drowned?' I said.

She gave me a single frightened glance.

'Don't tell anyone,' she whispered. 'No, I ran away. I was a silly, melodramatic girl. I left my scarf and my hat on the sea wall and I walked to Burbridge and went back to London. I was so young. We were both so very young. I never dreamed that he– poor, poor boy!

'We came down here to live on love and pennies when I was nineteen and he was twenty-two,' she went on softly. 'We thought we'd live on the edge of the world together and be happy. He was happy, but I couldn't bear it after a while, it wasn't what I'd been used to and I dared not tell him. I didn't want to break his illusion, you see, so I did the silly thing I did do. I ran away and pretended to be drowned. My cousin took me in and hushed it up. We never told, even when it came out in the papers that he had–'

'Shot himself?' I asked brutally.

'Yes,' she whispered, and shut her eyes. 'Poor boy, he was so gentle, so romantic, so much in love.'

I went over to the window. The marsh lay wild and sad and lonely in front of me. Presently I turned to her. She was so old, so pathetic, so helpless. I felt very cross with her.

'Look here,' I said, 'you mustn't come here again.'

'Oh, no–no, I won't. I do promise that.'

I felt silly.

'You can come, I suppose,' I said. 'Anybody can; but you mustn't peer out of the window in a sun-bonnet, because you're terrifying people. You used to wear the sun-bonnet here then, did you?'

Her lips quivered.

'He liked it,' she said. 'He said it made me look so charming. Oh, dear, I have been silly. Suppose people find out? Suppose it gets in the papers?'

'You won't be able to keep it a secret,' I said. 'There's that man downstairs as well as–'

She interrupted me.

'What man is that?'

'I think he's from the *Gazette*,' I said. 'He wouldn't come into the house. He's the man I was with when you looked out of the window at me.'

She stepped back from me and I saw fear in her eyes.

'You were alone,' she said. 'I saw you talking to someone, but no one was there. That's why I stared at you. You were quite alone.'

Her stupidity infuriated me.

'Don't be silly,' I said. 'He was a boy, really. Tall and thin, with fair hair and a pale face, and a raincoat buttoned up to his chin.'

I got no further. I saw the horror grow in her eyes and in her little wizened birdlike face.

'He came,' she said, huskily. 'He came.'

There was a long pause in which the world heeled over and those dreadful poignant words came back to me: 'Why should the woman come? It was the man who had hell here.'

The little old lady plucked my sleeve. Her face was trembling. 'Did he see me?' she said. 'Did he see me?'

I looked her full in the face and lied.

'No,' I said shakily. 'No. Come along. You'll be late for tea.'

The Correspondents

IN the 'eighties of the last century, when Robert Braine was a divinity student at Cambridge, Philip Dell was the only other person in the world who recognised him as a hero.

The two men parted one June day on the long, miserable station at the foot of the hill and never saw each other again, yet their curious relationship persisted for the rest of their long lives.

When Philip was ordained Robert wrote him from Paris and, doubtless because of the gravity of the occasion, forbore to give more than a hint of his own doings, which even so seemed to have a slightly romantic and worldly flavour.

But when Philip wrote a couple of years later to his friend's home address in Wiltshire, saying that his brief curacy in the north of London was at an end and that he had been offered a remote living in the Norfolk marshes, he received a longer and more enlightening letter in return a month or two afterwards.

In his own note Philip had shyly mentioned his approaching marriage.

'Dorothy is a dear, gentle girl who has been leading our choir,' he had written, his neat hand and precise vocabulary betraying nothing of the tremendous emotional upheaval of his heart.

> 'I have talked to her earnestly and have warned her of the dullness, and what I fear may sometimes even be the real hardship of our new life in a vast, draughty vicarage with none of the amenities of present-day civilisation, but she, dear sweet creature that she is, is prepared to go through it all for my sake.'

Robert's letter arrived when the Dells had settled down in their marshland fastness twenty miles from a railway station and as far from the world as if they had gone missioning to China.

'I like your wife's name,' he wrote, 'and I trust you will give her my sincere regards. Forgive me if I say I admire your courage. Frankly, the idea of marriage terrifies me. If you lived my life, my dear fellow, you'd understand me. I almost hesitate to tell you about myself, indeed to a certain extent I am afraid I may not, for the particular branch of the service to which I now belong is devilish secretive.

'You will probably be astonished to hear that I have been living in a humble part of Berlin for the past six months and am off to Belgrade in a day or so.

'When I was in Germany the exigencies of my profession decreed that I should become for the time being a baker in the employ of a certain peculiarly interesting restaurateur, but in my leisure hours, which were damnably few, believe me, I used to revert to my normal character and mingle with more congenial society.

'I met Irna in the house of a certain Baroness and danced with her whenever I got the chance, for beauties of her calibre do not blossom under our leaden skies, believe me. Just at the moment when I was beginning to lose my sleep over the girl, her fiancé, an insufferable Prussian in the Imperial Guard, had the disastrous notion of following me home when I left the ball given in honour of Beaconsfield, who was over for the conference. Imagine my discomfiture when he walked into the bakehouse and found me up to the elbows in dough, utterly incapable of making the true explanation.

'That was the end of that romance. For a while I was heartbroken, but I gradually came to realise my Heaven-sent escape. I think little Greta, the laundress, may have helped matters, but you are a full-fledged parson now so I won't tell you about her.'

Mrs Dell read the letter after her husband and blushed at it.

'An odious man,' she said. 'I can't believe he was ever a great friend of yours.'

'He not only was, but still is, my love.' Philip spoke with that mild obstinacy which grew on him in later years. 'He was an extraordinary fellow, and remains so, it appears. A man like Robert was destined to have adventures. We mustn't let ourselves get narrow down here. A man in the Secret Service has demands made upon him which are much greater than those put upon the ordinary stick-in-the-mud, like myself. A certain worldliness in Robert is inevitable.'

'A stick-in-the-mud?' Dorothy looked at her husband sharply, and her grey eyes were hurt and dubious. 'I thought this was to be our great adventure, Philip?'

The Vicar of Pelham Wick swept aside the accounts of the Industrious Ladies' Guild which littered his desk and took his wife in his arms.

'I was speaking loosely, my dear,' he said. 'For me this life of ours is a tremendous adventure, the only great adventure I could ever have.'

And then because he was an honest man, albeit a tactful one, he added under his breath:

'But I am not Robert and never shall be.'

Philip replied to Robert's letter in due course. He sent it to the old Wiltshire address and marked it 'Please forward'. He wrote very simply, trying to keep any disloyal note of envy out of his quiet paragraphs.

'My dear fellow,' he wrote, 'I enjoyed your letter. It brought a dash of colour into this placid close. I hardly know what to tell you in return. My cat has built herself a nest like a starling twenty feet up in the ivy on the church and it took three of us–Tom, my gardener; George, the churchwarden; and myself–to get her and her family to safety. There we were, risking our necks and trembling with conscious heroism, while my wife stood below covering her eyes lest one of the tabby babes should fall to destruction. This is the kind of excitement I get down here.

'However, everything is relative.

'My wife and I see very little company, which is perhaps just as well just now.'

Philip hesitated long over this final sentence, his delicacy fighting with his great pride and the secret emotional triumph which was consuming him. In the end he left it as it was, remembering that Dorothy was sensitive.

Robert's reply arrived nearly two years later.

'What a mad world it is!' he wrote on the thin foreign paper whose crackling sheets brought the very stuff of romance into the shabby vicarage dining-room.

'I am in Paris.

'A most extraordinary thing happened to me. I met Irna again. She is now calling herself Ernestine and is the wife of a man who bids fair to make a name for himself in French politics. Apparently my famous bakery escapade put a stop to her projected marriage with the insufferable young Guardee and I was a little apprehensive at first because I had already heard most of the story.

'However, she soon put me at my ease and actually thanked me for my share in the business. I must confess I find her charming. I danced with her at the Imperial Russian Embassy last night and could not help noticing that there was not a man in the room who did not envy me.

'Her husband is clever but too old for her. He is the typical bourgeois politician, gross, palefaced and volatile. I saw him glance at her once or twice last night and I wondered.

'Later. Wiltshire.

'I put away this note meaning to finish it in a day or so, but much water has flowed under the bridge since then—rather dirty water some of it, I am afraid. I hope I am not going to shock you by this chapter in my chronicles, but you must regard yourself as my father-confessor. Well, as you may imagine, I saw a great deal of Madame Ernestine in the days immediately following our dance, and at last, as seemed inevitable when we met, she softened noticeably towards me and I heard the true story of her monstrous marriage.

'The man was a brute and he submitted her to such treatment as I will not harrow you by recounting. I was more than sorry for her and I may have been a little indiscreet in my attentions, but at any rate you may be assured I did nothing to merit the astonishing behaviour of the husband.

'He insulted me in a public place in front of a great many of my more distinguished friends, thus forcing me to retaliate, and before I knew what had happened I found myself with a duel on my hands!

'This was a fair, if at first a slightly ridiculous, business, and, God forgive me, I was inclined to treat the whole thing as a thundering lark, but I was not so lighthearted, believe me, when my shot pierced the fellow's chest and he collapsed dying in his seconds' arms.

'The whole thing was hushed up as much as possible, thanks to my distinguished associates, but I had to get out of the country as quickly as I could and I received a severe wigging from my superior officers in London.

'I am now rushing off to St Petersburg as a penance. I heard nothing from Ernestine and can get no word from her. If you can bring yourself to reply to such a rapscallion, write to my brother's address and he will send on all letters.'

Philip thought it prudent to conceal Robert's communication from Dorothy, but he read it several times himself, for he was still a young man.

He wrote back the following spring when he was happier.

'We have a son,' he stated baldly in the midst of a spate of gentle meanderings about his work, the weather and his beloved countryfolk. 'I have called him Philip Nathaniel Henry Robert. Our first baby, also a son, died six hours after birth.'

It was the shortest paragraph in the letter and told nothing of the intense emotional drama of that mercifully far-off night twenty-two months before when the dark garden had flickered with the uncertain light of hurricane lanterns bobbing to and fro from the gate, and there had been hushed voices and low, heart-rending sounds in the creaky old house.

On that occasion the doctor's gig had remained in the stable yard until the grey morning had come, bringing bitterness and disillusion and despair with it.

For a considerable time there was no reply from Robert the elder, but one day a long parcel arrived containing a very fine ivory-headed cane pierced for a tassel, and with a card bearing the inscription '*For Robert the Younger with his reprobate Uncle's love.*'

There was also a brief note for Philip.

> 'The enclosed stick was given me by the lineal descendant of René de Chevreuse, Duc de Pouilly, whose ancestor had it as a gift from Louis XVI. I did him a trifling service in Beauvais and he insisted that I took it. It was his dearest possession.'

Philip wrote a suitable letter of thanks and hung the stick on the drawing-room wall, where it remained, an object of the deepest veneration, for over thirty years, lending a touch of romantic enchantment to an otherwise prosaic if comfortable room.

From these beginnings the correspondence continued a leisurely course down the years. Philip's letters remained gentle, pleasant chronicles of a quiet, useful life unstirred by any remarkable occurrence. In his hands even the sensational affair at Cherry's farm, which began with a double murder and ended with a conviction and a hanging, became a balanced, brief account of a rustic tragedy.

And that much more personal disaster, the death of old George, the churchwarden, in the early days of War, which ended a deep friendship and saddened the blossom whiteness of the spring for ever for the Vicar of Pelham Wick, was never mentioned at all.

Robert, on the other hand, made his colourful experiences live. As the years went on he became a legendary figure.

Ernestine, too, became a heroine. Her daughter turned up in wartime Paris and was miraculously saved from death as a spy by the intercession of her mother and the influence of Robert himself. His youth and vigour were perennial.

The last letter from Robert to reach the Vicarage arrived ten years later. It had all the old fire, if also some of the old floridness of style which the writer had never bothered himself to correct.

'The bad penny turns up once more,' he wrote happily, 'looking a great deal the worse for wear, I am afraid, but still as sound as ever, thank God. I am writing this in the train coming home from Geneva.

'My travels this time have taken me to Palestine, Rome and Prague, where I think I can truthfully say I did useful work—although my Viennese experience was perhaps not quite so satisfactory, if I must be honest. Still, I got around and shall be off to Washington in a week or two. Not bad for an old 'un, eh?

'I called at Juan-les-Pins on my way out and had a few days with Ernestine in her lovely villa. I lost my heart to her once more. Even at sixty-five she is lovely. And although I did not approve of the greasy-haired young puppies who console her widowhood (her third husband the Comte del Montator died two years ago, as I may have told you), I found her a stimulating companion. What gaiety! What youth!

'She was kind enough to say she still thought of me as a young man, and, God bless her, I believe she does.

'When I left her I found myself strangely dissatisfied with my life. Perhaps I should have settled down. I have lived, yet what have I now? No honours, no fortune, no companion for my age. Only my magnificent memories. Still, in my normal moments these suffice me. I said I had lived; I have, you know.'

Three months after this, and before Philip had found time to reply, a telegram from Wiltshire arrived.

'*Robert Braine sinking*,' it said briefly. '*Would greatly appreciate it if you could come*.' And it was signed '*Ernestine*'.

The news struck a note of flat calamity, such as had not been sounded at the Vicarage of Pelham Wick for many years. The hero was dying. It was the end of an era, the passing of Romance.

As Philip stood helplessly by, watching Dorothy packing his necessities, he found that he was reacting to the emergency in an unusual way. Robert's dying affected him as his living had done. Philip had not been to London for ten years, and never to Wiltshire, and he contemplated the journey now with excitement.

Nor was this the cold, blank sense of loss that old George's death had brought with it. Robert's death was high tragedy: two friends parted for a lifetime, but still friends and united at a death-bed. It was poignant, almost exhilarating.

As Dorothy fastened the suitcase her eyes were shining.

'I'm glad *she* went to him,' she said.

'Ah, Ernestine,' said Philip softly and shook his head.

All through the long confusing journey, with its terrifying passage through the City, he thought of Robert and he was ashamed of himself for being so old. Two years of Robert's memories would fill a column: his own life might be written in a chapter.

It was dark when he arrived at the small country railway station and the grim-faced youth who met him explained that there was very little time. After a terrifying ride, he climbed out on to a moss-grown drive and walked up two shallow steps to an old elm door, which stood open.

As he stood hesitating a light flickered at the far end of the stone hall and an old woman came forward, an oil lamp held high over her head.

'Mr Dell?' she said in a harsh, respectful voice with a country twang in it. 'Will you come in here, please, sir?'

He followed her into a dusty study and she set the lamp down on a table. She was a tall, gaunt woman and her manner was authoritative, after the way of very old servants.

'I didn't like to tell you at the door, sir,' she said, 'but he's gone. He dropped off an hour ago.'

Philip nodded. It seemed he had expected the news. Yet he was conscious of a sense of deep disappointment. Robert was gone. The dramatic reunion was not to be. The elderly housekeeper insisted on taking him upstairs to the big overcrowded bedroom where books, ornaments and little wicker tables besieged an enormous patriarchal bed.

The old man who sat beside it rose respectfully as they entered and the woman glanced at Philip.

'This is my husband, sir,' she said. 'We've looked after the poor Master for fifty years.'

Philip was puzzled.

'I only knew Mr Robert,' he said. 'I never met his brother.'

'That would be Mr Richard,' observed the housekeeper placidly. 'He died when I was a girl. Mr Robert's been what you might call a recluse all his life. I don't think he's been outside the garden these twenty years. We took the liberty of sending for you, sir, because you were the only person he ever wrote to. He was a wonderful, quiet, thoughtful man, were Mr Robert. He'd take the services at one time, but when the curate came he retired, as you might say.'

Philip stood very still.

'Was Mr Robert the vicar of the parish?' he inquired unsteadily.

The woman blinked at him.

'Why, o' course he were, sir,' she said. 'Just like his father and grandfather were before him. They were all wonderful retiring gentlemen. Never took but little interest in the parish. It was always as if their thoughts were far away. And Mr Robert he was just the same.'

A great inspiration came to Philip.

'You,' he said to the woman, 'you are Ernestine?'

'Yes, sir,' she said primly. 'My surname was Ernest and the Master's mother thought it unsuitable for a woman, so she called me Irna in the German fashion, and afterwards the Master changed it to Ernestine. When I married John here we'd all got used to it ... Would you care to see the Master's face, sir? He were a very old man.'

'No,' said Philip suddenly. 'No. I'd rather think of him as I remember him.'

The old servants bowed to his very natural request.

Dorothy came to meet Philip at Norwich station.

'How tragic missing him after all,' she said. 'Still, I'm so glad you went, dear. Tell me, did you see Ernestine?'

To the best of his knowledge Philip had never told a direct lie in his life, but truth is a graceful mistress, capable of many disguises.

'Yes,' he said softly. 'I saw her. Only for a moment. She went away almost as soon as I recognised her.'

'What was she like?'

Dorothy's old eyes were bright and childlike in her excitement. Philip put his thin arm round her.

'A creature of romance,' he said, 'but not the type who could ever have satisfied me.'

He Preferred Them Sad

OF all the unpleasant people I have ever met I think Mr Walter Cough took the ultimate palm for downright greasy villainy.

I met him years ago in the days when I was earning a precarious living along with a crowd of other art-students in a nest of picturesque, but draughty, studio rooms overlooking the Bayswater Canal.

We had a joint agent at that time, a lazy, pink-faced young man as impecunious as we were. When one barren Friday he dropped in to say that if I would design a letter heading incorporating four angels, a couple of cornucopias, a mountain or so, and the title of a certain company in Old English caps, and take my sketch to Mr Walter Cough, Inkermann Avenue, by six o'clock that evening, there was a very good chance that I should receive cash on the spot for my trouble, I got down to work immediately.

I did not like Walter Cough when I first set eyes on him in his smug little sitting-room with the cotton curtains, the plastic flowers and the overwhelming smell of stale cooking.

After he had insulted my drawing and beaten me down for it I liked him still less. But afterwards he grew friendly and told me about his nefarious profession.

I conceived a positive loathing for him and would have taken my work away in a fine burst of outraged virtue had I had my bus fare back to the studio and something to eat when I got there.

As it was, I took the money rather shamefacedly and he went on talking.

He was a plump, pale man nearing fifty-five, with an unctuous manner which gave place at times to a ghoulish humour larded over with conceit.

He was eating when I came in. It was a dreadful meal, consisting of ham, bloaters and jam washed down with great cupfuls of black tea from a pale blue enamel pot.

He didn't offer me any, but kept me standing in front of him with my drawing propped up against a sticky jampot. He wouldn't make up his mind about it at first and I was wondering why, because there was not much in it to like or dislike, when it occurred to me that he was keeping me as long as he could because he wanted an audience. Since I wanted to sell the drawing I encouraged him to talk.

'You didn't want the address of your office on it, did you?' I ventured.

He chuckled and winked at me.

'This is the only office I've got and the only office I need,' he said. 'That's the beauty of my business. It's the only warehouse, too.' He waved a podgy hand to the great cupboard in the corner. 'That's my stock in there. I do my business by sheer personality. You'd be surprised what a lot of mugs there are in the world. There's one born every minute, that's what Shakespeare says. Ever heard of Shakespeare?'

I said I had but that I didn't recognise the quotation.

'I was in the gutter once,' he went on, his eyes popping at me. 'You wouldn't think that to look at me now, would you?'

I didn't think it would be politic to tell him what I thought, looking at him then, and doubtless he took my silence for admiration for he nodded at me with great complacency.

'I used my head,' he said. 'Open that cupboard over there. Go on, open it.'

I did as I was told, and when the cupboard door creaked open I found that it was full of the most villainously bound red and gold hymn-books I had ever seen. I fancied myself as something of a connoisseur in book production at that time, and as I examined one of the dreadfully printed little slabs of cheap paper, which crackled open amid a positive shower of dried glue, I was shocked and almost gave myself away.

It was a dreadful production. The cover was gaudy and vulgar, imitation leather embossed with cheap gilding and embellished with little tin clasps. Even the hymns themselves were bad and had been filched, I suspected, from some mid-Victorian production long fallen into disuse.

'What d'you think of it?' said Mr Cough. 'It's not worth a guinea is it?'

'Good heavens, no,' I said involuntarily.

He laughed and put a generous helping of jam on to the edge of a plate from which he had been eating cold bacon.

'That's what I sell 'em for,' he said. 'I won't tell you what I pay for 'em, but it's less than a tenth of that amount, less than a tenth. I sell 'em by the half-dozen.'

'Whoever to?' I said, and my genuine bewilderment delighted him so much that he couldn't help telling me. He put down his knife.

'Now it's no good thinking you can do the same,' he said. 'Get that clean out of your head before I begin. You haven't got the brains and you haven't got the personality, and you never will. But I can do it. I sell 'em to relations.'

'Your relations?'

That made him laugh so much that I thought he was going to choke.

'Oh, no!' he said. 'I haven't got any relations. Not mine. You've got less brains than I thought you 'ad. I sell 'em to the relations of people who've died. Every morning I buy up all the local papers and I look for the announcements of people who've popped off. Then I trot round to the 'ouse–you've got to go at once; it's no good waiting till the shock's passed off–I knock at the door and I ask to see the party who's dead.

'Well perhaps some sorrowing relative comes to the door and tells me the news. Then I pretend to be very upset. I say I'm very sorry. I explain that it's very awkward for me, because the dear departed has ordered six hymn-books from me, had 'em specially bound. It was going to be a surprise present, I tell 'em.

'Well, you'd be surprised how they fall for it. Nine times out of ten I get my money on the spot. It's partly to get rid of me, partly because they're in the mood. It's as easy as falling off a log if you know how to do it. You'd never do it, though, not in a million years.'

'No,' I said rather weakly. 'No, I don't think I should.'

The story was so very shocking that I could hardly speak to him.

'Some of 'em ask me for a receipt,' said Mr Cough. 'That's why I'm 'aving this heading. Of course some of 'em don't bother. They just give me my money and off I go. It's my knowledge of psychology that does the trick. I go at the right moment you see, as soon as I see the announcement.'

'You say nine out of ten?' I said. 'Doesn't the odd one prove rather difficult at times?'

A thoughtful expression passed over his face.

'Oh I have awkward moments,' he agreed after a pause, 'but I'm very smart. I'm quick-witted. I know when to fade away.

'Sometimes, of course, there's been a mistake. That doesn't happen often, but when it does it gives you a bit of a shock. I'm very careful meself but sometimes the papers get a name wrong and you find yourself askin' to see the husband when it's the wife who's dead.'

He really was insufferable. As I stood looking at him I thought he was the most revolting specimen I had ever seen in my life, and looking back from this distance I am inclined to be of the same opinion.

'Had a good day to-day?' I inquired sarcastically.

'Not bad,' he said, helping himself to another cup of tea. 'Only one dud. That was in a house in Putney, rather a nice old 'ouse near the river. I couldn't get the woman to understand what I was talking about. Thinking it over, I fancy she must have been a foreigner. It was annoying because the old man who had died–Parkinson, his name was–seemed to be a wealthy bird from what I could read in the paper. There was quite a bit about his philanthropy.'

I changed the subject, and we got back to haggling about the drawing. I had actually got the money in my pocket when there was a tap on the door and the landlady admitted a visitor. He was a tall, thin, distinguished old gentleman with very bright blue eyes and he stood hesitating in the doorway with a rather simple smile on his face.

'I'm so sorry to intrude,' he said, 'but I want to speak to Mr Walter Cough.'

My host got up, wiping his mouth hastily with a handkerchief. He was the professional salesman at once, bright, friendly, almost a little obsequious.

'Glad to see you, sir,' he said. 'What can I do for you? Won't you sit down?'

I made way to leave but Mr Cough indicated that he wanted me to stay and I drifted into a corner where I stood watching them. The newcomer seemed delighted.

'I'm so glad to have found you,' he said. 'When Mrs Simmez told me that I'd missed you this morning, I was so disappointed. She said you had some beautiful hymnbooks and I did want to see them. Oh, forgive me, I haven't introduced myself. This is my card.'

He fumbled in his pocket and brought out an ancient wallet.

'Here we are,' he said. 'Mr William Parkinson, Chantrey Hall, Putney. It ought to have the name of the street on it, but I've been there so many years that everybody knows me.'

I glanced at Walter Cough out of the corner of my eye. The whole thing looked a bit fishy to me and, after my brief acquaintance with him, I hoped he was going to get caught. He looked a little put out but not at all suspicious, I was glad to see.

'I did come round this morning,' he said cautiously. 'A Mr Earnshaw – told me that you might be interested to see the new hymn-book I've just brought out. It's a beautiful thing, well worth the money.'

'I don't remember Mr Earnshaw,' said the visitor, blinking thoughtfully, 'but whoever he is he's quite right. A most awkward thing has happened to me. A local paper has published my obituary notice. I have been very ill, but their interest in me was a little premature.

'This is the first time I've been out for some weeks. There's a little chapel I'm very interested in at the moment and I was going there tonight. In view of everything I thought it would be seemly to make a small present to the place, and when Mrs Simmez told me that someone had been round to show me some hymnbooks it seemed to me that they had been sent by providence. She remembered your name and I looked you up in the telephone book. Have you one of the volumes here?'

I was glad to see Mr Cough looked a little shamefaced as he produced that dreadful book, but Mr Parkinson was not as shocked as I had been. On the contrary he seemed delighted with it.

'The old hymnal of my boyhood,' he said, 'and what lovely binding! This is delightful. I can't think of anything more fitting. I should have written you, of course, but the matter is rather urgent. That's why I came myself. Have you got fifty copies of this?'

I thought Mr Cough was going to faint.

'Well yes, I have,' he said. 'They're rather expensive, you know, but one has to pay for a production like that.'

'One does indeed,' said the old man, turning over the monstrosity with an admiration that made me feel a little sick.

'A guinea' said Walter Cough defiantly.

'Really?' said the visitor. 'Yes, well, it's not dear for a present, is it? Let me see, that'll be £52.10.0. I think you ought to deliver for that.'

'Oh, I'd be happy to,' said Walter Cough in a tone in which I thought I detected a trace of hysteria. 'Any time day or night I'd be happy to. Anything to oblige.'

Mr Parkinson glanced at the clock on the mantelpiece.

'Half-past six,' he said. 'I should like them there by eight at the latest. Shall we say a quarter to eight? Bring them to the chapel. I don't know if you know Baghdad Road?'

'I'll find it.' Walter Cough was a little too enthusiastic and I thought the visitor must notice his jubilation. However, he was a very old man and there was a simplicity in his bright blue eyes which was the very essence of guilelessness.

'Get off the bus at the Fellowship Arms, Baghdad Road, and walk down about a hundred yards,' he said. 'There you'll find quite a narrow footpath between two houses. If you go down there a little way you'll come to a gate in a brick wall. It won't be open but it won't be locked. If you go through there you'll find yourself in a garden. You'll see the chapel at once.

'Take the books to the side door and I'll be waiting for you. it's quite a small place. I don't want people to know the present comes from me, so I'd like to get the books put round before the others arrive. Will you do that? I'll give you the money there. You'd like cash, wouldn't you? At a quarter to eight, then.'

Walter Cough showed him out with a perfectly straight face, but when he came back he laughed until he was nearly sick. I have never heard anyone laugh so long or so offensively.

'Didn't I handle him?' he said. 'He's one in a million. They're not all like that. That's a bit o'jam. I've never had that happen to me before. Now p'raps that's learnt you. There's a lot of truth in what the poet says. There *is* a mug born every minute, a real mug. You can't say he bought with his eyes shut. He saw it and he *liked* it. That's the miracle of this game. A real mug is a genuine mug, he's a mug all through. He likes being done. He's satisfied. Now you run along, my dear.'

I left him counting out fifty hymn-books from the great cupboard in the corner, and as I trudged down the road to look for a bus I felt very bitter.

I heard of Mr Walter Cough again the following morning when I picked up our communal newspaper. A little paragraph at the bottom of one of the news pages caught my attention.

'Man Found Dead on Chapel Steps.'

I read the paragraph with interest. 'Walter Cough, 56, itinerant bookseller, of Inkermann Avenue, was found dead on the steps of a mortuary chapel in Baghdad Road, Putney, late last night. Cough was a stranger to the district and is thought to have had a seizure. He was carrying a large parcel of books at the time.'

For two or three days I wondered about Mr Walter Cough. The whole incident had left a very unpleasant impression on my mind and at last, when I could control the impulse no longer, I went down to Putney and inquired my way to Chantrey Hall.

It was a large, old-fashioned suburban house standing by itself in a big garden in a backwater which was quiet and forgotten. I didn't like to go in, naturally, but I hung about outside the iron railings which bordered the garden and spoke to an old man who was sweeping up leaves on the other side of the low privet hedge.

'Excuse me,' I said rather nervously, 'but does Mr William Parkinson live here?'

The gardener straightened his back and surveyed me with not unfriendly interest.

'You've come too late, miss,' he said. 'He's dead.'

I suppose I looked rather pale because he hastened to soften down the baldness of the announcement.

'Yes, the poor old boy died last Wednesday,' he said, 'a week ago today. He was ill for a long time. They had him down at the nursing home. His wife went to stay with relations and the house has been shut up for several days now. There's no one in but Miss Simmez who caretakes.'

I stood there helplessly. It had been Friday when I had visited Walter Cough and if Mr Parkinson had died on Wednesday . . . ?

'Is the funeral over?' I said unsteadily.

He nodded. 'Yes. They had it from the mortuary chapel in Baghdad Road. There was hundreds came to it.'

'I daresay there were,' I murmured. 'He was a great philanthropist, wasn't he?'

My informant sighed.

'He was,' he said. 'But he was wonderful sharp. A wonderful sharp old man, that he was. There weren't nobody ever got the better of him.'

The Unseen Door

IT was London, it was hot and it was Sunday afternoon. The billiard room in Prinny's Club, Pall Mall, which has often been likened to a mausoleum, had unexpectedly become one.

Superintendent Stanislaus Oates glanced down at the body again and swore softly to Mr Albert Campion who had just been admitted.

'I hate miracles!' he said.

Campion drew the sheet gently back from the terrible face.

'Our friend here could hardly have been taken by this one,' he murmured, his pale eyes growing grim behind his horn rimmed spectacles. 'Strangled? Oh yes, I see–from behind. Powerful fingers. Horrid. Who done it?'

'I know who ought to have done it.' Oates was savage. 'I know who's been threatening to do it for months and yet he wasn't here. That's why I sent for you. You like this four-dimensional stuff. I don't. See anyone in the hall as you came up?'

'About forty police experts and two very shaken old gentlemen, both on the fragile side. Who are they? Witnesses?'

The Superintendent sighed. 'Listen,' he commanded. 'This club is partly closed for cleaning. The only two rooms unlocked are the vestibule downstairs and this billiard room up here. The only two people in the place are Bowser, the doorkeeper, and Chetty, the little lame billiard marker.'

'The two I mentioned?'

'Yes. Bowser has been in the vestibule all the time. He's a great character in clubland. Knows everybody and has a reputation for infallibility. You couldn't break him down in the witness box.'

'I've heard of him. He gave me a particularly baleful stare as I came in.'

'That's his way. Does it to everybody. He's become a bit affected as these old figureheads do in time. He's been a power here for forty years, remember. Surly old chap, but he never forgets a face.'

'Beastly for him. And who's this?' Campion indicated the white mound at their feet. 'Just a poor wretched member?'

'That,' Oates spoke dryly, 'is Robert Fenderson, the man who exposed William Merton.'

Campion was silent. The story of the Merton crash, which had entailed the arrest of the flamboyant financier after a thousand small speculators had faced ruin, was still fresh in everyone's mind. Merton had been taken to the cells shouting threats at Judge, jury and witnesses alike, and photographs of his heavy jaw and sultry eyes had appeared in every newspaper.

'Merton broke jail last night.'

'Did he, by Jove!' Campion's brows rose. 'Was he a member here once?'

'Until his arrest. Knows the place like his own house. More than that, someone sent Fenderson a phony message this morning telling him to meet the club secretary here this afternoon at three. The secretary is away this weekend and knows nothing about it. I tell you Campion, it's an open and shut case—only Merton hasn't been here unless he flew in by the windows.'

Campion glanced at the casements bolted against the heat.

'He hardly flew out again.'

'Exactly, and there's nowhere for him to be hidden. Bowser swears that he went all over the club after lunch and found it deserted. Since then he's been on the door all the time. During the afternoon only one member came in, and that was Fenderson. The only other living soul to cross the threshold was Chetty, who is far too frail to have strangled a cat, let alone a man with a neck like Fenderson's. Bowser has a perfect view from his box of the street door, the staircase and this door. He insists he has neither slept nor left his seat. He's unshakeable.'

'Has the unyielding Bowser a soft spot for Merton?'

Oates was nettled. 'I thought of that at once, naturally,' he said acidly, 'but the evidence is all the other way. One could even suspect Bowser of having a grudge against the chap. Merton made a complaint about him just before the crash. It was a stupid, petty quarrel–something about who should say "Good morning" first, member or club servant? Merton is like that, very self important and a born bully. Bowser is a graceless, taciturn old chap, but I swear he's speaking the truth. He hasn't seen Merton this afternoon.'

Mr Campion glanced round the spacious room, its walls lined with cue-racks and an occasional bookcase.

'All of which leaves us with the lame marker, I take it,' he ventured.

'The perishing little fool!' The Superintendent exploded. 'He isn't helping. He's gone to pieces and is trying to say he hasn't been here this afternoon. He lives in the mews at the back of the building, and he's trying to say he played hooky after lunch today–says he thought no one would be in to play. Actually any-one can see what did happen. He dropped in, found Fenderson didn't want a game, and went out again very sensibly. Now he doesn't want to appear as the last man to see the poor chap alive. I've told him he's doing himself no good by lying. Hang it all. Bowser *saw* him.'

'And so . . . ?'

'And so there must be another way into this room, but I'm damned if I see it.' The Superintendent stalked over to the win-dows again and Campion stood watching him.

'I'd like a word with Bowser,' he murmured at last.

'Have it. Have it by all means.' Oates was exasperated. 'I've put him through it very thoroughly. You'll never shake him.'

Campion said nothing, but waited until the doorkeeper came in a few minutes later, stalking gravely behind the sergeant who had been sent to fetch him. Bowser was a typical man of trust, a little shaky now and in his seventies, but still an imposing figure with a wooden expression on a proud old face, chiefly remarkable for its firm mouth and bristling white eyebrows. He glowered at Campion and did not speak, but at the first question a faint smile softened his lips.

'How many times have I seen Chetty come into the club in my

life, sir? Why, I shouldn't like to say–several thousand, must be.'

'Has he always been lame?'

'Why yes, sir. It's a deformity of the hip he's had all his life. He couldn't have done this, sir, any more than I could–neither of us has the strength.'

'I see.' Mr Campion went over to a bookcase at the far end of the long room and came back presently with something in his hand.

'Mr Bowser,' he said slowly, 'look at this. I suggest to you that it is a photograph of the man you really saw come in and go out of the club this afternoon when Mr Fenderson was already here.'

The old man's hand shook so violently that he could scarcely take the sheet, but he seized it at last and with an effort held it steady. He stared at it for a long time before returning it.

'No sir,' he said firmly, 'that face is unknown to me. Chetty came in and went out. No one else, and that's the truth, sir.'

'I believe you think it is, Bowser.' Mr Campion spoke gently and his lean face wore a curious expression in which pity predominated. 'Here's your unseen door, Superintendent,' he spoke softly. Oates snatched the paper and turned it over.

'Good God! What's this?' he demanded. 'It's a blank brown page–from the back of a book, isn't it?'

Mr Campion met his eyes.

'Bowser has just told us it's a face he doesn't know,' he murmured. 'You see, Oates, Bowser doesn't recognise faces, he recognises voices. That's why he glares until people speak. Bowser didn't *see* Chetty this afternoon, he heard his very distinctive step–a step which Merton could imitate very easily. I fancy you'll find that when there was that little unpleasantness earlier in the year, Merton guessed something which no one else in the club has known. When did it come on, Bowser?'

The old man stood trembling before them.

'I–I didn't want to have to retire from the club, sir,' he blurted out pathetically. 'I knew everyone's voice. I could still do my work. It's only got really bad in the last six months–my daughter comes and fetches me home at night. It *was* Chetty's step, sir, and I knew he could never have done it.'

'Blind!' The word escaped the Superintendent huskily. 'Good Lord! Campion, how did you know?'

It was some time before Mr Campion could be prevailed upon to tell him, and when he did he was slightly diffident.

'When I first passed through the hall,' he said, 'Bowser glared at me as I told you, but as I came upstairs I heard him say to a constable: "Another detective, I suppose?".'

He paused, and his smile was engaging as he flicked an imaginary speck from an immaculate sleeve.

'I wondered then if there was something queer about his eyesight—no offence, of course, no offence in the world'

Bird Thou never Wert

I bought the cage for a bird which never came. My young nephew promised me a parrot and wrote to me from Teneriffe to say it was on its way. A psittacosis scare plus the authorities, however, combined to frustrate his generosity.

It was during the period between the letter from Peter and the disappointing official communication that I acquired the cage and had it sent up to my flat. Even in appearance it was no ordinary contraption. I have a struggling weakness for the baroque and when I saw the lovely monstrosity, part pagoda, part miniature bandstand, hanging in the window of my favourite junk shop I went in and bought it hastily before my good sense could curb my enthusiasm.

In the living-room of my flat it appeared even more arresting than it had done in Robb's shop. It was very large, for one thing, much larger than I had suspected, and it took up the whole of the circular table in the corner by the second window. There was no other place to put it, and finally it remained there looking very odd beside my prim bookcases and restrained prints: even I was a little taken aback.

I thought perhaps my Roman shawl might cover the cage until Polly or Oliver put in an appearance. After all, bird-cages are frequently covered at night.

I had to go out that evening until a little after nine o'clock, but when I returned I got out the shawl and draped it over the cage. It looked charming, I thought. The brilliant stripes of colour were just what that rather dull corner needed.

Having admired the effect, I sat down at my bureau to correct some proofs. It was an early autumn evening and my windows were closed against the sharpness in the air. The square below is always quiet, but that evening it was silent, and no sound of traffic reached me over the tops of the plane trees, which were casting their last leaves against the violet sky.

I had corrected two galleys and was beginning the third when the thing happened. Behind me in the room someone coughed.

It was not a faint sound, nothing that could be explained away by a mouse in the skirting or a loose window sash: it was a cough, human, personal and very loud, a cough of definite utility. I swung round, my pencil in my hand. Let me say at once that I am not a nervous woman. If I hear a noise at night I take a torch and investigate. My first feeling, I remember, was one of resentment at having my privacy disturbed. Then I saw that my room was still empty.

I got up resolutely. No one in my family has ever suffered from hallucinations and I was disturbed. The whole thing would have to be explained.

I was halfway across the room to the other window to see whether by some trick of acoustics the sound could have been projected into the room from the square below when the second thing happened.

'Dear-est,' said a charming feminine voice which yet had more than a trace of exasperation in it, '*must* you?'

I own I stood petrified. The voice was so near.

'Must,' replied a male voice and giggled.

It was the giggle which paralysed me. It was so authentic, if I may use such a term, so obviously some real person's private, individual giggle, and it was beside me in my ear.

'Brute,' answered the woman's voice faintly.

Then there came another sound, the unmistakable rustling of feathers. I stared at the gaudy mound on the round table. The folds of the shawl did not move, but from beneath them came a quiet bird whistle, ending in a rather imperfect replica of a human sneeze.

Instantly my mind seized on an explanation, improbable enough, but better than the one I was forced to accept afterwards. I whipped off the shawl fully expecting a miracle to have occurred and a beady black eye in a wicked grey head to confront me.

To say I was disappointed is a ridiculous under-statement. The cage was just as I had last seen it, clean, empty and rather vulgarly ornate.

I stood for some time, the shawl in my hand. The room was quiet and normal. The electric fire glowed warmly.

Throwing the shawl upon a chair, I went out to the kitchenette and did a thing I very rarely do at night. I made myself a cup of tea. There is a little mirror over the sink and I caught sight of my face in it. The sight shocked me into my senses again. I looked haggard and as though I had seen a ghost, whereas, of course, I knew I had merely been the victim of some foolish practical joke.

I went back to the living-room at last, my mind full of hidden radios and concealed tape recorders. I certainly made a thorough search. I found nothing at all. The room was just as it had always been. My somewhat austere type of furnishing, a relic of my Cambridge days, afforded very few hiding places.

Thoroughly alarmed, I decided to go to bed at once and call in upon my doctor in the morning. I threw the shawl over the cage again and bent to switch off the fire.

'George–really! I might as well be married to an ape . . . '

The woman's voice, so charming and distinctive with its slight Scots accent, arrested me in the very act of stooping and I remained crouching over the stove, the hairs prickling on my scalp.

'Un-apeily married,' replied the male voice which I had heard before. It spoke with idiotic relish and chuckled again.

This time the laughter ended abruptly, and an obviously parrot voice remarked hoarsely:

'My name is John Wellington Wells,' adding immediately a collection of shrill whistles, a cuckoo call and a realistic hiccup.

Now thoroughly frightened, but preserving, thank heavens, a modicum of common sense, I got up from the hearthrug and advanced stealthily upon the cage. There was no doubt about it–the voices came from beneath the shawl.

Even as I approached I could hear the thing, whatever it was, preparing its ghastly impersonations.

'George dar-ling . . .' It was the woman's voice this time, perfectly reproduced in every intonation, I felt sure.

Cautiously I raised a corner of the shawl and peered beneath. There was a squawk of rage, a rattle, and then silence. The cage was empty. I saw nothing, not even a shadow.

Alone in my sitting-room with my skin creeping, I made a series of experiments. Looking back on it I know it was one of the most dreadful hours I have spent, but I am a strong-minded woman and I did not go to my room until I had found out the all-significant fact and had proved it.

The manifestation, or whatever you care to call it, only occurred when the cage was covered. It was nothing to do with the shawl. A blanket served equally well. Light did not seem to affect it, nor did position. As soon as the cage was covered the dreadful idiot parrot voice within began again.

There were no more impersonations that evening, only whistles, catcalls and three lines of a hymn repeated in a sing-song.

At last I took myself in hand. I left the cage uncovered and passed a fitful night in my bedroom behind a locked door.

The following day I could not bring myself to confide in anyone. Frankly, I did not fancy the task of telling such an utterly ridiculous story.

As soon as I was alone in the flat, after the daily woman had left, I got out the shawl and covered the cage again. This time there was no result. The cage remained quiet.

My first feeling was one of intense relief, followed by extreme irritation with myself for permitting my imagination to run away with me. I went out to a lecture that night, still considerably shaken by what I could only feel was a very disturbing trick of the brain.

I arrived home a little after ten and as soon as I came into the hall I heard the two voices. I stood with my hand on the sitting-room latch, my heart thumping. My instinct was to turn and run for assistance, but there is an obstinate something in my nature which I can only call pride, and eventually I pulled myself together, opened the door and switched on the light.

A guilty silence greeted my arrival. The room was cold and empty. On the table stood the cage, covered by its multicoloured hood. I closed the door, and as I walked towards the table I distinctly heard the odd rasping noise that a parrot makes as it rubs its beak on the wood of its perch.

I had stretched up my hand to pull the shawl away when the voice within began to speak again. Never shall I forget that strange reported conversation. First of all the woman's voice, soft, educated, endearing, and then the man's, jovially wheezy and shaken now and again with foolish laughter.

'George, don't–don't. My dear, be serious for once. Be a little sensible. You're not dignified, darling. You're not even amusing. You're silly.'

'Perhaps I come from the Scilly Isles.' This followed by the insufferable chuckle.

Then the woman's voice again, near breaking-point this time.

'George, really, I can't stand it! You're such a fool. So puerile. I tell you I can't stand it. These incessant lunatic jokes aren't faintly funny. Dearest, pull yourself together.'

There was a pause, followed by an explosion of partly controlled laughter.

'Yo-ho, heave ho,' sang the male voice, and the parrot, or whatever it was, added a hoarse guffaw or two of its own.

'Really! . . .' There were tears in the woman's voice and a dangerous edge of hysteria. 'I can't stand it any longer. I've been thinking about what I'm going to do for months now. I knew you'd drive me to it in the end. My nerves have snapped, I tell you. Look, George, look, I've got a gun in my hand. Look at it! If I were to pull the trigger . . .'

'There'd be a loud report,' sang the male voice, quoting evidently, from some comic song.

'George, I'm going to –I'm going to–'

In its effort to reproduce the whispered exasperation in the feminine voice the bird whistled with ghastly effect.

The answering male giggle was positively insane in its stupidity. 'I'd rather have a nice cup of tea,' the voice sang.

The gunshot startled me half out of my senses. I have heard a parrot imitate the popping of a cork and been amazed by it, but this was quite different. It sounded as a shot must sound when heard through a telephone. There was the first sharp crack and then the faint repercussions all uncannily reproduced and emphasised by that dreadful, devilish bird.

The scream which followed was equally convincing, and I felt my throat contract, but the peak of horror came afterwards in that soft, broken-hearted little moan and the single murmured word, so appalling in its economy.

'Dead.'

I think I must have fainted. When I came to myself I was lying upon the rug, the shawl clutched in my hand, and above me, on the table, the enormous ornamental cage, empty and innocent as when I had purchased it.

I did not sleep at all that night. In the morning I rose, determined to take the cage back to Robb's immediately. I was haunted by the tragedy I had overheard so strangely, a tragedy made even more horrible by the awful element of low comedy which had dominated it.

I am naturally an inquisitive woman, but in this instance I was determined to make no inquiries. I did not want to know to whom the cage had belonged before. I did not care. I did not want to think of my dreadful experience again.

I actually had my hat on when I remembered Mrs Beckwithston's appointment. She was the sister of the Bishop of Mold, and although we had corresponded frequently we had never met. I knew her to be a kind woman, completely taken up with her good works, and when she had written me that she was passing through London on her way to France, and had asked if I could possibly see her at an unusually early hour, I had written back to invite her to breakfast. It was only my daily woman's hasty preparations in the kitchenette which reminded me that I expected a visitor.

I went into the sitting-room and looked at the cage. Uncovered, it was certainly ugly but I knew not dangerous. I steeled myself to keep it in the house an hour longer.

Mrs Beckwithston was punctual. The moment the bell rang

I hurried out into the hall to meet her. However, my daily was before me and from the open front door I heard my visitor inquiring whether I was at home.

I did not scream, but my blood froze and I felt my face congealing. It was *the* voice. I should have recognised it anywhere by its timbre and the soft rolling of the R's. I stood trembling, convinced that I was going mad. Mrs Beckwithston, whom I knew well, at least by repute, was, I was certain, the woman whose part in a terrible tragedy I had overheard in my own room only the night before.

I stared at her. She had a very ordinary pale face with no distinctive features, little make-up and was dressed entirely in black.

Breakfast was a terrible meal. I'm afraid I barely spoke and when I did my words sounded distrait even to myself.

My guest, however, was completely at her ease. She chatted pleasantly about our common interests, congratulated me on my flat, and betrayed a personality that was altogether charming. Yet every time she spoke, at every syllable which left her sympathetic lips, I was reminded horribly of my experiences of the past two days.

When at last the meal was nearly over there was a second ring at my doorbell and she looked up.

'That will be my husband,' she said. 'You don't mind, do you? I told him to call in here for me. He's been to the agency for our tickets.'

I felt a fine perspiration break out all over my face and with what seemed an enormous effort I turned my head towards the door. It opened. My daily woman murmured something and then there came floating in to me from the hall that personal, individual giggle I knew so well.

'My dear,' said Mrs Beckwithston to me, 'this is George.'

They must have thought me demented. I was. I goggled at the man. He was round and short and devastatingly jolly.

'Some—some tea?' I stammered when even I noticed that the atmosphere was becoming strained.

'Splendid,' he ejaculated, and, turning to his wife, he threw out his hands. His voice was jocular. I knew exactly what it was going to be like even before I heard it, smug, bantering, ineffably foolish, 'Give me to drink, Ambrosia. And, sweet Barm . . . a nice cup of tea would do as well as anything. I thought of that coming along in the cab. Rather nicer punctuation than the usual, don't you think, or don't you?'

'Darling, *must* you?' said Mrs Beckwithston plaintively and actually laughed.

So did I, immoderately and rather wildly, I fear.

They left at last. The man went out first, but his wife turned back.

'I wonder,' she said. 'I do hope you will forgive me for asking such a thing, but where did you get that cage?'

I felt the blood singing in my ears as I told her.

'A second-hand shop?' she exclaimed. 'Well, then of course it really must be the same. How extraordinary!'

She went over and touched the infernal thing lovingly.

'It is!' she said joyfully. 'I recognise it by that little nick on the brass there. Oh, my dear, I'm so glad *you've* got it. It belonged to our poor Johnny. We were so sad when he died, we couldn't bear to keep it. He was the sweetest bird. So clever! He used to imitate George and me until you'd really think it was ourselves speaking. I *must* tell George.'

The husband was recalled and he too recognised the cage and was facetious on the subject of coincidences. They stood together, two respectable middle-aged persons, and eulogised their dead pet. He was amazing. So excruciatingly funny. So lifelike. So droll. So unexpected.

Mrs Beckwithston sighed over his memory.

'He really loved us,' she said. 'He was a true friend.'

They were on the doorstep by this time and George Beckwithston, whose eyes were sad, looked up.

'Ah, poor Johnny, he had only one fault. You remember, Marion?'

Mrs Beckwithston smiled again.

'I do,' she said tolerantly. 'It seems absurd to say it of a parrot, but Johnny really was half-human. And there was just this one little thing. He was–forgive such a forceful word, but there really is no other for it–such a dreadful *liar*, poor darling. I'm sure he hasn't gone to heaven.'

The Same to Us

IT was particularly unfortunate for Mrs Christopher Molesworth that she should have had burglars on the Sunday night of what was, perhaps, the crowningly triumphant week-end of her career as a hostess.

As a hostess Mrs Molesworth was a connoisseur. She chose her guests with a nice discrimination, disdaining everything but the most rare. Mere notoriety was no passport to Molesworth Court.

Nor did mere friendship obtain many crumbs from the Molesworth table, though the ability to please and do one's piece might possibly earn one a bed when the lion of the hour promised to be dull, uncomfortable and liable to be bored.

That was how young Petterboy came to be there at the great week-end. He was diplomatic, presentable, near enough a tee-totaller to be absolutely trustworthy, even at the end of the evening, and he spoke a little Chinese.

This last accomplishment had done him but little good before, save with very young girls at parties, who relieved their discomfort at having no conversation by persuading him to tell them how to ask for their baggage to be taken ashore at Hong Kong, or to ascertain the way to the bathroom at a Peking hotel.

However, now the accomplishment was really useful, for it obtained for him an invitation to Mrs Molesworth's greatest week-end party.

This party was so select that it numbered but six all told. There were the Molesworths themselves – Christopher Molesworth was an M.P., rode to hounds, and backed up his wife in much the same way as a decent black frame backs up a coloured print.

Then there was Petterboy himself, the Feison brothers, who looked so restful and talked only if necessary, and finally the guest of all time, the gem of a magnificent collection, the catch of a lifetime, Dr Koo Fin, the Chinese scientist himself – Dr Koo

Fin, the Einstein of the East, the man with the Theory. After quitting his native Peking he had only left his house in New England on one memorable occasion when he delivered a lecture in Washington to an audience which was unable to comprehend a word. His works were translated but since they were largely concerned with higher mathematics the task was comparatively simple.

Mrs Molesworth had every reason to congratulate herself on her capture. 'The Chinese Einstein', as the newspapers had nicknamed him, was hardly a social bird. His shyness was proverbial, as was also his dislike and mistrust of women. It was this last foible which accounted for the absence of femininity at Mrs Molesworth's party. Her own presence was unavoidable, of course, but she wore her severest gowns, and took a mental vow to speak as little as necessary. It is quite conceivable that had Mrs Molesworth been able to change her sex she would have done so nobly for that week-end alone.

She had met the sage at a very select supper party after his only lecture in London. It was the same lecture which had thrown Washington into a state of bewilderment. Since Dr Koo Fin arrived he had been photographed more often than any film star. His name and his round Chinese face were better known than those of the principals in the latest *cause célèbre*, and already television comedians referred to his great objectivity theory in their patter.

Apart from that one lecture, however, and the supper party after it, he had been seen nowhere else save in his own closely guarded suite in his hotel.

How Mrs Molesworth got herself invited to the supper party, and how, once there, she persuaded the sage to consent to visit Molesworth Court, is one of those minor miracles which do sometimes occur. Her enemies made many unworthy conjectures, but, since the university professors in charge of the proceedings on that occasion were not likely to have been corrupted by money or love, it is probable that Mrs Molesworth moved the mountain by faith in herself alone.

The guest chamber prepared for Dr Koo Fin was the third room in the west wing. This architectural monstrosity contained four bedrooms, each furnished with french windows leading on to the same balcony.

Young Petterboy occupied the room at the end of the row. It was one of the best in the house, as a matter of fact, but had no bathroom attached, since this had been converted by Mrs Molesworth, who had the second chamber, into a gigantic clothes press. After all, as she said, it was her own house.

Dr Koo Fin arrived on the Saturday by train, like a lesser person. He shook hands with Mrs Molesworth and Christopher and young Petterboy and the Feisons as if he actually shared their own intelligence, and smiled at them all in his bland, utterly-too Chinese way.

From the first he was a tremendous success. He ate little, drank less, spoke not at all, but he nodded appreciatively at young Petterboy's halting Chinese, and grunted once or twice most charmingly when someone inadvertently addressed him in English. Altogether he was Mrs Molesworth's conception of a perfect guest.

On the Sunday morning Mrs Molesworth actually received a compliment from him, and saw herself in a giddy flash the most talked-of woman in the cocktail parties of the coming week.

The charming incident occurred just before lunch. The sage rose abruptly from his chair on the lawn, and as the whole house party watched him with awe, anxious not to miss a single recountable incident, he stalked boldly across the nearest flower bed, trampling violas and London Pride with the true dreamer's magnificent disregard for physical obstacles, and, plucking the head off a huge rose from Christopher's favourite standard, trampled back with it in triumph and laid it in Mrs Molesworth's lap.

Then, as she sat in ecstasy, he returned quietly to his seat and considered her affably. For the first time in her life Mrs Molesworth was really thrilled. She told a number of people so afterwards.

However, on the Sunday night there were burglars. It was sickeningly awkward. Mrs Molesworth had a diamond star, two sets of ear-rings, a bracelet and five rings, all set in platinum, and she kept them in a wall safe under a picture in her bedroom. On the Sunday night, after the rose incident, she gave up the self-effacement programme and came down to dinner in full war paint. The Molesworths always dressed on Sunday and she certainly looked devastatingly feminine, all blue mist and diamonds.

It was the more successful evening of the two. The sage revealed an engaging talent for making card houses, and he also played five-finger exercises on the piano. The great simplicity of the man was never better displayed. Finally, dazed, honoured and happy, the house party went to bed.

Mrs Molesworth removed her jewellery and placed it in the safe, but unfortunately did not lock it at once. Instead, she discovered that she had dropped an ear-ring, and went down to look for it in the drawing-room. When at last she returned without it the safe was empty. It really was devastatingly awkward, and the resourceful Christopher, hastily summoned from his room in the main wing, confessed himself in a quandary.

The servants, discreetly roused, whispered that they had heard nothing and gave unimpeachable alibis. There remained the guests. Mrs Molesworth wept. For such a thing to happen at any time was terrible enough, but for it to occur on such an occasion was more than she could bear. One thing she and Christopher agreed: the sage must never guess . . . must never dream . . .

There remained the Feisons and the unfortunate young Petterboy. The Feisons were ruled out almost at once. From the fact that the window catch in Mrs Molesworth's room was burst, it was fairly obvious that the thief had entered from the balcony; therefore, had either of the Feisons passed that way from their rooms they would have had to pass the sage, who slept with his window wide. So there was only young Petterboy. It seemed fairly obvious.

Finally, after a great deal of consultation, Christopher went to speak to him as man to man, and came back fifteen minutes later hot and uncommunicative.

Mrs Molesworth dried her eyes, put on her newest negligée, and, sweeping aside her fears and her husband's objections, went in to speak to young Petterboy like a mother. Poor young Petterboy gave up laughing at her after ten minutes, suddenly got angry, and demanded that the sage too should be asked if he had 'heard anything'. Then he forgot himself completely, and vulgarly suggested sending for the police.

Mrs Molesworth nearly lost her head, recovered herself in time, apologised by innuendo, and crept back disconsolately to Christopher and bed.

The night passed most wretchedly.

In the morning poor young Petterboy cornered his hostess and repeated his requests of the night before. But the sage was departing by the 11.12 and Mrs Molesworth was driving with him to the station. In that moment of her triumph the diamonds seemed relatively unimportant to Elvira Molesworth, who had inherited the Cribbage fortune a year before. Indeed, she kissed poor young Petterboy and said it really didn't matter, and hadn't they had a wonderful, wonderful week-end? And that he must come down again some time soon.

The Feisons said good-bye to the sage, and as Mrs Molesworth was going with him, made their adieux to her as well. As the formalities had been accomplished there seemed no point in staying, and Christopher saw them off in their car, with poor young Petterboy leading the way in his.

As he was standing on the lawn waving somewhat perfunctorily to the departing cars, the post arrived. One letter for his wife bore the crest of the Doctor's hotel, and Christopher, with one of those intuitions which made him such a successful husband, tore it open.

It was quite short, but in the circumstances, wonderfully enlightening:

'Dear Madam,

In going through Dr Koo Fin's memoranda, I find to my horror that he promised to visit you this week-end. I know you will forgive Dr Koo Fin when you hear that he never takes part in social occasions. As you know, his arduous work occupies his entire time. I know it is inexcusable of me not to have let you know before now, but it is only a moment since I discovered that the Doctor had made the engagement.

I do hope his absence has not put you to any inconvenience, and that you will pardon this atrocious slip.

I have the honour to remain, Madam,

Yours most apologetically

Lo Pei Fu

Secretary.

P.S. The Doctor should have written himself, but, as you know, his English is not good. He begs to be reminded to you and hopes for your forgiveness.

As Christopher raised his eyes from the note his wife returned. She stopped the car in the drive and came running across the lawn towards him.

'Darling, wasn't it wonderful?' she said, throwing herself into his arms with an abandonment she did not often display to him.

'What's in the post?' she went on, disengaging herself.

Christopher slipped the letter he had been reading into his pocket with unobtrusive skill.

'Nothing, my dear,' he said gallantly. 'Nothing at all.' He was amazingly fond of his wife.

Mrs Molesworth wrinkled her white forehead.

'Darling,' she said, 'now about my jewellery. Wasn't it too odious for such a thing to happen when that dear, sweet old man was here: what shall we do?'

Christopher drew her arm through his own. 'I think, my dear,' he said firmly, 'you'd better leave all that to me. We mustn't have a scandal.'

'Oh, no,' said Mrs Molesworth, her eyes growing round with alarm. 'Oh, no; that would spoil everything.'

In a first class compartment on the London train the elderly Chinese turned over the miscellaneous collection of jewellery which lay in a large silk handkerchief on his knee. His smile was child-like, bland and faintly wondering. After a while he folded the handkerchief over its treasure and placed the package in his breast pocket.

Then he leaned back against the upholstery and looked out of the window. The green undulating landscape was pleasant. The fields were neat and well tilled. The sky was blue, the sunlight beautiful. It was a lovely land.

He sighed and marvelled in his heart that it could be the home of a race of cultivated barbarians to whom, providing that height, weight and age were relatively the same, all Chinese actually did look alike.

She Heard it on
the Radio

BEFORE Miss Amber died she lived for eight or nine years in a small darkish room with a very high ceiling at the back of the dilapidated house where we students had lodgings.

She was a compact and tidy little body, so exquisitely happy that you were instantly aware of it if you so much as passed her on the stairs or brushed by her in the dank, unpainted hall.

She was sixty-one or two when I knew her, and she earned a small weekly wage in a coal office in a side street. It was one of those London backwaters which seem to have been left over from the stuffy intimacy of the last century.

Every evening at a quarter to six she came hurrying down the street, her long black coat, which she wore both in winter and summer, flapping in the wind. She usually carried three carrier bags, one brown and two white ones, on these occasions; and she would pant upstairs with them, fit her key in the scratched yellow door and disappear into her small high-ceilinged cell until ten minutes past eight in the morning, when she would trot out again to the coal office, plump and smiling and utterly content.

On Sunday mornings she turned out her room, leaving the door wide open, so that as we came by we could see that grim, clean prison which was twilit even in the summer because the blank wall of the house next door was considerably too near her window.

On Sunday afternoons she shut the door and was not seen again until ten minutes past eight on Monday morning, when she hurried out to work once more.

We were art students then. There were about a dozen of us scattered over the house, all very noisy, young and traditionally poor. We accepted Miss Amber as part of the landscape.

I was the first of our gang to become aware of her as a person. A series of late afternoon lectures decreed that I should arrive at the tube station an hour later than usual on two days of the week and my walk home led me past the multiple store at the precise moment that Miss Amber came out with the largest and last of her two white bags.

Naturally we walked along together and she chatted affably the whole way in her soft high voice, which always gave me the uncomfortable feeling that it was very seldom used.

She was neither brusquely rude nor embarrassingly frank, which I have since discovered are the two more usual peculiarities of the very lonely people of the world. She talked very quietly and without affectation of the ordinary things of life, revealing a store of unexpected information on all sorts of subjects.

I found her a most delightful and comforting companion. She was wise, sophisticated without being worldly, intelligent, balanced and informed. I began to look out for her neat figure with anticipation.

Now and again I was tempted to confide in her some of my own more pressing problems and I found her not only sympathetic but also helpful and sane in her advice, which was unusual in my experience.

Our bi-weekly walks had gone on for a couple of months before it occurred to me to wonder at this remarkable contentment of hers, this strange unfed fulfilment.

It was only when she chanced to say one day that she had no friends or relations that I realised she had no acquaintances or business associates either, and, moreover, never seemed to have had any, and the woman confronted me as a phenomenon.

Once I was aware of this she worried me as the unexpected has always worried me, inspiring a passionate curiosity I have never been able to control.

Miss Amber talked, thought, and felt like a woman who was in the midst of an interesting family life with friends, hobbies and objects of affection to absorb and interest her. Yet I knew she had none of these things and, as far as I could see, had never had any of them. I began to pump her shamelessly.

She was not exactly reticent, but she was shy. The first glimmer

came to me when she had referred in the course of conversation
to a piece of society gossip some three months old. It had been a
fairly common rumour, but not much had appeared in print, and
as a young woman very conscious of living in the knowledgeable
set I was rather surprised to find that she knew more than I did.

'That's interesting,' I said. 'Where did you hear that?'

She hesitated and frowned.

'I'm not quite sure,' she said. 'Could it have been on the radio?'

'Hardly,' I said and laughed, but the word had given me a clue.
'You listen in a lot, do you? I never hear a radio in your room.'

Her face lit up.

'I listen all the time,' she said. 'I've got earphones. They are
very comfortable. As soon as I've had my supper I get into bed
and pop them on and I listen until I go to sleep. I don't know
what I'd do without my radio. It's such a wonderful thing. I'm
never lonely now.'

'You've been lonely, then?' I demanded with all the brutal
avidity of the collector.

'Oh yes,' she said and sighed. 'Oh yes. Three years ago, before
I got my radio. I was very lonely then. I had no one to talk to at
all. I never got a new point of view. It was terrible, like being
shut outside a house, you know.'

'You hear talks and music and things, don't you?' I inquired
then.

She was dubious.

'Not much music,' she admitted finally. 'I don't understand
music very well. I hear the old songs, of course. I like the talks and
I like the announcer best, when he tells you things.'

I tried to press her further because I thought she must have
confused the announcer with some chatty commentator on current affairs. We had reached the gate by that time and she was in
a hurry to get back to her bed and her earphones.

The next time I saw her, however, I continued my rather
vulgar investigations. On this occasion I found her in more com-
municative mood.

'Last night he was tremendously interesting; they all were,' she said. 'It was like going home, it really was. The children, too. They don't often have children, but these were charming. They sang and said their pieces and afterwards I heard them playing games.'

I thought I understood and permitted myself to get a little sentimental over the spectacle of this lonely little woman listening in to some programme for children. Unconsciously she added to my mental picture by remarking placidly:

'It was my caramel night, too. I did enjoy it.'

I suppose I looked startled, for she blushed and laughed.

'I have a little treat every night when I'm listening in,' she said. 'Sometimes a cup of milk cocoa, sometimes caramels, and sometimes a cigarette. Oh, I do myself very well. I have a lovely time. They tell you to.'

I stared at her stupidly.

'Who do?'

She shrugged her shoulders.

'The people who broadcast. Not all of them of course, but sometimes somebody slips something homely like that in. I get little recipes, too. Different ways to cook my eggs and that sort of thing.'

My impression of Miss Amber underwent a change. I began to think I saw the straggling flaw in her sane, equable temperament. I thought she must take the programmes personally, considering each comedian's aside or commentator's little archness as a direct kindness to herself. In my youth and ignorance I thought it very sad.

Once she had got into the habit of talking to me about her one real interest in life, she seldom spoke of anything else.

The mysterious gossipy commentator, whom she insisted on referring to as 'the announcer', was easily her favourite. She was charming about him in a naïve fashion that was half apologetic because she was neither a foolish nor unduly sentimental old woman.

'I would like to have had a son like that,' she said one day. 'That *would* have given me pleasure.'

She told me the story of her life one day in a word or two, and the cold empty tragedy of it touched me and then rather excited me, because I was young enough to dramatise it.

'I was engaged for fourteen years,' she said. 'We never had enough to marry on. He was such a dear good man. He had relations to support and he wouldn't marry me until we could have a home and I could have a baby. We both wanted to have a baby, a son, you know.

'When I was thirty-five his mother died and we thought we might manage it, but there was a 'flu epidemic and he caught it and went too. So I had to go on with my job. For years after that I was so lonely. I was right down once. I had silly ideas about leaving the gas on and that sort of thing. And then I got my radio set. I paid all I had for it, three pounds, but it's never gone wrong and I've been really very happy ever since.'

She smiled at me and her round face was bright and contented, so that I saw she was telling the literal truth.

'It was extraordinarily cheap,' I said hastily. 'Where did you get it?'

'I bought it off a man who came into the shop,' she said. 'Quite a rough-looking person. I thought at first he'd cheated me, because it didn't seem to work, but that was because I hadn't turned the knobs properly. Suddenly I got it right and it's been right ever since.'

I told the others about Miss Amber and because we were all very raw her tragedy had a fine fascination for us. We were a very ordinary set of young jugginses just going through that particular period of development when conscious virtue is at its most priggish worst.

We decided, over modest mugs of cheap Chianti, that something must be done about the old woman. At this distance I do not see why, exactly. Miss Amber was certainly a good deal happier than we were, or at least much more consistently so.

Mercifully Miss Amber was unaware of our interest. She did not need our pity and she did not notice it. She had her own amusement.

At the height of our excitement the idea of the new set was born. Someone pointed out that any radio set of three or four years of age must be pretty bad by modern standards, so we whipped round to buy Miss Amber a new one.

Finally we got it. It was a handy-sized set which could be plugged into the wall socket by her bed. We all got back early one evening, bribed the landlady to open the door of Miss Amber's room, and had it all fixed up and blaring like a fairground organ by the time she came back from work.

I remember to this day that half proud, half apprehensive thrill which I for one experienced as we leant over the banisters and saw her coming down the lower hall.

I remember, too, her terrified expression as she realised the ghastly noise was coming from her own little sanctuary. But, as I have said, she was a wise, sane little body and when she turned and saw our solemn young faces and round, embarrassed but excited eyes, she played her part magnificently.

'Oh, I am pleased!' she said. 'Oh, I am! I am grateful, I am indeed. You shouldn't. I can't thank you, I can't indeed.'

All that evening we sat proudly in our rooms and read our books, painted our pictures, made our clothes and talked our delirious never-ending talk, and as we glowed with virtue we heard the gusts of band and concert music floating up from downstairs.

The next night it was the same, the next and the next, but on the fourth evening, when most of us had gone to a dance, there was silence. There was silence the next night too, and we were perturbed. Our present seemed to have gone wrong. Our expert on the subject, a cheerful red-headed young man called Fry, went down at last, tapped on the door, and after a pause was admitted. The music began again almost at once, and he came out laughing.

The old dear had muddled the tuning, he explained, and went back to his etching in the studio under the roof.

The radio programme went through to the end that night, but next evening the set went wrong again, and after that there followed an awkward period when Fry was always at work upon it. He said all women were fools where delicate machinery was concerned, but that Miss Amber was an idiot.

After a while the more discerning among us began to entertain unhappy suspicions, which were confirmed one evening when Fry stalked into my room, where a gathering was taking place.

'You know, the old fool doesn't like it,' he said wrathfully. 'She prefers those dreadful old headphones. I even offered to fix them on the new set, but she wouldn't have it. She was almost in tears, demented old lunatic!'

It was practically our first experience of the ingratitude that is the inevitable portion of the obstinately well-meaning, and we were indignant because we were also very hurt. Providentially for Miss Amber, however, we had our pride.

Later on, the new set somehow got into Fry's studio and was afterwards sold.

Miss Amber made a pathetic little apology to me one day when she met me on the steps.

'I'd got used to my headphones,' she said. 'It was so kind of all you young people, but it wasn't the same. It wasn't the same at all.'

After that episode, life in the house went on as before. We were torn and tried, invigorated and exalted by our exciting communal life, and she lived quietly and dully, going out to work every day and returning to her strangely satisfying headphones and caramels at night.

Then one night she died.

The landlady found her in bed. The battered little radio set was by her side and the phones were still over her ears. The doctor who called in said she had been ill for a long time.

She had few belongings, no debts, and a small insurance policy to cover her funeral. The odds and ends in her room, what there were of them, became the property of the landlady.

Some weeks after Miss Amber had vanished off the face of the earth as if she had never been, and her room had been re-let, Fry called me into his studio one day. His brown eyes were shocked and only half amused.

'I say,' he said, 'that old bird *was* crazy. Look here.'

He pointed to a shabby radio case on the untidy table. It was little bigger than a shoe-box, and the lid, which had once been tacked down, was now prised open and its contents revealed. There was only a large and ordinary brick. The horrible, mean little fraud of the 'rough-looking' man who had come into Miss Amber's coal office was at last exposed.

Fry was spluttering, as he always did when excited.

'Mrs Thingummy downstairs asked me to have a look at this,' he explained. 'She swears Miss Amber used to plug her earphones into it and listen to all sorts of gossipy programmes with cookery recipes and heaven knows what in them, and the landlady wanted to hear them too. I couldn't get a sound out of it, so I opened it up and this is what I found. Don't you see, she couldn't have heard anything at all! She was mad all the time, mad as a coot!'

I said nothing then, but I have remembered the incident all this time because, you see, Miss Amber was not mad. She was the sanest, happiest little woman I ever knew, and what world she listened in to and derived her untarnishable delight from I do not dare to think.

The Man with the Sack

THERE was a personal letter under the pile of greeting cards sent off a week too soon by earnest citizens who had taken the Postmaster-General's annual warning a shade too seriously.

Mr Campion tore it open and a cry from Sheila Turrett's heart fell out.

'My darling Albert, Please come for Christmas. It's going to be poisonous. Mother has some queer ideas in her head and the Welkins are frightful. Mike is a dear. At least I like him and you will too. He is Mike Peters, the son of Ripley Peters who had to go to jail when the firm crashed. But it's not Mike's fault, is it? After all, a good many fathers ought to go to jail only they don't get caught. I don't mean George, of course, bless him (you ought to come if only for his sake. He's like a depression leaving the Azores. It's the thought of the Welkins, poor pet). I don't like to ask you to waste your time on our troubles, but Ada Welkin is lousy with diamonds and Mother seems to think that Mike might pinch them, his father having been to jail. Darling, if you are faintly decent do come and back us up. After all, it is Christmas. Yours always (if you come) Sheila. P.S. I'm in love with Mike.'

On Christmas Eve the weather decided to be seasonable; a freezing overhead fog turned the city into night and the illuminated shop fronts had the traditional festive appearance even in the morning. It was more than just cold. The damp atmosphere soaked into the bones relentlessly and Mr Campion's recollection of Pharaoh's Court, rising gaunt and bleak amid three hundred acres of ploughed clay and barren salting, all as flat as the estuary beyond, was not enhanced by the chill.

The thought of Sheila and her father cheered him a little, almost but not quite offsetting the prospect of Lady Mae in anxious mood. Buttoning himself into his thickest overcoat, he hoped for the best.

The railway station was a happy pandemonium. Everybody who could not visit the East coast for the holiday was, it seemed, sending presents there, and Mr Campion, reminded of the custom, glanced anxiously at his suitcase, wondering if the box of cigars for George was too large or the casket of perfume for Mae too modest and if Sheila was still young enough to eat chocolates.

He caught the train with ease, no great feat since it was three-quarters of an hour late, and was sitting in his corner idly watching the hurrying throng on the platform when he caught sight of Charlie Spring. He recognised the face instantly, but the name came to him slowly from the sifting of his memory.

Jail had done Mr Spring a certain amount of good, Mr Campion reflected as his glance took in the other man's square shoulders and developed chest. He had been a weedy wreck six months ago standing in the dock with the light from the roof shining down upon his low forehead, beneath which there peered out the stupidest eyes in the world.

At the moment he seemed very pleased with himself, a bad omen for the rest of the community, but Mr Campion was not interested. It was Christmas and he had troubles of his own. However, from force of habit he made a mental note of the man and observed that he boarded the train a little lower down. Mr Campion frowned. There was something about Charlie Spring which he had known and which now eluded him. He tried to remember the last and only time he had seen him. He himself had been in court as an observer and had heard Mr Spring sentenced for breaking and entering just before his own case had been called. He remembered the flat official voice of the police detective who gave evidence. But there was something else, something definite and personal about the man which kept bobbing about in the back of his mind, escaping him completely whenever he tried to pin it down. It worried him vaguely, as such things do, all the way to Chelmsworth.

Charlie had left the train at Ipswich in the company of some one hundred and fifty fellow travellers. Mr Campion spotted him as he passed the window, walking swiftly, his head bent and a large new suitcase in his hand.

It occurred to Campion that the man was not dressed in character.

He seemed to remember him as a dilapidated but somewhat gaudy figure in a dirty check suit and a pink shirt, whereas at the moment his newish greatcoat was a model of sobriety and unobtrusiveness. Yet, it was no sartorial peculiarity that haunted his memory. It was something odd about the man, some idiosyncrasy, something slightly funny.

Still faintly irritated, Mr Campion travelled a further ten miles to Chelmsworth. Few country railway stations present a rustic picturesqueness, even in summer, but at any time in the year Chelmsworth was remarkable for its windswept desolation. Mr Campion alighted on a narrow slab of concrete, artificially raised above the level of the small town in the valley, and drew a draught of heady rain and brine-soaked air into his lungs. He was experiencing the first shock of finding it not unattractive when there was a clatter on the concrete and a small russet-clad figure appeared before him. He was aware of honey-brown eyes, red cheeks, white teeth, and a stray curl of red hair escaping from a rakish tweed cap in which a sprig of holly had been pinned.

'Bless you,' said Sheila Turrett fervently. 'Come on. We're hours late for lunch, they'll all be champing like boarding house pests.'

She linked her arm through his and dragged him along.

'You're more than a hero to come. I am so grateful and so is George. Perhaps it'll start being Christmas now you're here, which it hasn't been so far in spite of the weather. Isn't it glorious?'

Mr Campion was forced to admit that there was a certain exhilaration in the air, a certain indefinable charm in the grey brown shadows chasing in endless succession over the flat landscape.

'There'll be snow tonight.' The girl glanced up at the feather-bed sky. 'Isn't it grand? Christmas always makes me feel so excited. I've got you a present. Remember to bring one for me?'

'I'm your guest,' said Mr Campion with dignity. 'I have a small packet of plain chocolate for you on Christmas morning, but I wish it to be a surprise.'

Sheila climbed into the car. 'Anything will be welcome except diamonds,' she said cheerfully. 'Ada Welkin's getting diamonds, twelve thousand pounds' worth, all to hang round a neck that would disgrace a crocodile. I'm sorry to sound so catty, but we've had these diamonds all through every meal since she came down.'

Mr Campion clambered into the car beside her.

'Dear me,' he said. 'I had hoped for a merry Christmas, peace and good will and all that. Village children bursting their lungs and everybody else's eardrums in their attempts at religious song, while I listened replete with vast quantities of indigestible food.'

Sheila laughed. 'You're going to get your dear little village kids all right,' she said. 'Not even Ada Welkin could dissuade mother from the Pharaoh's Court annual Christmas party. You'll have just time to sleep off your lunch, swallow a cup of tea, and then it's all hands in the music room. There's the mothers to entertain too, of course.'

Mr Campion stirred and sighed gently as he adjusted his spectacles.

'I remember now,' he murmured. 'George said something about it once. It's a traditional function, isn't it?'

'More or less.' Sheila spoke absently. 'Mother revived it with modern improvements some years ago. They have a tea and a Christmas tree and a Santa Claus to hand round the presents.'

The prospect seemed to depress her and she relapsed into gloomy silence as the car shot over the dry, windswept roads.

Mr Campion regarded her covertly. She had grown into a very pretty girl indeed, he decided, but he hoped the 'son in the Peters crash' was worth the worry he saw in her forehead.

'What about the young gentleman with the erring father?' he ventured diffidently. 'Is he at Pharaoh's Court now?'

'Mike?' She brightened visibly. 'Oh yes, rather. He's been there for the best part of a week. George honestly likes him and I thought for one heavenly moment that he was going to cut the ice with mother, but that was before the Welkins came. Since then, of course, it hasn't been easy. They came a day early, too, which is typical of them. They've been here two days already. The son is the nastiest, the old man runs him close and Ada is ghastly.'

'Horrid for them,' said Mr Campion mildly.

Sheila did not smile.

'You'll spot it at once when you see Ada,' she said, 'so I may as well tell you. They're fantastically rich and mother has been goat-touting. It's got to be faced.'

'Goat-touting?'

Sheila nodded earnestly.

'Yes. Lots of society women do it. You must have seen the little ads in the personal columns: "Lady of title will chaperone young girl or arrange parties for an older woman". Or "Lady X would entertain suitable guest for the London season". In other words, Lady X will tout around any socially ambitious goat in exchange for a nice large, fat fee. It's horrid, but I'm afraid that is how mother got hold of Ada in the first place. She had some pretty heavy bridge losses at one time. George doesn't know a thing about it, of course, poor darling—and mustn't. He'd be so shocked. I don't know how he accounts for the Welkins.'

Mr Campion said nothing. It was like Mae Turrett, he reflected, to visit her sins upon her family. Sheila was hurrying on.

'We've never seen the others before,' she said breathlessly.

'Mother gave two parties for Ada in the season and they had a box at the Opera to show some of the diamonds. I couldn't understand why they wanted to drag the menfolk into it until they got here. Then it was disgustingly plain.'

Mr Campion pricked up his ears.

'So nice for the dear children to get to know each other?' he suggested.

'Something like that.'

Mr Campion sighed deeply.

Sheila negotiated a right-angled turn. Her forehead was wrinkled and her eyes thoughtful.

'This'll show you the sort of man Kenneth Welkin is,' she said.

'It's so petty and stupid that I'm almost ashamed to mention it, but it does show you. We've had a rather difficult time amusing the Welkins. This morning, when Mike and I were putting the final touches to the decorations, we asked Kenneth to help us. There was some stupid business over the mistletoe. Kenneth had been laying down the law about where it was to hang and we were a bit tired of him already when he started a lot of silly horseplay. I don't mind being kissed under the mistletoe, of course, but –well, it's the way you do these things, isn't it?'

She stamped on the accelerator to emphasise her point, and Mr Campion, not a nervous man, clutched the side of the car.

'Sorry,' said Sheila and went on with her story. 'I tried to wiggle away after a bit, but when he wouldn't let me go Mike suddenly lost his temper and told him to behave himself or he'd damn well knock his head off. It was awfully melodramatic and stupid, but it might have passed off and been forgotten if Kenneth hadn't made a scene. First he said he wouldn't be talked to like that, and then he made a reference to Mike's father, which was unforgivable. I thought they were going to have a fight. Then, right in the middle of it, Mother fluttered in with a Santa Claus costume. She looked at Mike and said, 'You'd better try it on, dear, I want you to be most realistic this afternoon." Before he could reply, Kenneth butted in. He looked like a spoilt kid, all pink and furious. "I didn't know you were going to be Father Christmas," he said.'

Sheila Turrett paused for breath, her eyes wide.

'Well, can you imagine anything so idiotic?' she went on. 'Mike had offered to do the job when he first came down because he wanted to make himself useful. Like everyone else, he regarded it as a chore. It never dawned on him that anyone would want to do it. Mother was surprised, too, I think. However, she just laughed and said, "You must fight it out between you" and fluttered away again, leaving us all three standing there. Kenneth picked up the costume. "It's from Harridge's," he said. "My mother was with Lady Mae when she ordered it. I thought it was fixed up then that I was to wear it."'

Mr Campion laughed. He felt very old.

'I suppose Master Michael stepped aside and Master Kenneth appears as St Nicholas?' he murmured.

'Well no, not exactly.' Sheila sounded a little embarrassed. 'Mike was still angry, you see, so he suddenly decided to be obstinate. Mother had asked him to do the job, he said, and he was going to do it. I thought they were going to have an open row about it, which would have been quite too absurd, but at that moment the most idiotic thing of all happened. Old Mr Welkin, who had been prowling about listening as usual, came in and told Kenneth he was to "give way" to Mike—literally, in so many words! It all sounds perfectly mad now I've told it to you, yet Mike is rather a darling.'

Mr Campion detected a certain wistfulness in her final phrase and frowned.

Pharaoh's Court looked mellow and inviting as they came up the drive some minutes later. The old house had captured the spirit of the season and Mr Campion stepped out of a cold grey world into an entrance hall where the blaze from the hearth flickered on the glossy leaves of the holly festooned along the carved beams of the ceiling.

George Turrett, grey-haired and cherubic, was waiting for them. He grasped the visitor's hand with fervour. 'So glad you've come,' he murmured. 'Devilish glad to see you, Campion.'

His extreme earnestness was apparent and Sheila put an arm round his neck.

'It's a human face in the wilderness, isn't it, darling?' she said.

Sir George's guilty protest was cut short as Mr Campion was shown upstairs to his room.

He saw the clock as he came down again a moment or so later. It burst upon him as he turned a corner in the corridor and came upon it standing on a console table. Even in his haste it arrested him. Mae Turrett had something of a reputation for interior decoration, but large country houses have a way of collecting furnishing oddities, however rigorous their owner's taste may be.

Although he was not as a rule over-sensitive to artistic monstrosities, Mr Campion paused in respectful astonishment before this example of the mid-Victorian baroque. A bewildered looking bronze lady, clad in a pink marble nightgown, was seated upon a gilt ormolu log, one end of which had been replaced by a blue and white enamel clock face. As he stared the contraption chimed loudly and aggressively.

He passed on and forgot all about the clock as soon as he entered the dining-room. Mae Turrett sprang at him with little affected cries which he took to indicate a hostess's delight.

'Albert *dear!*' she said breathlessly. 'How marvellous to see you! Aren't we wonderfully festive? The gardener assures me it's going to snow tonight, in fact he's virtually promised it. I do love a real old family party at Christmas, don't you? Just our very own selves . . . too lovely! Let me introduce you to a very dear friend of mine: Mrs Welkin–Mr Campion.'

Campion was aware of a large middle-aged woman with drooping cheeks and stupid eyes who sniggered at him and looked away again.

Lunch was not a jolly meal by any means. Even Lady Turrett's cultivated chatter died down every now and again. However, Mr Campion had ample opportunity to observe the strangers of whom he had heard so much.

Mike Peters was a sturdy silent youngster with a brief smile and a determined chin. It was obvious that he knew what he wanted and was going for it steadily. Mr Campion found himself wishing him luck.

Since much criticism before a meeting may easily defeat its own ends, Mr Campion had been prepared to find the Welkin family pleasant but misunderstood people, round pegs in a very square hole. He was mistaken. Kenneth Welkin, a fresh faced, angry eyed young man, sat next to Sheila and sulked throughout the meal. The only remark he addressed to Mr Campion was to ask what make of car he drove and to disapprove loudly of the answer to his question.

A closer inspection of Mrs Welkin did not dispel Mr Campion's first impression, but her husband interested him. Edward Welkin was a large man with a face that would have been distinguished had it not been for the eyes, which were too shrewd, and the mouth, which was too coarse. His attitude towards his hostess was conspicuously different from his wife's, which was ingratiating, and his son's, which was uneasy and defensive. The most obvious thing about him was that he completely alien. George he regarded quite clearly as a nincompoop and Lady Turrett as a woman who so far had given his wife value for money. To everyone else he was sublimely indifferent.

His tweeds, of the best old-gentleman variety, had their effect ruined by the astonishing quantity of jewellery he chose to display at the same time. He wore two signet rings, one with an agate and one with a sapphire, and an immense jewelled tiepin, while out of his waistcoat pocket peeped a gold and onyx pen with a pencil to match, strapped together in a bright green leather case. They were both of them as thick round as his forefinger and looked at first glance like the insignia of some obscure order.

Just before they rose from the table Mrs Welkin cleared her throat.

'As you are going to have a crowd of tenants this evening, Mae, I don't think I'll wear it, do you?' she said with a giggle and a glance at Mr Campion.

'Wear what, dear?' Lady Turrett spoke absently and Mrs Welkin looked hurt.

'The necklace,' she said reverently.

'Your diamonds? Good heavens, no! Most unsuitable.' The words escaped involuntarily, but in a moment her ladyship was mistress of herself and the situation. 'Wear something very simple,' she said with a mechanical smile. 'I'm afraid it's going to be very hard work for us all. Mike, you do know exactly what to do, don't you? At the end of the evening, just before they go home, you put on the costume and come into the little ante-room which leads off the platform. You go straight up to the tree and cut the presents off, while all the rest of us stand round to receive them and pass them on to the children.'

Mrs Welkin bridled. 'I should have liked to have worn them,' she said petulantly. 'Still, if you say it's not safe . . .'

'Mother didn't say it wasn't safe, Mrs Welkin,' said Sheila sharply. 'She said it wasn't suitable.'

Mrs Welkin blushed angrily.

'You're not very polite, young lady,' she said, 'and if it's a question of suitability, where's the suitability in Mr Peters playing Santa Claus when it was promised to Kenny?'

The mixture of muddled logic and resentment startled everyone. Sir George looked helplessly at his wife, Kenneth Welkin turned savagely on his mother, and Edward Welkin settled rather than saved the situation.

'That'll do,' he said in a voice of thunder. 'That's all been fixed, Ada. I don't want to hear any more from either of you on the subject.'

The table broke up with relief. Sir George tugged Campion's arm.

'Cigar—library,' he murmured and faded quietly away.

Campion followed him.

There were Christmas decorations in the book-filled study and, as he settled himself in a wing chair before a fire of logs and attended to the tip of a Romeo y Julieta, Mr Campion felt once more the return of the Christmas spirit.

Sir George was anxious about his daughter's happiness.

'I like young Peters,' he said earnestly. 'Fellow can't help his father's troubles.'

Mr Campion agreed with him and the older man went on.

'The boy Mike's an engineer,' he said, 'and makin' good at his job slowly, and Sheila seems fond of him, but Mae talks about hereditary dishonesty. Taint may be there. What do you think?'

Mr Campion had no time to reply to this somewhat unlikely theory. There was a flutter and a rustle outside the door and a moment later Mr Welkin senior came in with a flustered lady. George got up and held out his hand.

'Ah, Miss Hare,' he said. 'Glad to see you. Come on your annual visit of mercy?'

Miss Hare, who was large and inclined to be hearty, laughed.

'I've come cadging again, if that's what you mean, Sir George,' she said cheerfully, and went on, nodding to Mr Campion as if they had just been introduced. 'Every Christmas I come round collecting for my old women. There are four of 'em in the alms-house by the church. I only ask for a shilling or two to buy them some little extra for the Christmas treat. I don't want much. Just a shilling or two.'

She glanced at a small notebook in her hand.

'You gave me ten shillings last year, Sir George.'

He produced the required sum and Campion felt in his pocket.

'Half-a-crown would be ample,' said Miss Hare encouragingly. 'Oh, that's very nice of you. I assure you it won't be wasted.'

She took the coin and was turning to Welkin when he stepped forward.

'I'd like to do the thing properly,' he said. 'Anybody got a pen?'

He took out a cheque book and sat down at George's desk uninvited.

Miss Hare protested. 'Oh no, really,' she said, 'you don't under-stand. This is just for an extra treat. I collect it nearly all in six-pences.'

'Anybody got a pen?' repeated Mr Welkin.

Campion glanced at the elaborate display in the man's own waistcoat pocket, but before he could mention it George had meekly handed over his own fountain pen.

Mr Welkin wrote a cheque and handed it to Miss Hare without troubling to blot it.

'Ten pounds?' said the startled lady. 'Oh, but really . . !'

'Nonsense. Run along.' Mr Welkin clapped her familiarly on the shoulder. 'It's Christmas time,' he said, glancing at George and Campion. 'I believe in doing a bit of good at Christmas time –if you can afford it.'

Miss Hare glanced round her helplessly.

'It's very–very kind of you,' she said, 'but half-a-crown would have been ample.'

She fled. Welkin threw George's pen on to the desk.

'That's the way I like to do it,' he said.

George coughed and there was a faraway expression in his eyes. 'Yes, I–er–I see you do,' he said and sat down. Welkin went out.

Neither Mr Campion nor his host mentioned the incident. Campion frowned. Now he had two minor problems on his conscience. One was the old matter of the piece of information concerning Charlie Spring which he had forgotten, the other was a peculiarity of Mr Welkin's which puzzled him mightily.

The Pharaoh's Court children's party had been in full swing for what seemed to Mr Campion to be the best part of a fortnight. It was half-past seven in the evening and the relics of an enormous tea had been cleared away, leaving the music room full of replete but still energetic children and their mothers, dancing and playing games with enthusiasm.

Mr Campion, who had danced, buttled, and even performed a few conjuring tricks, bethought him of a box of his favourite cigarettes in his suitcase upstairs and, feeling only a little guilty at leaving George still working like a hero, he stole away and hurried to his room.

The main body of the house was deserted. Even the Welkins were at work in the music room, while the staff were concentrated in the kitchen washing up.

Mr Campion found his cigarettes, lit one, and pottered for a moment or two, reflecting that the Christmases of his youth were much the same as those of today, but not so long from hour to hour. He felt virtuous, happy and positively oozing with goodwill. The promised snow was falling, great soft flakes plopping softly against his window.

At last, when his conscience decreed that he could absent himself no longer, he switched off the light and stepped into the corridor, to come face to face with Father Christmas. The saint looked as weary as he himself had been and was stooping under the great sack on his shoulders. Mr Campion admired Harridge's costume. The boots were glossy, the tunic with its wool border satisfyingly red, while the benevolent mask with its cottonwool beard was almost lifelike.

He stepped aside to let the venerable figure pass and, because it seemed the moment for jocularity, said lightly:

'What have you got in the bag, Guv'nor?'

Had he uttered a spell of high enchantment, the simple words could not have had a more astonishing effect. The figure uttered an inarticulate cry, dropped the sack, which fell with a crash at Mr Campion's feet, and fled like a shadow.

For a moment Mr Campion stood paralysed with astonishment. By the time he had pulled himself together the crimson figure had disappeared down the staircase. He bent over the sack and thrust in his hand. Something hard and heavy met his fingers and he brought it out. It was the pink marble, bronze and ormolu clock.

He stood looking at his find and a sigh of satisfaction escaped him. One of the problems that had been worrying him all day had been solved.

It was twenty minutes later before he reappeared in the music room. No one saw him come in, for the attention of the entire room was focused upon the platform. There, surrounded by enthusiastic assistants, was Father Christmas again, peacefully snipping presents off the tree.

Campion took careful stock of him. The costume, he decided, was identical, the same high boots, the same tunic, the same mask. He tried to remember the fleeting figure in the corridor upstairs, but the costume was a deceptive one and he found it difficult.

After a time he found a secluded chair and sat down to await developments. They came.

As the last of the visitors departed and Lady Turrett threw herself into an armchair with a sigh of happy exhaustion, Pouter, the Pharaoh's Court butler, came quietly into the room and muttered a few words into his master's ear. From where he sat Mr Campion heard George's astonished 'God bless my soul!' and rose immediately to join him. But although he moved swiftly Mr Welkin was before him and, as Campion reached the group, his voice resounded round the room.

'A burglary? While we've been playing the fool in here? What's gone, man? What's gone?'

Pouter, who objected to the form of address, regarded his master's guest coldly.

'A clock from the first floor west corridor, a silver-plated salver, a copper loving cup from the hall, and a brass Buddha and a gilt pomander box from the first floor landing, as far as we can ascertain, sir,' he said.

'Bless my soul!' said George again. 'How extraordinary!'

'Extraordinary be damned!' ejaculated Welkin. 'We've got valuables here. Ada!'

'The necklace!' shrieked Mrs Welkin, consternation suddenly welling up in her eyes. 'My necklace!'

She scuttled out of the room and Sheila came forward with Santa Claus, who had taken off his mask and pushed back his hood to reveal the features of Mike Peters.

Lady Turrett did not stir from her chair, and Kenneth Welkin, white faced and bewildered, stared down at her.

'There's been a burglary,' he said. 'Here, in this house.'

Mae Turrett smiled at him vaguely. 'George and Pouter will see to it,' she said. 'I'm tired.'

'Tired!' shouted Edward Welkin. 'If my wife's diamonds—'

He got no further. Ada Welkin tottered into the room, an empty steel dispatch case in her trembling hands.

'They've gone,' she said, her voice rising in hysteria. 'They've gone. My diamonds . . . my room's been turned upside down. They've been taken. The necklace has gone.'

It was Mike who had sufficient presence of mind to support her to a chair before she collapsed. Her husband shot a shrewd, preoccupied glance at her, shouted to his son to 'Look after your mother, boy!' and took command of the situation.

'You, Pigeon, get all the servants, everyone who's in this house, to come here in double quick time, see? I've been robbed.'

Pouter looked at his master in mute appeal and George coughed.

'In a moment, Mr Welkin,' he said. 'In a moment. Let us find out what we can first. Pouter, go and see if any stranger is known to have been about the house or grounds this evening, will you, please?'

The manservant went out instantly and Welkin raged.

'You may think you know what you are doing,' he said, 'but my way was the best. You're giving the thief time to get away, and time's precious, let me tell you. I've got to get the police up here?'

'The police?' Sheila was aghast.

He gaped at her. 'Of course, young woman. Do you think I'm going to lose twelve thousand pounds? The stones were insured, of course, but what company would pay up if I hadn't called in the police? I'll go and phone up now.'

'Wait a moment, please,' said George, his quiet voice only a little ruffled. 'Here's Pouter again. Well?'

The butler looked profoundly uncomfortable.

'Two maids say, sir,' he said, 'they saw a man running down the drive just before the Christmas tree was begun.' He hesitated. 'They–they say, sir, he was dressed as Father Christmas. They both say it, sir.'

Everyone looked at Mike and Sheila's cheeks flamed.

'Well?' she demanded.

Mr Welkin laughed. 'So that's how it was done,' he said. 'The young man was clever, but he was seen.'

Mike moved forward. His face was pale and his eyes were dangerous. George laid a hand upon his arm.

'Wait,' he commanded. 'Mr Welkin, you'll have to explain, you know.'

Mr Welkin kept his temper. He seemed almost amused.

'Well, it's perfectly simple, isn't it?' he said. 'This fellow has been wandering about in this disguise all the evening. He couldn't come in here because her ladyship wanted him to be a surprise to the children, but he had the rest of the house to himself. He went round lifting up anything he fancied, including my diamonds. Suppose he had been met? No one would think anything of it. Father Christmas always carried a sack. Then he went off down the drive where he met a confederate, handed over the stuff, and came back to the party.'

Mike began to speak but Mr Campion decided it was time to intervene.

'I say, George,' he said, 'if you and Mr Welkin would come along to the library I've got a suggestion I'd like to make.'

Welkin wavered. 'I'll listen to you, Campion, but I want my diamonds back and I want the police. I'll give you five minutes, no longer.'

The library was in darkness when the three men entered, and Campion waited until they were all in the room before he switched on the main light. There was a moment of bewildered silence. One corner of the room looked like a stall in a market. There the entire contents of the sack, which had come so unexpectedly into Mr Campion's possession, was neatly spread out. George's cherubic face darkened.

'What's this?' he demanded. 'A damned silly joke?'

Mr Campion shook his head. 'I'm afraid not. I've just collected this from a gentleman in fancy dress whom I met in the corridor upstairs,' he said. 'What would you say, Mr Welkin?'

The man stared at him doggedly. 'Where are my diamonds? That's my only interest. I don't care about this junk.'

Campion smiled faintly. 'He's right, you know, George,' he said. 'Junk's the word. It came back to me as soon as I saw it. Poor Charlie Spring–I recognised him, Mr Welkin–never had a successful coup in his life because he can't help stealing gaudy junk.'

Edward Welkin stood stiffly by the desk.

'I don't understand you,' he said. 'My diamonds have been stolen and I want to call the police.'

Mr Campion took off his spectacles. 'I shouldn't if I were you,' he said. 'No you don't–!'

On the last words Mr Campion lept forward and there was a brief struggle. When it was over Mr Welkin was lying on the floor beside the marble and ormolu clock and Mr Campion was grasping the gold pen and pencil in the leather holder which until a moment before had rested in the man's waistcoat pocket.

Welkin scrambled to his feet. His face was purple and his eyes a little frightened. He attempted to bluster.

'You'll find yourself in court for assault,' he said. 'Give me my property.'

'Certainly. All of it,' agreed Mr Campion obligingly. 'Your dummy pen, your dummy pencil, and in the receptacle which they conceal, your wife's diamonds.'

On the last word he drew the case apart and a glittering string fell out in his hand.

There was a long, long pause.

Welkin stood sullenly in the middle of the room.

'Well?' he said at last. 'What are you two going to do about it?'

Mr Campion glanced at George, who was standing by the desk, an expression of incredulity amounting almost to stupefaction upon his mild face.

'If I might suggest,' he murmured, 'I think he might take his family and spend a jolly Christmas somewhere else, don't you? It would save a lot of trouble.'

Welkin held out his hand.

'Very well. I'll take my diamonds.'

Mr Campion shook his head. 'As you go out of the house,' he said with a faint smile. 'I shouldn't like them to be–lost again.'

Welkin shrugged his shoulders. 'You win,' he said briefly. 'I'll go and tell Ada to pack.'

He went out of the room and as the door closed behind him George sat down.

'Hanged if I understand it . . .' he began, 'his own son Kenneth was going to play Santa Claus, or at least seemed to expect to.'

Campion nodded. 'I know,' he said. 'If Kenneth had been playing Father Christmas and the same thing happened I think you would have found that the young man had a pretty convincing alibi established for him. You must remember the thief was not meant to be seen. He was only furnished with the costume in case he was.'

His host took the diamonds and turned them over. He was slow of comprehension.

'Why steal his own property?' he demanded.

Mr Campion sighed. 'You have such a blameless mind, George, that the wickedness of some of your fellow men must be a constant source of astonishment to you.' He paused. 'Did you hear our friend Welkin say that he had insured this necklace?'

George's eyebrows rose. 'God bless my soul!' he said. 'What a feller! In our house, too,' he added as an afterthought. 'How did you spot it, Campion?'

Mr Campion explained. 'I knew Charlie Spring had a peculiarity but I couldn't think what it was until I pulled that clock out of the bag. Then I remembered his penchant for the baroque and his sad habit of mistaking it for the valuable. That ruled out the diamonds. They wouldn't be large enough for Charlie. When that came back to me, I recollected his other failing. He never works alone. When Mr Spring appears on a job it always means he has a confederate in the house. With these two facts in my hand the rest was fairly obvious.'

'You spotted the pen was a dummy when Miss Hare came this afternoon?'

Mr Campion grinned. 'Well, it was odd the man didn't use his own pen, wasn't it?' he said. 'When he ignored it, I guessed. That kind of cache is fairly common, especially in the States. They're made for carrying valuables and are usually shabby plastic things which no one would steal in the ordinary way. However, there was nothing shabby about Mr Welkin–except his behaviour.'

George poured out a couple of drinks. 'Difficult feller,' he observed. 'Didn't like him from the start. No conversation. I started him on shootin', but he wasn't interested, mentioned huntin' and he gaped at me, went on to fishin' and he yawned. Couldn't think of anything to talk to him about. Feller hadn't any conversation at all.'

The Secret

THE key fidgeted in the lock, grated, and was silent. Then the door swung quietly open, admitting a wave of cold air from the staircase of the block.

The man who was hatless and curiously short of breath stepped inside and, thrusting out his hand, groped for the familiar switch.

The next moment he was standing in his wet raincoat, gazing about him, at first in surprise and afterwards in the cold dismay of a realised fear.

After a few minutes of silent contemplation he pulled himself together and, glancing down at the key in his hand, tiptoed across the garish carpet to a small occasional table in the corner.

Having set the key in a prominent position on the polished surface, he granted the room a second glance, turned away shuddering and made for the door again.

He was a young man, but the strain of the last few months had told upon him and the bitter experience of the past few minutes had not helped.

His brown eyes were darker than they had been and his face was drawn.

His fingers were on the light switch again when he turned and saw her. She had risen from the depths of the big chesterfield pulled across the hearth, and even in that moment of crisis he wondered that she should be there alone in the dark with no fire on a chill night, the rain teeming down in cold fury outside.

The girl was very small, almost a child, with sleek brown hair which hung loosely round her shapely head. She was fragile, and still looked as though the least breath would blow her away.

That curious, almost ethereal fragility had increased, he noticed. She too had not found it so easy then.

She did not speak, but stood looking at him, her eyes bright and shy, her lips questioning.

Now that the moment had come words deserted him. He had rehearsed this meeting so often that at the crucial moment, like a stale actor on the stage, he had forgotten his part.

'I thought you'd left here,' he said helplessly. 'I was going away.'

Still she did not speak, and suddenly he lost control. His careful explanations and well-thought-out arguments were swept away by his urgent need. He stumbled towards her.

'I've come back,' he said. 'O Jenny, I've come back.'

She drew away from him, not resentfully but gently, almost, it seemed, reluctantly.

He saw her movement and stiffened.

'I know . . . I'm sorry,' he said dully, and sat down on the arm of the couch, his shoulders drooping.

Now that he was still she moved closer, perching herself on the farther arm of the couch, her feet on the seat, her arms clasping her knees.

They sat for a long time in silence and the room was very cold.

At last he looked up and met her eyes.

'I'm not a bad fellow, Jenny,' he said, 'Only ordinary.'

She stirred, moved towards him and drew back again.

'You've only just come back to London?' she said, and her voice was quiet and thin and very gentle, as it had always been.

He nodded. 'Last night. I had some sleep at a hotel, and then all day I've been wandering about trying to prevent myself from clearing off again. I knew I couldn't expect you to welcome me with open arms, but I thought I might just see you and find out if there was half a chance of patching things up. Is there?'

'You want to come back?' she said, and there was something in her voice that he did not understand.

He looked at her sharply. 'You're not angry, are you?'

'Angry? Oh no,' she said and looked down at her feet.

Once again he stretched out his hand to her, but she eluded him, shrinking away from his touch as though she were afraid of it, but he had the odd impression that it was not himself of whom she was afraid.

He thought he understood, and plunged into the story that had to be told.

'She left me,' he said jerkily. 'A fellow on the boat had more money. I was glad. I knew I'd made a mistake even then. After that I changed my route and went up-country. I've been there ever since. I thought I'd get over it at first. I didn't want to come sneaking back to tell you I'd made a fool of myself. I soon got over that, though. I love you, Jenny. I can't live without you.'

He glanced at her and saw that she was hanging on his words, a passionate sympathy in her eyes. He went on talking. It made it easier if he talked.

'I was up there alone for two months. I didn't even see a newspaper. Finally I made up my mind to come back. I felt I'd have more chance with you if I just turned up like this. Jenny, I ought to have married you. For my own sake I ought to have married you. I'd never have left you if we'd been married. It was only that irritating sense of freedom and yet the half-restraint with it. We were young, both of us; I want to marry you now. Will you let me?'

The girl shook her head. There were tears in her eyes and her whole body drooped as though she were overcome by some dreadful, secret tragedy.

'No,' she said. 'You can't do that. Not now. Never . . . never. Don't talk of it. Talk of usual things. How did you get in?'

'With my key. I've had it all this time. But I don't want to talk about usual things. I want you to marry me. I want to begin all over again.'

He had risen and came towards her, his arms outstretched.

'Jenny, don't look at me like that. What's the matter? Let me comfort you as I used. Do you remember?'

She started back from him.

'Don't touch me,' she whispered. 'Whatever you do, don't touch me. You mustn't love me, Geoff. You must go away.'

The couch was between them now and he knelt on it, pleading with her.

'I can't go. You still love me, Jenny. You never loved anyone but me. Do you remember how I found you down on the marshes? And that sunny day I came down to meet your people. And your father wanted to talk about politics but you took me out to show me the garden. And I kissed you down on the long green path behind the delphinium bank, where no one could see. Don't look at me like that, Jenny. What's the matter?'

She was staring at him, a tear trickling down her cheek.

'It's nothing,' she said and picked up the thread of his story.

'And then you brought me here that Sunday night. Do you remember? And there weren't any blankets, and I had your great-coat and a rug. It was the beginning of a new life for me.'

He closed his eyes. 'Oh don't, Jenny, please! Don't rub it in. You didn't see your people after . . . after I went?'

'No,' she said.

'Did you try to see them?'

'No.'

He turned away from her in an agony of self-reproach.

'Oh poor little Jenny! I didn't mean to behave like that. It was only that *she* just swept down on me and altered the whole world for the moment. It couldn't have lasted. I ought to have known that. I didn't think what it would be like for you. Oh my dear, you must come back to me. We'll be married as soon as we can arrange it, and then we'll go off on that trip we used to plan so often . . . pick up a car in Calais and go to Paris by road, and then strike south, just you and me.'

The girl shook her head. 'No. We can't go together. You mustn't want me to. Oh, my darling, you mustn't want me to.'

She spoke with such curious intensity that the realisation that something was seriously wrong forced itself upon his mind, something new, something for which he had not legislated.

'Why not?' he said.

She stood within a foot of him, her eyes fixed compellingly upon his face.

'Geoff,' she said, 'you must go away from here alone. I can't come with you. You must forget me, let your mind shut me out. It will be so much less hard for you, my dear.'

'No!' he said wildly. 'No. I love you. Don't send me away ...
please ... please don't send me away.'

'Go away,' she repeated. 'Go away quickly. Don't think of me.
Don't want me. When my name comes into your mind drive it
out. Don't think of me. I can never come.'

'You've said that before,' he said slowly. 'What is there to stop
you?'

'I can't tell you,' she said, drawing back from him, still speaking
in the same subdued, anxious tone. 'Don't try to find out.'

'There's some reason why you can't come? Some secret?'

She nodded, and the feeling of apprehension in the cold little
room struck into his heart.

'But my dear,' he said, 'if we love each other there's nothing
strong enough to hold us apart. Tell me about it.'

She had retreated to the centre of the room and was looking at
him wistfully and with infinite pathos in her face.

'I can't come,' she said brokenly. 'Oh my darling, I can't come.
You'll know soon, but not now ... not now, please. Don't make
it happen now.'

'But I must know,' he persisted. 'Don't you see, it means all
our life. Oh God, I can't let you go again!'

His voice broke helplessly on the last word and she swayed a
little towards him, her face twisted with pain.

'I love you,' she said. 'I have always loved you. For me you
were love. Believe that. But oh, my dear, I can't come with you
now. I can't.'

'Why? Why the mystery?' He was frightened now. 'Tell me.
I can bear it, whatever it is. Tell me.'

'Not now,' she implored. 'Not now. Oh, please, not now!'

The man glanced round the room and a faint enlightenment
came into his eyes.

'All this stuff is new, of course,' he said. 'I hardly recognised
our lacquer room. You're living with someone?'

'No,' she said faintly. 'No. Don't ask. Don't try to find out.'

He stared at her. The chill in the room was eating into his
bones.

'I don't understand. My lawyer sent you an allowance, didn't he? You haven't been poor, have you? I remember that frock you're wearing. It's old-fashioned now. Are you married?'

'No.'

'You're free, then?'

She nodded wearily. 'Free. Oh terribly, terribly free.'

'You can marry me, then?'

'No, never, Geoff.' She backed away from him. 'It's too late. We can never be married now. And remember, oh remember— afterwards, you mustn't think of me.'

She had retreated across the room now and was standing with her back to the heavy curtains which hung across the window. He followed her.

'I can't stand any more of this,' he said. 'I love you, you love me. I'm coming to kiss you. My dear, we belong to one another. There's nothing that can separate us.'

She stretched out her hand as though to ward him off, and her quiet voice was soft and breathless.

'Don't . . . don't. There is something between us, something enormous. I can't come. Oh Geoff, don't you see? I can't come.'

He stared at her and a fraction of the truth broke upon him.

'Jenny!' he said hoarsely, 'whose flat is this now?'

She was standing back against the curtains, and her whisper, although so soft, seemed to fill the room.

'Strangers.'

'Jenny!' The man was hysterical. 'What is the secret?'

A breath parted the curtains and she stepped back into their folds. Her voice was very sorrowful and had utter tragedy in its tone.

'Don't you understand . . . my dear . . . I killed myself.'

The curtains slipped over her and he leapt forward and swept them wide.

Beyond was the high white window with the dark rain lashing against the panes.

From outside the door came the sound of laughing voices as the owner of the flat set a key in the latch.

A Quarter of a Million

DETECTIVE SERGEANT RICHARDSON'S keen eye took in every detail of the man's appearance.

'There he is. Funny looking chap, isn't he? You wouldn't think a man with a face like that could get away with half a million.' He spoke softly and without turning his head, and the inconspicuous figure at his side grinned.

'You wouldn't think he could count to half a million, by the look of him,' Sergeant Murdoch observed.

'Probably can't,' said Richardson drily, and the two Yard detectives remained standing where they were on the quay, watching the stream of passengers hurrying down the gangway from the Channel steamer.

The man they were looking towards moved slowly away from the boat, almost as though he were loath to set foot on English ground. He was a strange-looking man, approaching sixty, heavily built and small-eyed. He was well dressed but his clothes sagged upon him, indicating suddenly lost weight. There was a stoop about his shoulders also and a certain furtiveness in his glance.

This was Joseph Thurtle, the man who three months before had been at the head of a large American cotton combine. The spectacular crash of the company and the subsequent revelation of its affairs had turned Mr Thurtle from a millionaire to a hunted fugitive.

The sensational story of his escape from the States with at least half a million sterling in negotiable securities had made front page news. Extradition warrants had followed him from country to country. He had fled from France to Italy, from Italy to Greece to North Africa, and now, as he set foot in England, he did so with the knowledge that the police must have prepared a suitable reception for him.

As he stepped off the boat he had looked behind him sharply. It was quite evident to the two men who watched that he expected a hand on his shoulder at any moment.

'Come on. We'll follow him through Customs.'

Richardson spoke quietly. A flicker of disgust passed across his red face.

'I don't like this method of Parker's,' he added. 'Why not arrest the man right away and put him out of his misery? This waiting for him at Victoria, so that he can have a snappy arrest with the Press standing round admiring is a bit cheap, to my mind.'

'Detective Inspector Parker is a bit cheap,' said Murdoch. 'You and I have been on this job for ten years, and I was thinking, have you ever before heard of or known a fellow with Parker's reputation at the Yard? He's an unpopular publicity hound. Come on! We'll keep an eye on this poor devil until he gets out of the train at Victoria feeling perfectly safe and walks straight into the arms of the unpleasant Parker and a battery of cameras.'

They sauntered into the crowd and, with the ease of long practice, edged their way through the jostling groups of passengers until they walked directly behind the man they shadowed.

There were many friends and relations awaiting passengers on the Folkestone Harbour station, but there was one young man among the throng who served in neither capacity. He was a shortish, round-faced, fair-haired individual with a foolish expression and rather blank, trusting blue eyes.

He observed Joseph Thurtle and sauntered forward casually as the man came hurrying down the platform. When he was within a few feet of Thurtle, however, he caught sight of the officials walking behind the financier. He hurried past the man and climbed into another compartment. To all outward appearances there had been nothing odd in his behaviour, and yet in that brief instant quite an important person had abandoned one plan and embarked upon another.

The fair young man sat himself in a corner, turned up the collar of his great coat, pulled his hat down over his eyes, and prepared to go to sleep.

Mr Joseph Thurtle, with his attendant spirits, settled himself in another compartment farther down the train. It was cold. The station looked damp and unattractive and as the train slid through the chalky tunnels on the upward run, some of the dank hopelessness of the day seemed to permeate the consciousness of every traveller.

Thurtle was afraid. He was also puzzled. He had felt that his landing in England was tantamount to handing himself over to the police, and coming over in the boat he had steeled himself to face an arrest upon the quay.

It had not come. He could not understand it. He leaned farther back into the cushions and peered out at the sodden landscape with weary, anxious eyes. He had played a dangerous game and he had lost. He wondered idly if life in prison was as bad or worse than current reports would have it.

The innocent old lady sitting opposite him thought he looked very tired, and wondered if he had found the crossing as trying as she herself had done.

Meanwhile, on Victoria station, Inspector Parker strode up and down the platform, his fingers caressing the handcuffs in his coat pocket. This situation he enjoyed. He was like that. His career had been one long line of rather unsavoury little triumphs which had forced him slowly to his present position.

There were camera men outside the station, and he was looking forward to a photograph of himself in the evening papers handcuffed to the celebrated absconding financier. It was against the rules, he knew. The superintendent would comment upon it unfavourably; but Inspector Parker privately considered that the publicity would be worth it. As he waited for the train he amused himself by imagining suitable captions beneath the picture.

Parker was pleased with himself. Soon after he had received Richardson's phone message from Folkestone saying that Thurtle had boarded the train, he had hurried down to the station, and incurred the totally unnecessary expense of keeping a taxi waiting outside so that he might walk straight into it with his charge.

As soon as the train was signalled, he retired to the ticket barrier and stood waiting for his man. The train came in, and immediately the partially deserted platform sprang to life, as carriage doors swung open and weary and excited travellers swarmed out, clamoured for their luggage, lost their children and rushed to and fro after the manner of their kind.

Richardson reached the barrier first. 'He's just coming, sir,' he said. 'You can't miss him. Black overcoat, check muffler, soft travelling hat.'

'All right, all right. You leave this to me, Richardson.'

Parker spoke testily, as though the man had been hindering him rather than giving him information.

Richardson surrendered his ticket and wandered over to the bookstall to wait for Murdoch. The faintly contemptuous expression which always came into his face after dealings with his chief was very apparent.

Thurtle came heavily down the platform towards the barrier. Most of the fire which had once made him such a dangerous force in the business world had long since died down. He was old, tired, and at the end of his tether.

Detective Inspector Parker pounced upon him as he stepped through the barrier.

'Joseph Thurtle!' he said.

The man swung round, and as he faced his captor there was an expression in his eyes which was almost relief. It had come at last, then. The wearing uncertainty was over. 'Yes,' he said quickly. 'Yes. You are a police officer, aren't you? Very well. I'll come with you, only don't make a scene here!'

D. I. Parker was a man who took an officious pride in his job. He recited the formula of arrest clearly and unnecessarily loudly, and then, producing his handcuffs, slipped a bracelet over the older man's right wrist.

'Surely that's unnecessary? I said I'd come with you.'

The man who had shunned publicity all his life glanced

nervously at the curious crowd which was beginning to collect.

'I'm sorry!' The inspector spoke curtly. The other bracelet of the handcuff was attached to his own wrist now, and together they walked across the platform, a small section of the crowd streaming after them.

On the top of the steps, in the archway to the station drive, D. I. Parker paused for an instant to glance behind him, ostensibly to look for Murdoch. It was only for a moment, but it gave the photographers time. A faint smile of satisfaction spread over the inspector's face, as he hurried over to his waiting taxi.

Had he been a little less pleased with himself, it is conceivable that he might have noticed a single swift glance which passed between the driver of the cab and a plumpish, fair young man, who had come out of the station by another door. It is also just possible that the inspector's sharp, well-trained eyes might have observed that the driver, although remarkably like was, indeed, not the actual man who had driven him from the Yard less than twenty minutes before.

'I suppose you're taking me to a police station?'

The crumpled, dejected prisoner, who sagged against the leather upholstery of the cab, turned an inquiring eye upon the lean and wiry man at his side. The two wrists, handcuffed together, lay upon the seat between them.

Inspector Parker vouchsafed no reply. The cab was passing Westminster Abbey. When they came upon the Embankment the traffic thinned because of the wide road and the cab gathered speed. The policeman sat up stiffly. His mind was far away, rehearsing just exactly what he was going to to say to Superintendent Wetherby. The job had been so simple that it was going to be difficult to introduce any element of self-congratulation.

He was still pondering on the problem when something occurred which materially altered the whole course of Inspector Parker's career.

A large moving-van stood by the side of the road, its doors gaping and its drawbridge apron down. It was growing dusk and, save for a bus and a few other taxis, there was very little traffic. The inspector was gazing through the glass, when the utterly incredible occurred. The cab driver slowed down, dropped into low gear, and, crouching over his wheel, suddenly swerved and charged straight at the back of the van.

There was a jolt as the front wheels hit the bottom of the apron, the engine roared as the cab took the strain, and the next minute they were plunged into darkness as they entered the van. The doors clanged to behind them and a figure swayed through the window towards them in the darkness and something hard and circular was pressed into his ribs.

'Sit still!'

The strange voice was calm, almost conversational. 'Don't start yelling or I'll fire.'

The inspector jerked the wrist of his prisoner. 'I suppose you think you're very clever, Thurtle,' he said. 'But this will mean another ten years on your sentence.'

'I don't understand.' The man's voice was genuinely afraid. 'I can't move myself.'

It was at this point that the inspector realised that a second assailant was leaning through the other window of the cab. Meanwhile, the van had begun to move. He could feel its wheels beneath him. The whole plot had been worked so smoothly and neatly that it was unlikely that anyone witnessing the incident would have guessed that anything was seriously wrong.

It took Inspector Parker some moments to grasp the enormity of the situation. Then he became angry. Only the gun muzzle in his ribs prevented him from becoming violent. He was not a timid man, however, and he leaned back against the cushions with at least a show of ease.

'I suppose you realise the penalties for this sort of thing?' he remarked.

The owner of the gun in his ribs laughed.

'The trouble with you cops is that you believe you're invulnerable,' he said. 'You shouldn't have handcuffed yourself to your prisoner. As it is, I'm afraid you'll have to come the whole way. And something tells me, Inspector Parker'—the voice was soft, almost caressing—'something tells me that you're going to find that very unhealthy indeed.'

'I don't know who you are,' said another voice out of the darkness, which the inspector recognised as his prisoner's, 'but you are doing me a great disservice. Why don't you let this man arrest me in peace?'

Once again the soft, explosive laugh, which was beginning to grate on the inspector, sounded in his ear.

'Good heavens!' the second man said. 'What do you think we are? A charity organisation? If you've come from the States, Mr Thurtle, you ought to know you've been hijacked. Perhaps you'd like me to translate for you, inspector? You're one firm, as it were, Mr Thurtle is another. And the bright lads who are taking you on this joy ride represent a third party who happens to be interested. Have you got that clear?'

The van swerved round a corner and in its depths Inspector Parker leaned back, the gun still in his ribs as he cursed beneath his breath.

At police headquarters Chief Detective Inspector Guthrie of C Division was talking to one of his more promising young men. 'Well, Fisher, we've found the taxi. Fortunately, Murdoch was able to identify the number. And we've found the moving-van. But the men, Thurtle, and Parker have vanished. This is a serious business for us. When a world-famous financier is arrested by a Yard inspector on Victoria station, and they both disappear, together with the taxi in which they are riding; that makes for newspaper crusades and questions in Parliament.'

The young man at the desk looked up from the plan which almost covered it. He was a big fair-haired officer with sharp grey eyes.

The Chief Detective Inspector continued: 'That WX-Fifteen district where we found the cab, is a vortex—a thieves' vortex. They just stand there and it swallows them up. It has happened time and again; only unlike a vortex they come up again—somewhere else.'

He walked across the room and stood looking over Fisher's shoulder.

'There you are!' he said, running his finger round an area marked in red on the large-scale plan. 'Here's Perry Street, Perry Square, Winton Street and Winton Mews and surrounding them Oxford Street, Tottenham Court Road, Charlotte Street, Goodge Street. Then in the centre is this interesting little patch, apparently as innocent as the Bank of England–and yet that is the spot. If a villain gets there he can disappear.'

Fisher passed his fingers through his fair hair. 'I'd just like to make sure, sir, exactly what has been done already.'

'Everything is in the file. You'll find all action undertaken during the last nine months there but I'll give you a brief résumé myself. I first noticed something odd about this particular district a little under a year ago. A jeweller's shop was broken into in Oxford Street. To all appearances it was an ordinary smash and grab carried out with clever team work. The two fellows who took most of the valuables went off in a car and were chased. They turned down St Francis Passage and got into Tottenham Court Road.'

Guthrie paused. 'The odd thing was, Fisher, that the raid was staged at night. We had a cordon right round the district looking for the Hendridge kidnappers. It was in the small hours and every car was stopped. The district was alive with police. These smash and grab raiders were seen to abandon their car at the corner of Goodge Street and turn into Perry Square. From that point they disappeared.

'Now that, I expect, is not a very extraordinary story to you, and it wasn't to me at the time. I thought it was poor police work and that our men had not been as smart as they might have been.

'But that was only the beginning. Since then, a peculiarly clever brand of organised crime in the West End has been on the increase. The villains have always used this method of escape, and the procession of incidents connected with this area came to the fore again last night with this kidnapping.

'That district has got to be laid open. The rat hole must be plugged. Now I want results. That is why you are handling the case. Take my advice and pin your faith to the WX-Fifteen district. That's where the solution of this mystery lies. We cannot surround this area and the crooks know we cannot.'

Bob Fisher bent over the plan. 'As I see it, sir,' he ventured, 'Winton Mews, where the cab and moving-van were found, seems to be the centre of interest. Both vehicles were stolen early yesterday morning. It's rather strange that the mews was built in the middle of a block like that, isn't it?'

'I don't think so. The two sides that face on to the square are modern. They are made up of flats and tailors' workrooms. The other two sides are older and consist of the original houses to which the mews used to belong. Some of these have shops on the ground floor. Then just across the road there's a block of luxury flats called Southwold Mansions and beside them is a yard leading to a warehouse.'

He bent over the other's shoulder and indicated on the plan the buildings he mentioned.

Fisher nodded comprehendingly. 'And all these places have been searched?'

'Searched!' Guthrie threw out his hand in an expressive gesture. 'Ask Ames if you want to hear about that. Here is some more background. This is Joe's café. He's a very honest fellow; reputed to put pea flour in the coffee. That is all that is known against him. Next there is the laundrette. Man and his wife run it. They let lodgings. We know all about them. The cigarette shop next door is clean, so is the music shop and the sandwich bar has nothing to hide. Now we come to the mews itself. Most of the garages are used by private owners, all respectable. We've gone over them. There isn't even a cellar under most of them.

'Only two are used as dwellings. This one here is a store room for the laundrette. The husband and wife sleep above. There's nothing there. Next door, of course, is old Mrs Wheeler. She's a fine old London character. She says she is a hundred and five next birthday. Bedridden, you know, and lives all alone except for welfare folk who hover around her and the tourists who come and have a look at her. We thought at one time that she might have done a little fortune telling but nothing more sinister.'

Fisher nodded.

'What's underneath this district?'

'There's the Underground, the Forty-Y sewer and the old Post Office tube now used by the Westbridge Stores to join its two branches for parcels delivery, so they can avoid the traffic from the Oxford Circus shop. There is no entrance, as far as we can see, to any of these underground ways from the WX-Fifteen district. But your first task is to recapture Thurtle. I don't think his friends are in it, by the way. I think it is private enterprise on the part of some other villains. Parker must be rescued and you must lay your hands upon the man who is organising this district – the man with the brains and the escape system.'

The phone rang and the older man picked it up.

'This is for you, Fisher,' he said. 'Sounds like a private call.'

Fisher took the call with a feeling of embarrassment.

'Bob, is that you at last. Look here, I'm in a flat – a furnished flat. I've taken it – not pinched it, you know, rented it. It's for my aunt, as a matter of fact. She's coming to town tomorrow and I don't think it'll suit her. You must come here and have a look at it, and I think you'll agree with me.'

In spite of his exasperation, Fisher smiled. The request was typical of George Box, that idle soul whom he had met on holiday earlier in the year, and whom he had bumped into several times since in the West End.

'Look here,' he said. 'I'm sorry. I can't manage it. I'm frightfully busy. Yes, busy. I can't talk now, either.'

'But, Bob, I say!' The tone was aggrieved. 'I'm putting something in your way. This is important. You come along. You'll regret it all your life if you don't. Listen, Bob!' The voice was lowered mysteriously. 'I can't say much over the phone, but I believe you'll find this a very interesting place.'

Fisher caught a fleeting glimpse of Guthrie's irritated expression, and he spoke severely into the mouthpiece.

'I'm sorry, Box, I'm busy,' he said. 'If you'll give me the

address I'll see what I can do later.' He pulled a scribbling pad towards him. 'Hello, yes–Three A Southwold Mansions, Perry Street.'

He stood staring at the address he had scribbled down and then turned and spoke into the phone with considerably more interest than before.

'Did you say Southwold?'

'Yes–Southwold Mansions. You come along!'

'Right. I will. Goodbye!'

Fisher put down the receiver to find Guthrie looking at him.

'That's a queer coincidence,' he said.

'Very odd,' agreed Fisher.

'Is your friend wealthy?' the older man said. 'Those are expensive flats. Dacre, the actor has one. A surgeon lives on the first floor and there's a stockbroker above him.'

Fisher smiled.

'Box has taken it for his aunt. I believe she's quite wealthy. I think I may drop in there tonight.'

'I think it would be wise,' Guthrie agreed. 'Eh, Davidson? What's the matter?'

The lugubrious man who had just entered said bluntly, 'Inspector Parker's been found, sir. He was discovered by a nature class with the back of his head blown out. The local police have got rid of the children but they're holding the boy who tripped over the body until we arrive. It is thought Parker was dumped from a car, the tracks are plain and they've followed them on to the main road where there's a lay-by. So far there is no trace of Thurtle.'

Chief Detective Guthrie sucked air through his clenched teeth.

'Murder, and one of our own men,' he said grimly. 'Get on to it, you two. It's arrests I want and quickly. Fisher, you can have Davidson for twenty-four hours after which time I want him back here.'

As the two men closed their Chief's door behind them Davidson allowed himself an epitaph for his deceased colleague: 'Poor old Parker. He'll never undertip another taxi man!'

Inspectors Davidson and Fisher had just come in from a search of that part of the forest where the body had been found. Their task had been fruitless and, a little dejected, they had retired to the police station to examine the clothes.

'Everything that was taken from the pockets is on this table,' the local inspector said.

Fisher stood looking at the usual collection of articles which Inspector Parker had been wont to carry about with him—his watch, a nail file, wallet, several odd pencils and a bunch of keys.

Davidson sighed. 'Nothing to help us among those,' he said gloomily. 'Let's look over the clothes.'

Together they examined the crumpled, bloodstained garments which had once clothed the perky, conceited inspector. It was a melancholy business. Although Fisher had attended to such a task many times in his career, he could never rid himself of a sense of distaste for the job. Suddenly an exclamation escaped him and Davidson and the local inspector glanced up. Fisher stood holding a scrap of dirty paper which he had extracted from Parker's left shoe. He spread it out on the table and they bent over it together.

The discovery was about three inches square, muddy and clearly marked with the imprint of a heel. It was evidently a page torn from a pad of forms. There was a single line of printing below the perforated edge. 'Hotel Formby', it ran. 'To be retained by owner.' Scribbled beneath were the figures '178'.

Davidson frowned and the local inspector looked puzzled.

'What do you make of that, Fisher?' Davidson spoke quietly. 'In his shoe, was it? What is it? Some hotel shoe-cleaning arrangement?'

Fisher shook his head.

'I don't think so. Why "to be retained by owner"? Have you ever stayed at a hotel where they gave you a receipt for your shoes?'

Davidson rubbed his chin. 'That's true. What do you make of it?'

Fisher answered. 'I assume that it didn't get into the shoe by mistake. Someone must have put it there deliberately, probably

Parker. The theory I'm inclined to favour is that Parker was imprisoned somewhere, looked round for something which might give him a clue to his whereabouts, and picked up this off the floor. Don't forget the muddy heel mark. Therefore I think our next step is the Hotel Formby. You know the place, don't you? It's in the Euston Road—a respectable establishment.'

Further examination of the dead man's belongings proving unproductive, the two Yard men left. As they went Davidson reviewed the facts of the case.

'Well,' he said. 'I think it's clear that Parker was shot before they got him out to the forest.'

'I don't think he was shot in cold blood,' said Fisher, his eyes on the road.

'You mean the angle of the bullet? Yes, I think perhaps you're right. He was shot from a distance. Probably he was trying to make a getaway, poor chap.'

The manager of the hotel received them not without some trepidation. He was a plump man, over middle age, with quick dark eyes and a small black imperial beard. The arrival of the two policemen in his well-run establishment was an unprecedented event, and he eyed them nervously. When they were seated in his office, Fisher drew out his notecase and, extracting the grubby scrap of paper, handed it to the manager.

'I wondered if you could tell me what that is, Mr Weller?'

The fastidious man picked up the paper between a thumb and forefinger. At first he seemed inclined to doubt if such a disreputable item could ever have had anything to do with the elegant Hotel Formby, but upon examination a frown spread over his forehead.

'Why, yes,' he said. 'There's nothing extraordinary about this— or at least I hope not.'

He shot an inquiring glance at the two inspectors, who remained completely wooden-faced and uncommunicative, waiting for him to continue.

'Oh, yes, it's quite simple,' he said. 'You see, we are rather cramped for space here, we have no garage belonging to the hotel. So in order to accommodate our guests, we have an arrangement with a big garage down the road whereby clients can leave their cars, but the charge is put through us and goes down on their bills in the ordinary way.

'Sometimes, when the garage is overcrowded, we patronise two or three other smaller establishments in the vicinity, and when this is done we make a practice of giving the owner of the car a slip like this. The duplicate half is handed in to the garage. Without this ticket no one can obtain his car.'

'I see. Then this is a garage ticket?'

Mr Weller deigned to glance at the offending paper once again. 'Exactly,' he said. 'A garage ticket belonging to a client who occupied room One-Seventy-Eight.'

A smile which he could only just hide flickered for an instant across Fisher's face as he shot a covert glance at his companion. Inspector Davidson grinned openly.

'Would it be possible to find out exactly who was the owner of this slip?' Fisher asked. 'This is an original, isn't it? Probably you have the carbon still in your pad.'

With an exaggerated sigh of exasperation the manager of the Hotel Formby pressed a bell and summoned his secretary. In a few moments the pad lay on the table in front of the detectives. Fisher turned over the leaves and a grunt of satisfaction escaped him.

'Here we are,' he said. 'Yes, this is it. And there's a date, too– February the twelfth. Now, Mr Weller, who occupied room One-Seventy-Eight on that date?'

The desk clerk was called and he came immediately, a pale, fair young man carrying a register. The identity of the owner of the garage ticket was revealed.

'Mr Richard Holt,' said the booking clerk. 'He's one of our oldest and most regular customers.'

'I've known Mr Holt for years,' said the manager. 'He's a manufacturer in Walsall and always stays here on his trips to London.'

'I'm afraid we must ask you for his address,' said Fisher. He turned to the clerk. 'Do you know anything about this ticket?'

The young man examined the slip with more interest than his employer had done.

'Yes, I think I do,' he said. 'I remember Mr Holt coming to me for garage accommodation rather late one evening. I phoned up our usual garage just down the road, but they were full up. I remember I had to make other arrangements for him.'

Fisher was pleased. Here at last was a witness who had a good memory and showed a genuine desire to be helpful. 'Can you tell me the name of the garage where the car was left?'

'I'm not sure. It must have been one of three. We have a resident chauffeur who fetches the cars from the garages for their owners. He might remember.'

There was a pause while the man was summoned and Fisher took advantage of it to get Mr Richard Holt's home address. The chauffeur was a harassed, plainly overworked individual who, besides driving the customers' cars, had the thankless task of odd-job man at the Hotel Formby. He did, however, remember Mr Holt's car.

'It was a Sunbeam Rapier,' he said. 'Not a new model. I put it in one of the three garages we use when the big one is full, but I couldn't say which now. I was very rushed, and it is some time ago. They'd probably know there, though.'

'I'll give you the addresses,' said the desk clerk helpfully and while he jotted them down the manager turned to Fisher with an appeal.

'Naturally, I don't know what business you are on, Inspector,' he said, 'but Mr Holt is a very old client of ours, and you understand that I was naturally loath to give you his address. If it would be possible for you to—er—discover what you have to without referring to me, I should be tremendously obliged.'

'Don't worry, sir. We don't say more than we have to.'

A moment later they stood on the pavement and Fisher ran his eye down the list of garages.

'Burchell's Garage, Albany Street, the Fairlop, Fitzroy Street and Knapp's Grafton Street. That's interesting, Davidson.'

'Grafton Street?'

They climbed into the car and Fisher, turning on the dashboard light, drew a roughly-made plan from his coat pocket.

'Look here,' he said. 'This is the diagram of the underground ways in the WX-Fifteen district. Here's the Forty-Y sewer, here's the railway, and here is the old post office tube now used by the stores. See what I mean? This tube runs right through this area, and comes out at Westbridge's other store in the Tottenham Court Road. On its way it runs beneath Grafton Street. I wonder. Anyway, let us go there first.'

Knapp's garage was an old stable, approached by a narrow brick way between an antique shop and the branch office of the electricity board. It looked uninviting, dark and none too prosperous. As they turned into the half-empty building a disreputable figure came out to meet them. He was small, rat-faced, and clad in garments which appeared to have been soaked in oil for many years. His one concession to smartness was a huge flat cap which he wore at a rakish angle.

'I'd like to speak to the manager, please.'

'I am the manager. And the proprietor, too. There's me name over the door–Thomas Knapp–and I'm not ashamed of it.'

'Remarkable,' said Fisher affably. 'Well, Mr Knapp, I am Inspector Fisher and this is Inspector Davidson.'

'I knew that before you told me,' said Mr Knapp. 'I didn't think you was in fancy dress.'

Fisher ignored the dig and went on.

'You sometimes garage cars for the Formby Hotel?'

'That's nothing to be ashamed of, I hope. Seems quite a nice hotel. The Formby's a place I wouldn't mind stayin' at meself.'

Fisher drew the ticket from his pocket and showed it, without, however, allowing it to leave his hand. 'Ever seen that before?'

Mr Knapp sniffed noisily. 'Might 'ave,' he said non-committally. 'It's the sort of thing anybody might 'ave seen before.'

'Well, do you recognise what it is?'

'Yus,' said Mr Knapp, after a pause which might have been the result of tremendous mental concentration on his part or mere caution. 'It's a ticket from the Formby for boarding a car.'

'That's right. Well, this ticket was given up in exchange for a Sunbeam Rapier on February the twelfth last. Wilkinson, the chauffeur of the Formby, thinks he may have brought it here.'

'Very likely,' said Mr Knapp.

'Well, did he?' asked Davidson. 'Did you house a Sunbeam Rapier from the Formby on the night of February the twelfth? And is that the ticket which was given up in exchange for the car?'

'Might 'ave been.' There was no way of telling from the expression on Mr Knapp's unlovely face whether he was telling all he knew or whether the subject had ceased to interest him.

'Better have a good think, my lad,' Fisher spoke sharply. 'This is important. You know who we are. We don't come round asking questions simply for fun.'

'Really,' said Mr Knapp with contempt. 'Well, I'll have to think then, won't I?'

'It wouldn't be a bad idea.'

The two detectives waited while Mr Knapp performed this unusual feat. 'No,' he said at last. 'No, I don't think I did. I wouldn't be sure, of course, but I don't think I did.'

Fisher's eyes narrowed.

'The car hasn't been stolen,' he said. 'There's no complaint about it. If it was here you needn't be afraid to say so.'

'Well, that's a nice thing to suggest!' said Mr Knapp with indignation. 'I'm doin' my best to 'elp you, aren't I? I say I don't think it was 'ere.'

'Don't you keep any records? How do you know what to charge the Formby?'

'I don't run up any accounts. It's cash on the nail. Course I keep records, flippin' tax men nosing about. I jots down the numbers of cars I puts up for the night and if the perishers gives me a piece of paper I gives it back again when they collect the car. All nice and tidy like.'

Fisher did not speak immediately. His eyes were taking in every detail of the draughty garage, and he had just caught sight of something lying among the litter which strewed the unswept floor. He bent down and picked it up. It was another ticket similar, save for the number, to the one he held. Mr Knapp grinned but there was a shifty expression in his crafty eyes.

'Lookin' for clues?' he inquired.

Fisher showed the piece of paper to Davidson. 'As you say,' he said turning to Knapp, 'all nice and tidy. Do you always keep your receipts on the floor?'

'I can't waste my time tidyin' up after customers,' said Mr Knapp. 'When a man gives me a receipt for a car 'e brought in the night before I let 'im 'ave it. And if the receipt falls on the floor I let it stay there. I don't spend me life cleanin' up.'

'So I see,' said Fisher.

Mr Knapp hesitated. 'Since you're so interested in me business, would you like to 'ave a look round?' he suggested. 'I've got a nice little place 'ere. I know you like to nose round a bit.'

He led them into the office at the back of the garage and into the small yard behind. The whole place was very untidy and dirty but although both the Yard men were on the alert, they saw nothing unexpected or unusual. There was a car pit with a truck standing over it. Fisher looked inside the vehicle but it was empty.

'Me and me mother lives in the attic above,' volunteered Mr Knapp confidentially. 'I don't keep any pets and I'm fully insured in case of fire. Anything else you'd like to know while you're about it? Just ask. Don't mind me.'

'Any cellars?'

Mr Knapp, who had turned aside to look at a pressure-gauge on a tyre, bent a little lower over the disc, but when he spoke his voice was as perky as ever. 'No,' he said. 'Nothing but drains and they're not too good. Would you like to have a look at the family album?'

Fisher grinned. 'We've got it all at the Yard, I expect,' he said, and nodding to the man the two detectives went out to their car.

'Well, what do you think?' asked Davidson. 'That man's got a record, no doubt, but I couldn't see anything out of order.'

'I don't know,' said Fisher slowly. 'Garages are such useful places for crooks. It's near the right area, too. I think I'll have it watched.'

Burchell's garage and the Fairlop both proved to be establishments in the charge of efficient ex-Service men who kept careful records of every car received from the Formby. They were positive that no Sunbeam Rapier had been housed by them on the night of February the twelfth.

'That brings us back to Mr Knapp,' said Davidson. 'Perhaps Thurtle shot Parker?'

Fisher shook his head. 'Not on your life,' he said. 'There's a very different man behind all this. Thurtle's a swindler, he took a big risk and came an almighty cropper but this fellow takes risks all the time.'

It was after midnight when Fisher at last found the time to present himself before the door of 3-A Southwold Mansions. The lights in the neat, well-kept hall were lowered to half strength, but the bright green door looked expensive and inviting.

In response to his ring the door was opened and Box's pink face appeared.

'So, you've come at last, have you?' he said. 'Come in. I was beginning to be afraid you'd backed out. Come in and have a drink.'

He was in pyjamas and dressing gown of many colours which blended in with his bright yellow hair. Fisher followed him into the main room of the suite. It was a big, ornate apartment, expensively furnished and comfortable. Box went over to a side table and mixed a drink for himself and his visitor, talking the whole time.

'I was afraid you hadn't taken me seriously. I had great difficulty in getting on to you at that place. You policemen always ought to be on the alert, you know—always eager to pick up a crumb or two of information which might lead you to big things. Have a cigarette? That box is full of them. The man I rented this flat from seemed to want to make me comfortable. He's left the whole place in running order.'

Fisher walked over to the window and sweeping aside the heavy lined curtains stood looking down. Perry Street, with its sinister yard, lay directly beneath him. Opposite was the narrow alley which led into Winton Square, with its small shops, unsavoury mews and curious reputation. Really, the view of WX-15 from the window at which he stood was extraordinarily complete. He was interrupted in his thoughts by Box, who thrust a glass into his hand.

'Well, what do you think of the flat?' he asked. 'It looks all right at first glance, doesn't it? If you were looking for a furnished flat for your aunt, wouldn't you say it was the very place?'

Fisher, whose only aunt was an impecunious and elderly spinster with strong teetotal convictions, grinned.

'I might,' he conceded. 'But seriously George, if you've brought me up here to congratulate you on your house hunting, you haven't been very intelligent.'

'Oh, but wait. I'm giving you a drink to brace you up.' Box's round face was momentarily serious. 'There's more to come. First of all, suppose you step in here?'

He led Fisher into an adjoining bedroom. It seemed an ordinary room, a little too elaborate for Fisher's own taste, but otherwise perfectly normal. Box was quivering with excitement, however.

'When I changed tonight, I dropped a cuff link,' he said. 'I was crawling about on the floor looking for it when I discovered this. Rather queer, isn't it?'

He pushed the bed aside and pointed to a ring set in the floor.

'Now look,' he commanded. He pulled it up and revealed a small square hole in the floor which contained, to Fisher's astonishment, three revolvers. Box rose to his feet.

'There you are,' he said. 'That's the first exhibit. Apparently my landlord likes to be ready for burglars. At the first alarm he can hop out of bed and go to meet them, a gun in each hand and one in his teeth. An impressive first appearance, I should think.'

Fisher shrugged his shoulders but his eyes were grave.

'Maybe just an idiosyncrasy,' he said. 'It certainly seems odd to leave them in a furnished flat.'

'Odd?' said his host. 'It's odd all right. You wait. Our next port of call is the kitchen. Here we have a service lift.'

The blue-tiled kitchenette had a wedge-shaped shaft built in across one corner, and in it was a small lift worked by ropes and unusually solid for such a contraption.

'This takes you right down to the back yard of the block,' Box said. 'Interesting, isn't it? It goes through the flat below, of course, but it doesn't have an outlet there.'

'How do you know?' Fisher inquired.

'Because I've been to see. I've ridden up and down in that thing twice. You'll find it more difficult because you haven't got my elegant proportions, but I did it quite easily. Look!'

He climbed into the hatch and sat there cross-legged, smiling out at his visitor. 'There you are,' he said. 'These ropes work at a touch.'

He grasped the rope at his side and moved himself up and down a few feet either way with ease. 'That isn't all,' he went on hastily, 'see this?'

He stretched out his hand and touched a switch on the inside of the panelling of the lift shaft. Instantly they were in darkness.

'See that?' Box's voice was triumphant. 'That turns out every light in the flat. And what's more, you can't turn them on again until this has been readjusted. You try!'

Using his torch, Fisher made the experiment. It was not until the switch had been put back that the flat was once more lit.

'Well, you're glad you came along, aren't you?' asked Box. Fisher smiled.

'I am, certainly. You must have had a joyous evening playing with these gadgets. Any more?'

'Only one thing I know of.' Box was as pleased as a child with a new toy. 'Come and stand in the sitting-room.'

They went back to the room Fisher had first seen, and Box indicated the fireplace. This was an over-decorated affair. The over mantle rose up to the ceiling and was made of lacquered wood ornamented with an inlay of mother of pearl in the form of a cherry branch in full blossom. The fireplace itself was set farther back in the wall, and there were small inglenooks built in on either side.

'What do you think of that?' Box demanded.

'Hideous,' said Fisher frankly. 'That decoration doesn't go with that design.'

Box grinned. 'Well, you stand and watch it, that's all.'

He went out of the room, leaving the door open, and from where Fisher stood he could see his dressing-gowned figure pass down the corridor and unlock the front door, through which he disappeared.

'Now,' said his exuberant voice. 'See the fireplace?'

Fisher glanced up. Each mother of pearl bud and flower was glowing with a ruby light. The effect was pleasant and somehow startling.

Box came back highly delighted.

'Did you notice it? Rather natty, isn't it? I saw it first when the man came to read the meter. It works very simply. Anybody standing on the doormat forms a contact which produces the illumination. Rather a jolly little flat, isn't it? Just the place for auntie.'

Fisher sat down in one of the deep armchairs before the fire-place.

'Look here, Box,' he said. 'How did you get hold of this place? How long have you been here?'

'I moved in about four o'clock this afternoon and I took the flat off a most respectable agent at eleven o'clock this morning. Apparently his client has gone abroad on a film contract. He's an actor. I forget the name. He left very suddenly and just threw the keys in at the agents and told them to let it. It's very cheap considering, and I snapped it up. Of course, I don't know if I should have been so certain it was just what auntie wanted if I'd noticed all the parlour tricks, but I didn't spot them until this evening. I rang up the agent but he'd packed up for the night. Then, of course, I just had to have someone in to see my display, so I got on to you. Would you like a history of my life now? Or perhaps, if we could think of a crowd we could ring up, we might throw a party. There must be a few people we know who haven't gone to bed yet.'

Fisher did not respond immediately. His mind was taken up with the strange disclosures he had just seen. Of course, there was just a chance that these elaborate signals and precautions were the property of a burglar-shy householder, alarmed by the recent increase in crime, but it hardly seemed likely.

Box broke into his thoughts.

'There's another bedroom over there you can have,' he said. 'Or don't the police ever sleep? I'm not a nervous man, you know, but there's something about this place that gives me the creeps. Do you notice it? There's a sort of—how shall I say?—expectant atmosphere about. Something most extraordinary.'

Fisher did not answer. He opened his mouth to speak, but at that instant there came an interruption so remarkable that it brought both young men to their feet. A prickly sensation ran down Fisher's spine.

From the fireplace someone had spoken. The voice had the curious metallic, yet hollow quality of a bad loudspeaker.

'Put out the lights,' it said. 'Put out the lights. We're coming up!'

As Fisher stood there wrestling with his surprise the voice came again. 'Put out the lights. We're coming up!'

Fisher was the first to pull himself together. He sprang forward into the wide, open fireplace and peered under the mantle. The explanation was instantly apparent. It *was* a loudspeaker. This then, was yet another of the many curious devices hidden in the flat. Even as he watched the disc it spoke again.

'Put out the lights. Hurry!'

Motioning Box to follow him, Fisher darted into the kitchen and pressed back the master switch. He had no doubt that there must be another such device more conveniently placed in the flat, but now was not the time to search for it. Then, keeping Box behind him, Fisher crept back to the main room. As they stood waiting in the darkness they could hear a little traffic in the street outside but otherwise there was not a sound. The flat seemed to be holding its breath.

Suddenly Box gripped the detective's arm and Fisher, who had his eyes fixed on the spot where he guessed the doorway must be, caught sight of the cherry branch picked out in crimson lights on the mantel. The warning was dramatic. Someone stood outside the green front door.

After what seemed like a full minute there was a faint click down the passage, followed by a rustling. Fisher laid a restraining hand on Box's arm. He was sufficiently experienced not to go leaping into a fight without first discovering the odds against him.

The silence was nerve-racking. The darkness seemed full of strange forms, there was no sound, no breath to tell them whether they were alone or not.

It was the crimson warning over the fireplace flashing out once again which was the first real indication that their visitors were leaving. Three times the lights flashed and then all was darkness.

Fisher pulled out his torch and swept it round the room. Nothing had been disturbed. They appeared to be alone. Box stepped back into the kitchen and a second later the lights were on again.

It was Fisher who first caught sight of the object down the end of the corridor just inside the front door. With a smothered exclamation he darted forward, Box at his heels. When they were within six paces of it, they pulled up short, and the two young men stood staring at this newest and most remarkable surprise the flat had to offer.

Half lying, half seated upon a heavy hall chair, her head thrown back, her eyes closed and her slim hands and ankles bound with cord, reclined a girl.

Fisher bent over her. 'Good heavens!' he said. 'Whatever next! Look here, you go and get her some water while I untie her.'

He turned his head as he spoke, and just for an instant he saw an expression on the other man's face. Fisher only caught a fleeting impression and in a moment it had passed from his mind as Box's face regained its normal colour and blissful appearance.

'Oh, yes. Yes, quite. I think that's a good idea. Should it be brandy? No, perhaps not. What a funny flat. I must tell the man tomorrow it won't suit auntie. Strange women popping in like this. She doesn't consider herself old-fashioned but she wouldn't like it. She's funny that way.'

He trotted off to the kitchen while Fisher unbound the cord which fastened the girl's wrists and ankles. She was beautiful. Her long red-brown hair flowed against her soft white skin, and her heavy dark lashes enhanced her pallor. Suddenly she opened her eyes and looked at him. Her first expression was one of surprise, which quickly turned to terror.

Before Fisher could speak, Box's inconsequential voice echoed from the kitchenette.

'Here, I say, Bob, half a minute! Come. Come at once, will you?'

There was an urgent note in the tone and Fisher turned instinctively. He found Box hanging over the lift.

'Listen,' Box said. 'Can you hear something?'

Fisher bent over the shaft.

'There's nothing there,' he said at length. 'What did you think you heard?'

'Someone screamed.' Box had lowered his voice and the effect was somewhat ludicrous. Fisher was inclined to be irritated. He took a glass from the shelf and filled it from under the tap.

'Come on,' he said. 'Don't forget the girl. She can probably put us wise to the whole thing.'

As he entered the passage he heard a sound which brought a curse to his lips. As soon as he came in sight of that empty chair he knew what had happened. The cords which had bound her lay on the floor and the front door hung wide. The girl was gone.

Fisher turned round and thrust the glass into Box's hand.

'Here, take this,' he commanded.

'I say, where are you going? Wait for me!'

Fisher glanced at him over his shoulder as he reached the door. 'I may just catch her. See you later.'

Box followed him to the doorway and then he frowned and, coming back slowly into the flat, shut the hall door behind him. For a moment he stood hesitating. Then he shrugged his shoulders and, placing the glass of water on the hall table, went back into the bedroom and began to dress with speed.

When he came out of the room, although his bland face was still good humoured a subtle difference had come over the expression in his eyes. They were no longer frank. Instead a purposeful look lingered in their depths. He went round the flat turning out the lights and then made his way to the kitchenette. He entered the lift with the air of one long accustomed to do so, and lowered himself swiftly into the yard below.

The dark coat which covered his trim form rendered him inconspicuous. He stood for a moment looking about him. Then, convinced that he was unobserved, he sent the lift back into position. Pulling his hat down over his eyes he stepped across the concrete and entered what appeared to be an area leading to a coal cellar.

The place was empty. It had been built in the days when the block of flats was a private house. The man seemed to know his way, for he used no torch and there were no street lights. He crept softly round the wall, and finally, discovering the door he sought, passed through it into yet another cellar.

He came out of this into an area precisely similar to the one by which he had entered. He stepped up into the street in a narrow turning on the opposite side of the road from the block of flats.

He stood listening but there were no unusual sounds above the hum of the traffic. Presently he set off down the pavement and turned into Winton Mews.

The narrow, unsavoury court was quiet, and no gleam of light showed from the windows above the garage doors. Box stepped forward and, moving up to the third door on the left, knocked twice, once loudly and once softly. Instantly it swung open, and he stepped into the darkness within.

'I wish you'd talk. You get on my nerves sitting there, Fishy Eyes!'

Mr Knapp stood at the end of the wooden table in the damp, ill-lighted cellar and looked at the man who sat opposite, his head resting upon his clasped hands, a dull expression upon his white face.

Joseph Thurtle had looked weary when he had stepped off the boat train at Victoria a little over twenty-four hours before, but in the interval he had become more haggard and drawn than would have seemed possible. He took no notice of the garage proprietor's opening gambit, but continued to stare straight in front of him.

'Leave 'im alone, Thos, can't you?' The speaker was a heavily built, red-faced individual, who lay sprawled upon a pile of newspapers spread out on a packing case in the corner of the cellar. 'Leave 'im to the boss!'

The other two occupants were cutting for coins on yet another box and they nodded their approval. One was a slender, dark young man and the other a splendidly proportioned, hard bitten looking giant of a man with three days' growth of honey-coloured hair on his chin.

Mr Knapp sniffed and wandered over to join the card players.

'I can't understand you, Jack,' he said, eyeing the dark young man. 'You sit here and play with Bill all day long. Don't you ever get tired of it?'

'Run away, Thos. You're interrupting!' Jack Simmons' voice was unexpectedly well modulated. 'Bill and I have done enough work for today. We don't get our fun as you do, tormenting the prisoner.'

'That's right.' The man addressed as Bill revealed a guttural Scandinavian accent. 'You go and worry Tim.' He indicated the big man in the corner.

'If he comes over here,' said that worthy with sudden violence, 'I'll break his skinny little neck.'

'All right. No offence, I 'ope!' Mr Knapp perched himself on the edge of the table and considered Joseph Thurtle once again.

Suddenly a rumbling roar shook the room in which they sat, but none of the men so much as batted an eyelid. They were used to the tube trains which hurtled past within a few feet of them. Joseph Thurtle stirred wearily where he sat, but the blank helpless look did not vanish from his eyes.

Then there was the sound of an electric bell and the company in the room glanced up. Mr Knapp slipped off the table and stood. A rough wooden door at the far end of the room swung open and a young man appeared. The collar of his dark coat was turned up and his hat was pulled well down over his eyes. He stood for a moment looking round at them, his plump face bland and inscrutable.

George Box, part-time theatre critic and part-time crook who had as yet escaped the attentions of the police, surveyed his assistants and his prisoner.

'Where's Casson?' he demanded.

'In the office.' Mr Knapp indicated a further door on the opposite side of the cellar. 'Mr Levine and Jamieson are there, too.'

Box nodded. The room he entered, although a cellar like the first, presented a very different appearance. Its walls had been painted and a fitted carpet covered the floor. It was also furnished for comfort.

The three men who lounged on the couch before the electric fire were different from their colleagues without. Here was the nucleus of the powerful organisation which caused Scotland Yard so much anxiety. There was Casson, a small wiry man with a toothbrush moustache, Jamieson, a quiet, grey-faced business man and Levine, perhaps the cleverest of the three. He was an elderly dapper Frenchman, irreproachably dressed in the latest fashion.

Box took off his hat and coat and threw them on a chair.

'Really, Casson,' he said mildly, 'I wish you wouldn't leave your lady friends about my flat without warning me. I had a visitor at the time, and it was very awkward. I've got nothing against the girl, mind you. It was only the way she intruded. You don't mind me mentioning it, do you?'

Casson started up in alarm.

'Oh! Who was there? I didn't know what to do with the girl. I couldn't very well have her here. The flat seemed the safest place to leave her.'

Box sat down on the arm of the couch.

'Suppose we get this thing straight,' he said, 'who on earth is she?'

Casson and Levine exchanged glances. In spite of Box's light manner there was something sinister in his tone, an implied reproach which they were quick to notice.

'We found her in the tube, hiding. She didn't give any account of herself, and it occurred to me that she might be dangerous.'

It was Levine who spoke, his slight French accent clipping the words.

Box smiled. 'I see. So you tied her up and left her in the flat for me to deal with? I recognised your voice, Casson, over the microphone. I only hope that Inspector Fisher didn't make a mental note of it also.'

'Inspector Fisher?'

All three men stared at him.

'In the flat? Then he knows?'

'Everything,' said Box complacently. 'He's seen some of the gadgets and was suitably impressed. I admit the sensational appearance of the girl was more than I'd bargained for.'

'But how did he get there? How did he find it?'

'I invited him, and I showed him.' Box's smile broadened.

Jamieson rose to his feet and peered into the round, smiling face.

'What are you playing at, Box?'

'Sit down. Don't worry. Let me explain. It occurred to me that the police activities in the WX-Fifteen district are beginning to irritate. Frankly, Jamieson, it is getting too hot. I considered the matter and decided that the best thing to do was to give them something to get their teeth into. I've been cultivating Fisher for some time, as you know. He holds the interesting theory that I'm an idle fool.'

Box paused for a moment, smiling, as if pleased by his own cleverness.

'This is our last job. We want the police fully occupied while we make our various get aways. Since we shall no longer require the flat I told him I'd rented it for an aunt of mine and that I thought there was something odd about it. At first he wasn't interested, but when I gave him the address he perked up his ears and came along this evening. I showed him over the place, and was just going to leave him to draw his own conclusion when the girl made her sensational entry. Now, Casson, she got away and Fisher went after her. If he catches her how much will she be able to tell him?'

'Not much,' said Casson quickly. 'Fortunately, not much. We didn't bring her here at all. We blindfolded her in the tube and took her up through the garage. She'd never recognise it again.'

'Who do you think she was? A policewoman?'

'No, I don't think so. She's too young for that. I can't imagine what she was doing.'

Box's eyes narrowed. 'You ought to have found out.'

The other three men were silent, and their leader rose and walked down the room.

'I've covered our tracks with regard to the flat. Blakeney put it in the hands of the agent this morning, and I took it out an hour later. If there's an inquiry in that direction, we're covered.' He paused. 'Now to work, since our friend in the next room has had about twelve hours to think it over, perhaps he may consider our proposition with a little more interest. Suppose we have him in.'

An ugly light came into Jamieson's eyes.

'The man's a fool,' he said. 'I'm in favour of using a certain amount of force. You'd almost believe he wants to serve his sentence.'

Box regarded his colleague with mild disapproval.

'My dear fellow, why so crude?' he said. 'Do remember we're business men, even if our methods are a little unorthodox. You keep reverting to the bang-him-on-the-head school of thought, I don't like it.'

'That's all very well, Box,' it was Casson who spoke, 'but we've got the fellow here, and as long as he's here he is a source of potential danger to us. If he's discovered, things could be very awkward indeed. Don't forget Parker!'

A regretful expression spread over Box's round, friendly face.

'That was a pity. I admit that,' he said. 'But the fellow was half out of the garage window. I agree with Bill it was the only thing he could have done. Besides, he knew too much. Now I think we'll concentrate on the business in hand. Let's sit round the table, shall we? Casson, I wonder if you'd mind bringing our obstinate guest in from the other room.'

Box took the head of the table, and Joseph Thurtle sat opposite him. His eyes were heavy, but there was still a sullen expression on his mouth, and his hands were clenched.

The other three men showed their reactions towards the situation in different ways. Jamieson was palpably nervous. The murder of Inspector Parker had shaken him and he was afraid. His fear made him savage, and he glared at their captive as though he could hardly keep his hands off him.

Levine was impassive, save for his bright black eyes which were fixed upon Thurtle's drawn face. Casson watched Box, grudging admiration in the half smile on his lips. That individual was the only one of the party who seemed completely at ease.

'Well, Mr Thurtle,' Box said, 'you look tired. I do hope you haven't found your companions in the other room too boring. It is astounding how irritating one's intellectual inferiors can be if one lives with them. Suppose we take up our conversation where we left it yesterday?'

'I don't want to treat with you. You can hand me over to the police, if you like. I'm at the end of my tether. I'm done.'

'Well!' continued Box. 'And I always thought you were an ambitious man. Come, come Mr Thurtle! This isn't the way to behave with friends who have gone to the extent of getting rid of a too attentive police officer and rescuing you. Suppose we talk business. You have a son in London, Mr Thurtle.'

For the first time during the conversation a flicker of animation came into the financier's dull eyes.

'He can't be here yet,' he said before he could check himself.

Box smiled.

'I'm glad to be able to give you the good news,' he said. 'Your son arrived at Southampton on board the *Elephantine* late last night. Naturally the authorities have no quarrel with him, and apart from a somewhat sketchy surveillance, they're leaving him alone. I imagine their interest in him would be considerably increased if they realised that he carries half a million about with him–that half million which you, Mr Thurtle, were clever enough to rescue from the crash.'

'That's a lie!'

The man was on his feet now facing his enemies. His eyes were blazing and he had all the dark defiance of an animal at bay in his quivering form.

'Well, well, well, why so defiant? You shouldn't protest so much. It makes people think. As I was saying before you interrupted me, I'm sure the authorities will be more interested in young Mr Thurtle when they hear the piece of information I shall be able to give them. In fact, I shouldn't be at all surprised if it didn't alter their view completely, and if young Mr Rupert Thurtle were to stand in the dock beside you.'

'But he's innocent,' the old man persisted. 'He didn't realise what he was doing, and I didn't enlighten him. The fault is mine–entirely mine–and I'm prepared to pay for it.'

'Well, let's hope the authorities will take the same view,' said Box pleasantly. 'I've often found, however,' he went on in a conversational tone, 'that's it's very difficult indeed to convince them of a thing like that. They're inclined to be obstinate. Officialdom, you know–the ruin of the country.'

Beads of sweat appeared on the financier's forehead. 'You're a fiend,' he said. 'What do you want me to do?'

Jamieson grunted. It was an expression of relief. Box's smile became, if possible, even more bland than before.

'I must say I prefer you in this kind of mood, Mr Thurtle,' he said. 'It brings out the softer side of your character, if I may say so. Well, now, suppose I outline this simple little proposition to you.

'In the first place, my friends and I are not greedy. We should hate you to think that. We are prepared to go shares with you—equal shares. Write a letter to your son instructing him to pay us half of the money he holds for you and we will release you. We will hand you over to him at any place he cares to name, so long as we are convinced that there is no police trap. Well, now, that's very fair isn't it?'

The financier sat down.

'No!' he said. 'I won't. You can do what you like but I'll never write that letter.'

Box shrugged his shoulders. 'What a pity,' he said. 'I can sympathise with you, of course. I can see your point of view and I'm inclined to admire it, but you see how it places me. I am a man of conscience. In fact, my conscience is very strong and very active. In order to chloroform it, shall we say, I require a quarter of a million pounds. If it is not forthcoming, and this confounded conscience of mine remains active, I shall have to go to the authorities in my capacity of a loyal citizen and tell them what I know. Your son is quite young, isn't he? It seems a pity. Twenty years, or even ten or fifteen, taken out of his life at this time will ruin him completely. What a pity!'

The clenched hands of the man who sat at the other end of the table moved involuntarily, and two bright spots of colour appeared in his ashen cheeks.

'I don't know who you are but you deserve to be hanged.'

'That's very uncivil and also you're behind the times. We don't hang people in England nowadays. We're civilised, no eye for an eye, tooth for a tooth stuff. We just shut 'em up in a little cell with all mod. cons.,' said Box pleasantly. 'Well, perhaps you wouldn't mind going back to the other room now. I must go and see the authorities.'

The older man remained where he was, his face working. At length a cry escaped him and he sprawled forward across the table.

'All right,' he said. 'All right. I'm beaten. I'll do it!'

Uttering a suppressed exclamation of triumph, Jamieson leaned forward across the table, but Box laid a restraining hand upon his arm.

'That's very wise of you, Mr Thurtle,' Box said softly. 'Very wise indeed. I was only putting my own case to you. My friends have devised other means of persuasion.'

He took a pen from his pocket and handed it politely to the stricken man. Casson brought notepaper and an envelope from a desk in the corner.

'One moment,' Box's face was very grave. 'I should like to point out to you, Mr Thurtle,' he said, in a voice unlike the bantering tone he had previously used, 'that we are not joking. Nor are we fools. Any attempt on your part to double cross us, to drop a concealed hint to your son or to frustrate us in any way and we'll have our revenge. It is very simple and we shall not hesitate.'

The other man looked up and met his eyes.

'I understand,' he said solemnly. 'You and I can take each other's words. Honour among thieves!' He laughed bitterly on the last words, and while Levine reddened angrily, Box's smile broadened.

'How true,' he said.

Thurtle wrote swiftly and when he had finished he handed the note to his captor. Box read it through aloud.

'I have been hijacked. I am held here for ransom. For heaven's sake, obey instructions, since my life depends upon it. Pay up to one half of what you hold. I dare not write any more, but do this for me. Yours, Dad.

'Yes, I think that'll do.' Box drew a paper from his pocket and put it on the table. 'This is a sample of your handwriting,' he said. 'I took the precaution of procuring it so that we should not have any hitch at the outset. Yes, that will do. I congratulate you, Mr Thurtle, on your intelligence.

'Now, since we are partners as it were, perhaps you would prefer to spend your time in here? It's warmer and more comfortable. I'm afraid one of us will have to remain with you, but I assure you you will find any of these gentlemen excellent company—quite different from the person Knapp, who, I admit, has all the hallmarks of a social failure.'

He put the two papers carefully in his pocket and went over to the door.

'Bill!' he said, 'I'm going out. Just make certain that everything is clear, will you?'

The words died on his lips, for at that moment Mr Knapp came hurrying into the room.

'I say,' he said. 'I thought I'd choked the police off, but there's a whole group of them round the garage.'

Box thrust out a hand and caught his shoulder.

'What's this?' he demanded sternly.

As he jerked the man towards him he revealed unexpected strength for one of his stature. Somewhat incoherently, Mr Knapp poured out the story of Fisher's visit to the garage.

'Look out, guv'nor,' he concluded. 'Your fingers ain't half bitin' into my shoulder! What do you think I am? Bloomin' rat or somethin'?'

'I wouldn't embarrass you by telling you in front of all these people,' said Box. His usual good humour had vanished and there was an element of anxiety in his voice. 'I thought the garage was safe. It's outside the area, and until now they haven't had a line on it. They got you on a car ticket from the Formby Hotel, you say? Well, I wonder how that happened?'

He stood thinking for some moments, and then a sudden expression of alarm flickered across his face.

'Parker!' he said. 'Parker was in that office alone for about five minutes. Knapp, you ought to clean up that place of yours. Your filthy shed and your disgusting business habits will be the finish of us.' As he flung the man from him he glanced round the group. Their faces were white and there was something very near panic in their eyes.

Box's nonchalance returned as if by magic.

'If it wasn't Fisher we might have something to worry about,' he said easily. 'But I assure you if you knew the man you wouldn't be alarmed. He's harmless, with about as much brains as an over-fed Pekingese. Oh, well, we must take to the tube!'

Casson went over to him. 'Be careful of the mews exit,' he murmured. 'There's a patrol which goes through there every twenty minutes.'

Box nodded. 'I just missed it as I came in,' he said. 'But don't worry. I think, in the circumstances, I shall take a trip on our emergency railway. Bill and Knapp can come with me just in case of accidents.'

Casson raised his eyebrows.

'The store?' he said softly. 'That's not very safe, is it?'

Box patted his shoulder.

'My dear chap!' he said. 'What an engaging person you are. I don't know whether it's occurred to you, but the whole method by which we live is not exactly renowned for safety.'

Casson looked after him as he went through the door. He had a great admiration for Box but there were times when he was afraid.

'Call this a joy ride? It gives me the creeps!'

Mr Knapp's unlovely voice was raised in the stuffy gloom. 'Just fancy what'd 'appen if someone was to set a parcel trolley in motion?' he asked. 'It'd come 'urtling down 'ere like one o'clock and where should we be then, I'd like to know?'

'Safely under it and out of this business for good,' said Box cheerfully.

The three men were walking down the post office tube now used by the two branches of Westbridge's Department stores. Box went in front with a torch. Mr Knapp trotted along at his elbow and Bill, the Swede, brought up the rear. They bent low to avoid the overhanging electric cables which propelled the swift parcel trucks from one store to the other.

Here and there along the line there were old 'stations' which marked the site of the long disused post offices. Mr Knapp's garage was one, and there was another beneath the modern block of Winton Street flats. But these had been long passed by the three men, and they now came to a bend beyond which was the faint light of a single electric bulb.

This was the end of the tube as it was now used–the dispatch department of Westbridge's Oxford Circus branch.

Box turned off his torch and spoke softly.

'Keep back! There's an armed watchman on the premises, and it's most important we shouldn't get caught tonight.'

'It's most important we shouldn't get caught any time, I 'ope,' said Mr Knapp truculently, and he shrank closer to the dusty sides of the tunnel.

The dispatch department was yet another of the old 'stations.' A low, concrete platform ran down to the rails, and five or six parcel trucks were drawn up at the far end. The single electric bulb, which was kept alight night and day, glowed over the ghostly and deserted scene.

Motioning to the others to follow him, Box crept forward across the concrete way and tried the doors leading into the back basement of the shop. They were unlocked, since the only approach to them was through the shop's private tunnel. He passed through silently, Mr Knapp, sniffing irritatingly, followed him, and Bill, a life preserver clenched in one mighty fist, came last.

Inside all was pitch dark and uncannily quiet. Box drew out his torch and flashed it round. They were in a large packing cellar, but the doors to the concrete staircase stood open, and they moved towards them.

They climbed up the stairs on silent, rubber-shod feet. At the first landing they paused. Had they been attempting a burglary nothing would have been more simple but since their intention was merely to get out, the problem was, perversely, more difficult.

The service doors were closed with iron bolts which would make a noise when moved. Moreover, they were probably well provided with burglar alarms.

Box seemed to have an uncanny gift of finding his way about, however, and he led the others down a corridor, passed great showrooms covered with merchandise under dust-sheet shrouds, and came at last to the thing he sought, a side door into the street.

It was at this moment that Mr Knapp caught his breath noisily, and Box, glancing over his shoulder, saw the flickering light of a torch coming towards them down the passage. It was the night watchman.

'He's armed,' Box whispered to Bill. 'Attend to him.' Then with all the coolness in the world, he bent over the lock which held the door.

Mr Knapp who, to do him credit, had more courage than would appear, stepped forward into the passage and tore off down it like a rabbit. The night watchman turned his torch full upon him, and his startled voice shattered the silence.

'Hands up, my lad! You're covered!'

Mr Knapp turned at the far end of the cul-de-sac, and the watchman, keeping his torch full upon him, advanced, his gun levelled. He passed within a few feet of Bill. For a second the life preserver hung in the air and then descended with a thud upon a spot just above the man's left ear. He went down without a groan and lay sprawling upon the ground, his gun and torch flying wide.

Mr Knapp came back grinning.

Box was still working on the catch which held the door. A new system of locks had recently been installed at Westbridge's and his task was not as simple as he had hoped.

It was at this moment that the disturbing thing happened. The lights went on all over the building. The effect was terrifying and Box started back from the door with an oath. At first he thought he had disturbed the mechanism of some new burglar alarm, but the next moment he knew he was wrong. He could hear the sound of voices and the tramp of feet.

He swung round on the frightened Knapp and Bill.

'Get back to the tube. Whatever you do, don't get caught. Go on! Beat it!'

They needed no second bidding, and the Swede lumbered off

the way they had come, while Mr Knapp seemed to have disappeared into the air at the first word of command.

Box himself stepped into one of the deserted showrooms, sprang lightly over a counter, and crouched there. He could hear people moving, and then the gruff voice of a police constable echoed from the passage he had just left.

'Hello, what's this? Quick! Here's the watchman laid out!'

There was a trample of feet, a certain amount of confused conversation, and then silence.

Box was no coward but neither was he a fool. He realised that an exhaustive search of the building would now be made. He crept along, keeping his head below the counter, and worked his way to the end of the showroom until there was only six feet of open space between him and the service stairs.

He raised himself cautiously and looked about him. At first he thought no one was in sight but a slight sound above him made him look up. A narrow balcony ran round the showroom, from which great double doors led into other departments. Two people stood upon this, deep in conversation. Their backs were towards him, and he knew himself to be undiscovered. What did startle him and sent an unaccustomed thrill of alarm through him was that he recognised them.

On the balcony was no other person than Bob Fisher and beside him was a girl. Even at that distance Box knew her. It was the young woman who had been left bound in his flat less than two hours before. Box crept away making for the tube.

Meanwhile, up on the balcony, Fisher continued his conversation with the girl with the red-gold hair.

'But they were here,' she said excitedly. 'There was someone here!'

'That's all right,' he said. 'We've got the place surrounded, and if there is still anyone left in the store we shall catch them. It was very lucky I caught up with you in Perry Street, Miss Bellew!'

Jean Bellew looked at him. 'I was a fool to run away,' she said, 'but I was so scared. The moment I was free I just took to my heels and ran. I didn't know where I was, and I had only the vaguest idea of how I got there.'

The detective nodded.

'I shall want a complete statement from you,' he remarked. 'I think I've got the facts fairly clear but one or two points remain. You work in the dispatch service here, don't you?'

She nodded assent. 'Yes; I'm going all through the business. My father is the manager of this branch.'

'I see. You noticed that someone had been tampering with your delivery trucks?'

She nodded again. 'I ought to have told the foreman right away. But I—I didn't think he'd take it seriously. I thought he would be difficult. Anyway, I decided to make my own investigations. Not a very intelligent thing to do, as it turned out.'

Fisher smiled. 'Well, not very wise perhaps when you are dealing with this kind of customer. So you went down the tube alone after closing hours this evening?'

'Yes. I had a torch, and I'm afraid I didn't think there was anything to worry about except perhaps rats. I seemed to walk for miles. I passed a disused platform and a good deal farther on I came to another. This one was much cleaner than the first, and—well, it looked used. So I climbed off the track to investigate. I went through an archway and found a stone flight of stairs. I went up, feeling that I couldn't be trespassing since, as far as I knew, the whole line belonged to the stores. Then I saw a door with a crack of light under it.'

She paused and drew in a deep breath.

'I pushed it open and went in. The next thing I knew, someone had thrown a cloth over my head and I was knocked to the ground. Then, with my head still covered, they bound my hands and ankles, and someone picked me up and carried me quite a long way. I struggled to get free, but it was impossible. Finally they put me down on a stone floor and I heard them whispering.'

'When you say "them", how many were there?'

'I don't know. Three, I imagine, or perhaps four.'

'Men?'

'Yes. I didn't hear a woman's voice.'

'Can you remember the voices? Anything they said?'

'They were whispering. I couldn't catch any words. I was then put in a car and driven through some streets. It was very stuffy and I had difficulty in breathing. I think I must have fainted because I don't remember any more until I saw you bending over me.'

'Well,' said Fisher, 'we'd better have all that written down. You can come back with me now.'

'As you say. But it is very late and I must phone my parents first as they may be anxious.'

Bob Fisher watched her go off down the balcony, but whatever he was thinking, it was put out of his mind by the arrival of a sergeant.

'Everything's quiet now, sir. They've taken to the tube. As far as we can see nothing has been touched, although of course, we can't be sure of that until the assistants arrive in the morning. The watchman is coming round nicely. He's still a bit dizzy. Says he knows there must have been two men but he only saw one. He can't give a very good description of him but he thinks he'll be able to remember better when his head clears. I've sent a couple of men down the tube. Is that right?'

'No,' said Fisher quickly. 'Call them back. I think our best way is to sit tight at the end of the tube, sergeant. If you go down a rat hole, you know, you drive the creatures out the other end; but if you sit quietly at the opening, that's when you catch your rats. We must concentrate on stopping up the holes.'

The sergeant went off to recall his men and Fisher strolled down to the main hall of the stores to wait for Jean Bellew. He was conscious of a secret glow of exultation. Things were beginning to move.

*　　*　　*

Casson strode up and down the room, his hands deep in his pockets, a frankly scared expression in his eyes.

'I don't like it, Box,' he was saying. 'It's dangerous.'

Thurtle had been relegated to the outer room again and Box, Casson and Levine were alone.

Jamieson came in a moment later. His face was very pale.

'We're trapped,' he said. 'It's happened at last. I always knew it would some day. The store ends of the tube are filled with police. The garage is watched most carefully, and there are three or four plainclothesmen actually in the mews.' His voice rose angrily. 'D'you realise it? We're caught. They'll get us.'

Box, perched on the edge of the table, grinned irritatingly at the other man. Two sharp lines of anxiety across his forehead were the only indication of strain which he bore.

'Don't get hysterical,' he said lightly. 'You haven't got the build for it, Jamieson. It makes you look foolish. Don't worry. We're very comfortable here, aren't we?'

The other man stared at him.

'Don't play the fool, Box,' he said. 'This isn't the time for it. We're up against something worse than anything we've ever tackled before. I tell you we're trapped!'

'I see no reason for getting excited just because we've got a few coppers hanging round the house, as it were.'

Box's tone was still light, although there was just the faint suggestion of anxiety in his voice.

'Don't worry,' he repeated. 'We've got out of worse scrapes than this. Besides, you mustn't forget our guest, the amiable Mr Thurtle, who is going to pay us so handsomely for his deliverance. It would be a pity to lose our heads just now when everything is going so well.'

'It's all very well to talk like this.' Levine had broken into the conversation. 'I am afraid you are just trying to encourage us, my friend. I am afraid that you, too, are alarmed. After all, you have in your pocket the letter to young Thurtle, but you have not yet been able to deliver it. Isn't that so?'

There was a suggestion of more colour in Box's round face at this announcement but he still seemed at ease.

'Of our exits it occurs to me that the mews is by far the most convenient,' he observed. 'I think I shall go out that way. After all, as you point out Levine, I really ought to deliver Mr Thurtle's message to his son. Yes, I think the mews.'

'But it's madness!' It was Casson who spoke. 'If you are caught you bring the whole hornet's nest down upon us.'

Box laughed. '*If* I'm caught. It's funny what a difference that one little word makes.'

He walked over to the desk in the corner and taking a small key from his pocket, unlocked a drawer in its depths. From this hiding place he took three glass globes, resembling golf balls, save that they were lined with a silvery substance. These he placed very carefully in the pocket of his coat. From another drawer he took out a gun, checked it, and slipped it into his hip pocket.

'What are you going to do?' Jamieson's eyes were fixed upon him questioningly.

It was one of George Box's foibles that he hardly ever carried a gun, but on the rare occasions when he did so, he seldom came back without using it.

'Be careful!' muttered Levine. 'Don't forget Parker. I saw in the evening papers that they've found the body.'

'Of course they've found the body,' said Box. 'The police are always finding bodies in Epping Forest. It's quite the fashionable spot to leave them. I don't think I shall ask any of you gentlemen to accompany me—you're too jumpy. I'll draw my recruits from the other room. I suggest that you sit round the fire and tell one another's fortunes by cards. You can expect me back in about an hour. By the way, if you hear a certain amount of noise upstairs, don't be alarmed. There's nothing whatever to be excited about.'

He went out and the three men in the room exchanged glances.

'He has courage,' said Levine.

'He's a fool,' said Jamieson.

'He likes to pretend he is a fool,' said Casson. 'I wish I had his stupidity.'

Meanwhile, in the outer room, Box had signalled to Simmons and Tim. They got up and followed him without a word. They stepped out of the room and into the dark, damp-smelling passage without.

It was very narrow and scarcely high enough for a man to stand upright. To their left was a flight of steps leading down to the tube, and opposite them a narrow tunnel wound upward.

Keeping his head low, Box advanced cautiously along this opening. It was dark and clammy with damp, but it was evident that they knew the way well, for they hurried along with apparent unconcern. At length the tunnel broadened into a square cavity with a very high roof. In this there was a ladder, stretching up into the gloom above. Box mounted it and they followed.

The top of the ladder rested against a wooden platform built on to the wall like a shelf. Box climbed on to it and his head came to within a few inches of the roof. He knocked upon the boards above very softly and waited. Almost at once the signal was answered. Three gentle thuds, followed by one loud one, sounded from the outside of the partition.

Tim clambered up beside Box and together they thrust back the heavy iron bolts that kept the trapdoor shut, and then let it carefully downwards. There was the sound of something heavy rustling to one side as they eased themselves up.

The hole through which they had entered lay directly beneath the lower half of a large bed, under which there was just room enough for them to creep out. In the bed, propped up among a nest of cushions, lay a little old woman. Her face was wrinkled but her black eyes were sharp. She greeted them with a wide, toothless grin and muttered an unintelligible remark.

Box beamed at her. 'Thank you, Mrs Wheeler,' he said. 'Sorry to disturb you.'

'Be careful.'

A voice spoke out of the gloom that enveloped the far end of the room, and the next moment a tall figure glided forward. A woman dressed in the uniform of a Sister of Mercy stood before them. She looked the part perfectly but a Mother Superior would have been surprised at her attitude.

'You can't go out there,' she said. 'It's dangerous. It's a good job you put me on watch. She's so old you never know what she might tell 'em. The police have been here three times tonight already. They've questioned everybody in the mews. They don't suspect us more than anyone else, but they've got their eyes on the whole place. For heaven's sake be careful.'

Box signalled to her to be quiet and tiptoed over towards the door. Opening a flap in the panelling, he peered out. The sight which met his eyes was not reassuring. Three men stood talking in the middle of the yard. He fancied he could see other men lurking at the only exit. But what particularly displeased him was the fact that the tallest of the three, not a dozen yards away from him, was Fisher himself. The man seemed to be ubiquitous.

Box swore under his breath. He had underestimated the energy of this apparently slow-witted young man. It was evident that he was tenacious, too – certainly not a man easily put off his purpose.

A sudden misgiving seized the watching crook. Perhaps he had been unwise in associating himself with the flat. Perhaps already Fisher knew too much. Box drew out his revolver.

Then he beckoned his two companions and gave them some muttered but explicit instructions.

'Look here, Grace,' he went on, turning to the woman. 'You lie low. They'll come here, but don't worry about that. Rave at 'em for disturbing the old woman, if you like, but don't forget to play your part. This is going to be a ticklish job, but the way we shall work it I don't think there's a chance in a million that they'll associate us with you if you act properly. Are you ready, Tim? Tackle low, remember.'

The big man grunted and Jack laughed softly.

'That's Fisher himself out there, isn't it?' he whispered. 'Will you get him?'

Box's hand closed over the butt of his gun.

'I might,' he whispered back. 'It occurs to me, Jack, that I might. Now, ready?'

He pulled the flap in the door open wider. His movements were so quiet that even those in the room could not hear him make the least sound. Having got the way clear and with a stream of cool air blowing in upon his face, Box felt in his coat pocket.

He drew out one of the silver balls and held it for a moment poised between thumb and forefinger. Then he raised his arm and there was a click far off across the yard as the pellet struck the bricks.

One of the three plainclothesmen swung round in its direction, but seeing nothing, he turned again to his companions. What he had not noticed in the darkness was the cloud of greyish mist arising from the broken missile.

Box hurled another of the smoke bombs, and another; one in the direction of the gateway, one farther down the yard. The effect was just what he had intended. Within a minute great clouds of smoke were belching out of the yard, with the detectives coughing and staggering in the midst of them. Someone was blowing a police whistle.

Box seized his opportunity. The moment the smoke became dense enough to cover him he threw open the door and, with his two companions, slipped out. The woman closed and barred the way behind them.

The difficulty of the smoke screen was that once in it, they were blinded themselves, but Box was undeterred. He pressed on towards the opening at the far end of the mews.

A figure loomed towards them and Box had the satisfaction of seeing Tim hurl himself upon the policeman and knock him to the ground. With Jack behind him he hurried forward. As he reached the entrance to the narrow way which led out of the mews into the street he caught a glimpse of a familiar figure towering up through the billowing smoke. It was Fisher, standing ready to seize any man who attempted to leave the yard.

Box raised his gun.

It was at that moment that the young inspector slipped off the kerb, stumbled and this saved his life. A bullet whirled by his head and flattened itself against the brickwork of the house behind him. Seeing his way was clear, the crook did not hesitate, but dashed through the passage into the street.

Jack would have followed him but he had reckoned without Fisher. From comparative safety Box, looking over his shoulder, saw the two men struggling. He fired again and heard Fisher cry out as he staggered and clapped his hand to his chest. Box waited for no more. He walked swiftly away in the direction of Oxford Circus.

The shots caused uniformed men to come hurrying to the scene. Turning a corner Box was nearly knocked over by one of them.

'I say, there's something very dangerous going on down there, constable,' he said, his voice squeaky with excitement. 'It looks as though a house is on fire in Winton Mews. I was going to have a look at it, but then I heard the shots, so I thought perhaps I'd better get out of the way.'

'You thought right, sir,' said the officer, who had no time for foolish young men. 'You get along.' As he spoke he continued down the street at the double. Box did not trouble to glance after him. Instead he strode on feeling particularly pleased with himself.

At Oxford Circus, he turned into a public call box and rang up Mr Rupert Thurtle at the American Hotel in Cornwall Street, where he was staying under the assumed name of Crayle. He was answered almost immediately and Box guessed that Thurtle junior had been finding it hard to sleep.

'Hullo, Mr Thurtle,' Box said softly.

There was no reply, during which the American was making up his mind whether to admit to the name or not.

Box continued speaking: 'I'm afraid I can't introduce myself very fully over the phone, but I am alone and I bring you a message from the "Old Wizard". Do you hear me? "Old Wizard". Could I see you at once?'

A smothered exclamation at the other end told him that the use of the family nickname had been successful.

'Right. Yes. When can you come?'

Box answered cautiously.

'I could be with you in under ten minutes. By the way, Mr Thurtle, I should advise you not to play any tricks. Communication with the police will be followed by the instant lodging with them of information concerning your luggage. Do you understand me?'

'I don't know who you are,' said Rupert Thurtle, 'but if you will come to this hotel at once I will see you alone. I shall not be foolish enough to talk with the police.'

Box hung up the receiver.

Twenty minutes later, a pale faced, dishevelled young man sat in his hotel bedroom reading and re-reading the message which Box had brought. Box, completely at ease, sat on the edge of the bed.

'Well?' he said at last. 'This is a business deal, Mr Thurtle. I hope you will not raise any objections to a scheme which your father has already approved.'

Rupert Thurtle passed a hand over his forehead. Then he looked up into the face of the man before him.

'This is my father's handwriting,' he said. 'And these are the words he would use. And yet the whole letter is unlike him.'

Box remained silent, and the other man went on:

'I don't know your name,' he said, 'and I don't expect it would help me if I did, but I feel there is something I must point out to you. That is, the money which you demand is the only weapon I have with which to defend my father legally. If I part with the money and he still falls into the hands of the police, all is lost.'

'In other words, you want to make certain that you are going to get the goods,' said Box easily.

'Yes, I want to make sure that, if I pay, my father will be a free man–at least so far as you are concerned.'

Box considered. 'How soon can you lay your hands on the money?' he inquired.

'Tomorrow morning.'

'It's in a safe deposit, I suppose?'

'Naturally.'

Box bent forward. 'At Lantern Bay, a little place on the coast just beyond Southampton, there is a motor yacht,' he said. 'Its captain is a discreet person called Tomlinson. I will see that he meets you at the Ship Hotel, saloon bar, at noon tomorrow. Take the money with you and wait on the boat. I shall bring your father down by car. Pay me the money there. And if you'll take my advice you will smuggle your father into southern Ireland.

'I warn you. Any attempt to doublecross me or my friends and—well, we are not particularly fond of your father. I don't suppose any of us would be heartbroken if the police discovered that in attempting to escape he had been accidentally drowned.'

The words were spoken lightly but Rupert Thurtle was left in no doubt as to Box's true meaning.

'Very well,' he said. 'Yes. I—I quite understand. Tomorrow at noon; then—my father.'

'Tomorrow,' Box agreed. 'A quarter of a million pounds.' With this, he nodded to young Thurtle and left.

It was nearly dawn when Box, a solitary figure, walked down Perry Street. Since he was alone, he had permitted the mask of bland good humour, which he usually wore, to drop from his face. He did not make the mistake of deceiving himself into thinking the situation was not bad.

For some time now he had been doing his best to return to his underground retreat where his assistants and prisoner awaited him. It was not simple. Both store entrances to the tube were guarded by police. The garage was being watched and Winton Mews still had uniformed men on duty. All the entrances were blocked.

For the time being he was checked.

He walked on slowly, his quick brain reviewing the situation. He was not sure what effect his shot had had on Fisher, or whether Jack Simmons had been successful in getting away. On the whole, Box rather fancied he had. That young man fought like a fiend and had the slipperiness of the proverbial eel.

Yes—at the moment the outlook was poor. At noon, young Rupert Thurtle would be waiting with the ransom. Somehow or other his father had to be spirited away from beneath the eyes of the police. It was then that Box, in passing, happened to glance up at the uninspired façade of Southwold Mansions. Every window in his flat was ablaze with light.

He stood there looking up and then, with the characteristic

recklessness which made him the personality he was, he turned in to the darkened entrance of the flats and went upstairs.

He thrust his latchkey into the lock, turned it and walked in. He closed the door noisily, threw his hat and coat down and strode into the main room.

He had prepared himself to meet any emergency, and nothing but the merest flicker of surprise showed itself when he caught sight of the figure sprawled in the chair in front of the fireplace. It was Fisher.

Fisher looked very white and his shoulder was bandaged. He was also wearing Box's dressing-gown.

'Hullo, Box,' he said. 'I say, I hope you don't mind me coming back here but I've got to hang about in this district, and I've had a bit of a scrap. It occurred to me that this was the most comfortable and convenient place to wait. I felt pretty sick when I found you weren't here, but the door was on the latch and so I walked in and made myself comfortable.'

Box stifled a desire to laugh. There was something very amusing in the situation. So his bullet had gone wide. He was angry with himself for that. He slipped back into the part which he always played in Fisher's company.

'Not at all – good idea,' he said. 'I say, what's the matter? Hurt yourself? Where have you been all this time? I've been careering round the streets looking for you and that girl. When I realised I'd missed you I didn't feel like coming back. I went on to an all-night café in Piccadilly.'

He walked over to the hearthrug and stood looking down with apparently friendly concern at the man he had attempted to kill such a short while before.

'What's all the drapery for?' he demanded, indicating the bandages.

Fisher grimaced.

'Nothing very much. We had a bit of a dust-up in Winton Mews and a fellow put a bullet through the fleshy part of my shoulder. It's nothing at all – merely a nuisance.'

Box's blue eyes grew round with astonishment.

'Really?' he said. 'Winton Mews? Why, that's quite near here, isn't it? Good heavens, this flat isn't at all the place for auntie. What's up? Did you catch the girl?'

'Yes,' Fisher replied. 'But that seems hours ago. She had an extraordinary story to tell. D'you know, Box, this flat of yours is owned by crooks?'

'Really?'

'I'm afraid so,' Fisher spoke slowly. 'I won't bother you with a lot of details, but there's an underground tunnel used by two stores as a parcels chute, and the girl was investigating a certain trouble they'd had with their dispatch service when she was kidnapped and brought up here.'

'Really!' said Box again. He was sitting on the edge of his chair with an expression of mingled excitement and alarm on his face. 'I say, I'll move out. I don't want to be mixed up with anything like this. Look here, what are you doing? Oh! I forgot, you bobbies are like doctors—you never tell, do you?'

The detective grinned. 'Not in the usual way,' he said, 'but as a matter of fact tonight I feel like a talk, it must be something to do with the dope they pumped into me at the hospital. Box, you can keep your mouth shut, can't you?'

'Me? I'm as silent as the grave and about as deep.'

'I believe I'm on the verge of a breakthrough. I don't know if you listen to the news at all but you must have heard of the disappearance of Joseph Thurtle, the financier.'

Box looked vague.

'Oh, yes,' he said, brightening up suddenly as his mind appeared to take hold of the problem. 'I do remember now. You fellows made a complete hash of his arrest, didn't you? There was an article in one of the papers—oh, very uncomplimentary. Are you on to this man?'

The blue eyes revealed nothing but ordinary interest and the hand that held the cigarette was steady.

'If I can only carry through my plan this morning, I shall have Thurtle in custody by one o'clock.'

Box bent forward to flick his ash into the fireplace.

'Sounds exciting,' he said. 'Can I hear?'

'We believe a villain kidnapped Thurtle with the idea of holding him for ransom. He's a mystery man. We've been looking for his hiding place for months but now I believe I've stumbled upon it. When that fellow shot me I had caught his assistant. The chap wriggled but I got him by the back of the jacket. Then my shoulder started to go numb and, although I clung on with one hand, my other hand was helpless. Before the sergeant could catch up with us the man had slipped out and streaked off down the road. I was just left with the coat which won't be much help.'

He lowered his voice.

'Their hide-out is in one of the old post office stations along the line of the disused tube and their exit is in the Mews.'

Box raised mild blue eyes to the other man's face.

'I can hardly believe it,' he said deliberately.

Fisher continued. 'I've narrowed it down,' he said complacently, 'and as soon as it's light I shall put my plan into action. It's very simple. These fellows have only three possible exits; either one of the stores and one other in Winton Mews. I've arranged for a strong force of police to wait at the beginning of the tunnel in each store.

'I shall have Winton Mews completely surrounded. When I give the signal my two posses will advance down the tube and flush out the crooks into Winton Mews.'

Box, who had been listening to this recital with his head held slightly on one side, regarded the man opposite him. 'I say,' he said, 'I didn't think you had it in you. I always imagined you coppers were bone from the neck up. I don't mean that offensively. It's the general idea, you know.'

Fisher went on with great satisfaction. 'It's not a bad plan,' he said, 'and I've got a hunch that it's going to succeed. I'm only waiting until it is light so there is no possible chance of anyone getting away in the mews. It sounds pretty fool-proof, doesn't it?'

'Yes,' said Box slowly. 'Unless–I say–of course, I don't know anything about these things, but are you sure you've got every exit covered? I mean, are you sure they can't get out some other way?'

'Certain,' Fisher sounded quite childishly pleased with himself. 'I thought at first there was another way out through a garage in Grafton Street, and I had the boys watching it until half an hour ago. Then it dawned upon me that we were wasting our time, a view also expressed by my superintendent who complained about the number of men I was tying up! I got a search warrant and examined the place thoroughly and satisfied myself there was nothing there. So I've withdrawn the guard.' He paused. 'If you don't mind, I shall wait here until it is light?'

'Of course. What an adventure. I've always wanted to be on a police raid. Do you want me to go climbing about sewers?' asked Box.

Fisher laughed. 'No, thanks. We're not co-opting civilians to do our dirty work. You'd better get some sleep.'

'Well, I'm not staying here,' said Box with sudden deliberation. 'This place is too darn peculiar for me. The agent can have his flat back. I'm going to sleep in my own bed. This isn't in my line at all. Finding a flat full of gadgets is one thing, but revolver shots and kidnappers just haven't got the same appeal in my young life. I'll ring you up later in the day and find out if you are still alive.'

Fisher looked uncomfortable. 'Look here. I can't turn you out like this,' he said.

'Nonsense! Anything to oblige a friend. You stay where you are, then if anything further happens in this unconventional flat it'll happen to you and not to me.'

Box went out into the hall, still talking. Outside the door he drew out his gun and hesitated. Finally, however, he shrugged his shoulders and began to laugh silently to himself. From his point of view the situation had its amusing side.

Mr Knapp, his pale, unpleasant face greasy with excitement,

leaned forward across the table in the 'office' where the gang was assembled.

'You're right, boss, the guard was withdrawn about three quarters of an hour ago.'

The faces of the others, who had spent a night trapped in their own fastness, were haggard, but there was a new light of hope in their eyes.

'Of course it was,' said Box testily. 'I've just come in that way. I tell you our young friend Fisher has surpassed himself. At the moment he is sitting up in the flat waiting for the light, and I have a fancy that it is going to descend upon him in a blinding flash.'

Perching himself on the edge of the table, he repeated the main substance of the detective's discourse. Levine began to laugh. Presently Jamieson joined him, and gradually the whole room echoed with their amusement. Box glanced at his watch.

'Knapp,' he asked. 'Are the cars ready?'

The little man nodded.

'All set, boss. There's the Cadillac and the Jensen. They'll both beat any police car on the roads.' He grinned. 'I've got a new set of number plates for every twenty miles if necessary.'

'Very well, then.' Box surveyed his forces. 'Tim, you'll drive the Cadillac and Jack the Jensen. Get into the chauffeur's uniforms and go on up to the cars and the rest of you clear up. Jamieson, you and Levine and Bill take the Jensen and Casson and I will look after Thurtle in the other. We're making for Lantern Bay, remember. Captain Tomlinson has orders to put out as soon as he gets young Rupert aboard. Then if he should have any idea of double-crossing us, our tracks are covered. We'll wait for them at Lantern Bay, hand over the prisoner, share the money and then everyone follows his own escape route as planned.'

As he spoke, he moved over to the desk and methodically took every scrap of paper out of it. Having satisfied himself that there was nothing left in the room which could possibly incriminate any of them, he signalled to Knapp, who brought a duster.

Meanwhile the others had donned wash-leather gloves, and within a few minutes every surface of the room had been wiped clear of fingerprints. It was a most methodical, careful piece of work, which any policeman could scarcely have helped appreciating. At last everything was ready. Box glanced at his watch. Five minutes to five.

'I fancy we have about half an hour to spare,' he remarked. 'Unless–hello!'

They paused, listening. Unusual sounds were issuing from the staircase which led down into the tube. The raid was beginning. Box was very cool, and his blue eyes were dancing. He seemed to be enjoying the situation.

'Come,' he said. 'We shall just do it, and in great style.'

He led the way down the staircase into the tunnel. Casson and Levine brought Thurtle along between them. He seemed to be completely apathetic.

Far away, from both ends of the tube, came the hollow sound of voices. The police were making no secret of their attack, and Box reflected, with a thrill of amusement, that Fisher had been so certain of success, so convinced that every exit was stopped.

After moving some thirty yards Box led the way through a door in the wall to a second stone staircase. Here the air was close and stifling. He hurried on to a square landing, leading out of which there was a second door.

He pushed this open cautiously, and entered into a small, cupboard-like apartment, where the air was surprisingly fresh. The reason for this became obvious when one glanced up to find that this was the inspection pit of Mr Knapp's garage, which had been built by the previous tenant by the simple expedient of cutting off the head of the cellar stairs.

Box pulled himself out lightly, and leaned back to help Levine hoist up their prisoner. It was not quite daylight, and it was still dark in the garage. The doors had been opened, however, and against the grey patch of light which they framed, the cars loomed out, dark and graceful.

The crooks moved swiftly. As soon as Box's head appeared above the inspection pit the uniformed figures in the drivers' seats started their engines, and Mr Knapp, who had been the last man up, spoke in a muffled whisper to his leader.

'Hurry, boss. I hear the trucks moving. I expect they're using them. It's going to be a near thing.'

Box chuckled.

'It's going to make them very sick,' he said. 'We shall wriggle out straight under their noses, net the money and get away with it.'

He sprang lightly into the back of the car, where Casson had already seated himself with Thurtle beside him. Mr Knapp settled himself on the floor at their feet.

'Let her go, Tim.'

The car leapt forward, and Box leaned back among the cushions, a smile of complete satisfaction spreading over his face. His eyes fell idly upon the shoulders of the man who had just brought the car swinging out of the garage. As he stared he noticed something which sent a chill down his spine.

Between the back of the chauffeur's collar and his cap was a tiny end of surgical bandage. The man who drove the car in which he and his prisoner rode so complacently had a wounded shoulder.

With a muttered exclamation, Box leaned forward and felt for his gun, but at that instant the car came to an abrupt stop. Box was thrown off balance and in that moment his chance of escape vanished.

Doors were pulled open and armed men appeared. From his position of vantage in the driver's seat Bob Fisher turned round. He smiled as he removed his cap.

The Jensen had been pulled up at the same time a little farther down the street, and the grinning detective who had taken Jack Simmons' place climbed out into the road.

The round-up was complete, neat and precise in every detail. The hidden police had swept down upon the cars immediately their drivers had brought them to a standstill.

Joseph Thurtle, alone unperturbed among the wrestling throng, permitted himself to be led quietly into a police car and driven this time without adventure to Scotland Yard. The other men put up a fight, but they were completely unprepared for the attack and proved no match for their assailants.

It was some time later when George Box was being driven to headquarters, with Fisher seated on one side and Davidson on the other, that the slightly puzzled expression returned to his blue eyes.

'I don't bear any grudge against you, Fisher,' he said affably. 'This is first blood to you. You laid a trap and I fell into it. I thought you underestimated my intelligence. It happens, I misjudged yours. But what I want to know is this: How did you spot me? When did you realise I wasn't quite the innocent friend who had rung you up to show you a peculiar flat?'

'You're under arrest. You take my advice and keep quiet,' said Inspector Davidson.

Box shook his head.

'Not at all,' he said. 'I'm naturally curious. After all, I think you owe it to me.'

Fisher turned, and for a moment, his shrewd grey eyes met those of the crook.

'Two little incidents,' he said, 'and one rather striking corroboration of the suspicion planted in my mind. When I looked over your entertaining flat, you told me you had only been in the place five or six hours. And yet every ash tray was filled with cigarette stubs. My naturally inquiring mind compelled me to have a look at them. They were all of your own particular brand, with the tips discoloured. You're a very wet smoker, Box. Perhaps that's why you only smoke them half-way through?

'Of course, that was a very small point, but it did occur to me that no human being could have smoked so much in a mere afternoon. That put me on my guard.'

He paused. 'Then, when the young woman made her sudden and startling appearance, I caught a glimpse of your face. I expected you to be surprised, astounded, bewildered–anything. Yet I saw none of these. You were angry. At the time I didn't understand.'

Box laughed unpleasantly.

'You're a brighter little detective than what I thought,' he said. 'Anything else? I'm afraid it doesn't strike me as being very conclusive so far.'

Fisher grinned.

'It was your generosity which undid you in the end,' he said. 'I think I told you that in the fracas in the mews one of my assailants slipped his jacket. That coat had a tailor's label with his client's name neatly written inside. Do you give all your old clothes away to your gang?'

Box swore.

The Pioneers

GINA BARING was going to leave her husband. They had discussed the move very carefully and with all the mutual consideration which had characterised every step of their eventful twelve years of married life.

Hitherto they had faced each obstacle in their joint path and had avoided it or surmounted it together, but now the time had come when it seemed to both that the wisest course lay in the dissolution of their partnership.

Gina Baring sat in her white and gold drawing-room and trembled. She was not aware that she was afraid, but that subconscious, almost physical intelligence which governs the senseless reactions of the body was in a state of panic.

The front part of her brain was busy thinking of Fergus Cappet, the man to whom her husband was so lightheartedly relinquishing her; or rather it was thinking of the uncomfortable armchairs in his dark book-lined living-room and wondering if he would permit her to change them for something less reproving to the flesh.

Over the Florentine mantelpiece her own portrait, painted before Jan Baring had become the fashionable A.R.A. he now was, smiled down at her with wide, confident eyes. Mrs Baring met the painted gaze and shivered without knowing why.

She and Jan were parting on the morrow. Their simple arrangements had already been made with due attention to the comfort and convenience of all concerned.

Tomorrow, Fergus, who was bohemian in the fine old-fashioned sense of that extraordinarily demoded word, would receive Gina Baring with that lack of formality which his two disastrous past experiences had taught him to prefer.

On her departure from home her husband had arranged to phone his solicitor and instruct the law to take its heavy-footed course. Then, on the day in which the Court should pronounce Jan a free man, he would marry Lynne Agnew.

The Barings had worked out every move together, as they had worked out the other serious steps in their lives, such steps as their rise from the studio in Soho to the flat in St John's Wood and afterwards their departure to Kensington, and from Kensington to their present home on the Kentish Downs.

It was a dignified programme, comfortable and eminently practical. Gina Baring knew that it would work admirably.

At the moment she was in a state of enforced calm. She was not considering the future or permitting herself to peer too closely at the immediate past.

When Fergus Cappet had taken her into his arms and his narrow, ugly mouth had trembled as he told her of his insufferable need for her, his appeal had come at a time when Lynne Agnew had already taken a definite place on Jan's horizon, so that Fergus had been a godsend to Gina Baring, providing as he did a blessed avenue of dignified escape.

Mrs Baring stirred on the couch. Lynne Agnew was coming to dinner. She had phoned to invite herself that morning and Jan had brought the intimation to his wife apologetically.

'I told her the Perneys were coming,' he had said rather helplessly: 'I explained that they were old friends we hadn't seen for seven or eight years; but she's made up her mind. It won't matter, will it?'

Gina Baring had looked into her husband's dark face and had smiled and reassured him. Privately she considered Lynne's gesture vulgar, precipitate, and unfortunately typical, but she did not say so. The Barings had always preserved a code of politeness which, while it made their daily relationship particularly comfortable, tended to keep them strangely unaware of each other's more intimate reactions.

Now, as Gina sat waiting for the Perneys to arrive on the evening train, she considered Lynne Agnew's attraction once again, and once again gave it up as incomprehensible. The entire cul-de-sac in which her own and Jan's life had suddenly come to a full stop was incomprehensible to her.

It had begun with the house. The house was the house of their dreams. In the days when they had worked together in the dusty little studio littered with the paraphernalia of Jan Baring's trade, the miscellaneous belongings of their myriad friends, and their own few possessions, they had conceived just such a dwelling and had furnished it in imagination with just such treasures as it now contained.

That was over ten years ago. Since then they had worked as only the obstinately successful artist knows how to work, and at last, through sweat and the bloodshed of reverses, had realised their sweet ambition.

Gina Baring's glance rested on the porcelain bowl they had brought from Marseilles, the candelabra they had picked up in Rome, the table that had come from the castle in Wales, and the puzzled expression in her round, grey eyes grew stronger.

Lynne Agnew had arrived on the scene with the house. She was a member of the country social set whose card of membership was the possession of reasonably sized property in the district, and the blonde widow had annexed Jan in a fashion so blatant and forthright that Mrs Baring had sat spellbound, scarcely believing her senses.

It had happened so suddenly. Jan had slipped into a vacant niche as the affluent celebrity of the neighbourhood and Gina had found herself without a place.

The little dinners at which one met the same people, heard the same gossip and exchanged the same half-digested views bored and bewildered her. She became aloof and unfriendly, while Jan, on the other hand, took to the life with unexpected enthusiasm.

He played bridge, he danced, he bought an expensive car and drove Mrs Agnew about in it and listened with apparent satisfaction to her secondhand sophistries.

At the moment when Gina Baring's astonishment had turned to bitterness and her discomfort become identified with shame, Fergus Cappet had appeared with his romantic and tragic appeal.

Tonight the Perneys were coming down from town for a snatched week-end, and tomorrow, when they had gone again, the Barings' marriage was ending as quietly and unobtrusively as it was possible to ensure.

Gina rose. It was nearly fifteen minutes past seven. In a moment now Jan would swing the car in at the drive gates and the Perneys would climb out to greet her.

She was not very clear in her mind about the Perneys. Victor had been a friend of Jan's in the early days. He had come to the gatherings, and towards the end of the time had often brought with him the little thing who was now his wife.

Gina Baring feared they might be a dull couple. She remembered those first years as a period of drudgery, only made possible by a youthful exuberance now as inexplicable as it was irrecoverable.

It was nearly eight years since she or Jan had seen either of them, and Victor's letter announcing his marriage and his intention of descending upon them had seemed very much of an irritating voice from the remote past.

Neither of the Barings had ever any desire to be rude, however, and since it was easier to put up with their old friends for a night than to go through the laborious business of an explanation, they had fixed an early date and fitted in their own arrangements accordingly.

Gina Baring saw the forthcoming evening as a last dull prelude to her new adventure, and did not look forward to it particularly. She heard the car drive up and, after glancing at herself in the round mirror, went out to greet her guests in Jan's house for the last time.

Her first glimpse of them interested her. The man was much as she remembered him. He was thicker, perhaps, and less untidy, but he had the same feckless, typically artistic face and the same youthful expression.

The girl had grown up. She was more assured but still vulnerable and Gina felt vaguely maternal towards them both.

She noticed that Jan was nervous. He hustled in with the suitcases and was inclined to talk loudly about trivialities. For the first time it occurred to her that the evening might have its embarrassing moments.

It was at this instant that Victor Perney caught sight of Gina, and her formal smile of welcome vanished before his whoop of delight.

'God!' he said. 'Darling! Oh, my lovely woman, what a *corker* of a house!'

She was in his arms and hugged and kissed like a long-lost mother before she could draw breath.

'Gina!' cried the girl behind him. 'Oh, Gina, you've grown lovely. I knew you would. We always said you would and you have. Oh, darlings, isn't this marvellous?'

Gina Baring was kissed again, and with a boisterous guest on either arm and followed by Jan, she was swept startled and breathless, into the breakfast-room, out into the garden and back through the french windows again.

Sally Perney paused on the threshold and stood hesitating, looking like some plump and delighted robin in her fashionable suit and bright sweater. Her quick turn of the head towards her husband was birdlike, too.

'Vic,' she said joyfully. 'Oh, Vic, they've done it. Look!'

Following her ecstatic gaze, Gina Baring had the odd experience of seeing her own room for the first time. The discovery that it really was lovely, as lovely as she and Jan could conceive a room, came to her with a sudden sense of comfort which was rudely dispelled immediately afterwards by her next thought, which was of the morrow.

Jan tried to take the situation in hand. His intelligent face was blank as he busied himself with drinks. He talked incessantly, asking questions without waiting for answers to them, and firing off little scraps of random information whenever there seemed to be the least fear of a lull in the conversation.

The Perneys were not in the least disconcerted by him. They were as unselfconscious as a pair of savages and as happy as children newly home from school. The extraordinary delight which they seemed to take, both in the house and in the Barings themselves, was bewildering to Gina at first, and afterwards, when she grew used to it, oddly stimulating in spite of the heartbreaking irony of the situation.

The Perneys examined the furniture, expressing frank approval and demanding the history of each piece, until at length even Jan unbent and condescended to honour them with one of his famous impersonations of old Cordigliani, the antique dealer in the Hampstead Road.

Gina found herself laughing, and Victor Perney threw an arm round her shoulders.

'Hell, it's good to see you two again,' he said with deep satisfaction. 'When we saw old Jan in the station we had an awful fear that you might have changed, but you haven't, you know. You're just the same. Just as you were ten years ago.'

Gina Baring shot a guilty glance at her husband, but he was not looking at her. He and Sally Perney were exploring the depths of the china cabinet and he had his back to the rest of the room. Presently he turned and spoke with studied casualness.

'By the way, you two. I hope you don't mind, we've got another guest for dinner. Mrs Lynne Agnew is coming along. We did our best to put her off, but she's a determined soul.'

The Perneys looked disappointed, but were disposed to be obliging.

'One of the local ladies?' inquired Victor, perching himself on the arm of a sofa. 'I suppose you can't get away from neighbours even here. What's she like?'

Jan refilled his glass carefully before speaking.

'Charming,' he said at last. 'I've got a portrait of her in this year's Academy.'

Sally looked up.

'A rather big thing with a blue background?' she demanded. 'I saw it. You did too, Vic. I pointed it out to you.'

'That's right. A nice thing. Rather more conventional than your usual stuff, but very pleasant. A grim-faced wench with flowers in her hair.'

Jan's dark face grew a shade more dusky.

'That's the one.'

Perney raised his glass.

'If she's a client, God bless her!' he said piously. 'God bless all sleek, yellow-haired, hard-mouthed women who want their portraits painted.'

He set down his glass and threw himself on the leopard-skin rug before the fireplace and buried his face in it like a child.

'I was at your wedding.' His smothered voice continued the conversation affably. 'Chianti and cake in Jan's studio. I was fifteen and got drunk as an owl on it. Now you're successful and I'm married and damn nearly successful myself. Isn't it miraculous? I say, have you ever done this, Jan? The fur on a leopard's head is the softest thing in the world. You try.'

In the end they all sampled it, one after the other, even Gina. It was remarkably soft. The short hair caressed their cheeks deliciously.

'A simple pleasure,' remarked Sally Perney, sitting back on her heels and laughing. 'I shouldn't like to do it on our dirty old hearthrug. We've got a real genuine Sheraton table though and a lovely Napoleon mirror with eagles. Next month, if all goes well, we'll buy a corner cupboard.'

Gina blinked. The girl's enthusiasm contained the genuine note. It echoed faintly down the years, as familiar and astonishing as the call of the first cuckoo in spring. Through the gush, the parrot-talk, the second-rate, the second-hand chatter of their new-won world, it trembled bugle-clear.

She glanced at Jan and he met her eyes and smiled with an amused tolerance which was just a little insincere.

Gina Baring turned away from him and tried to think of Fergus, Fergus who at any rate did want her, Fergus whose hungry, unhappy eyes were forever searching for that key to peace which must always lie hidden irrevocably beneath his own insufficiency. But her lips were unsteady.

It was very fortunate that Lynne Agnew should have chosen that precise moment to arrive. Her appearance caused a diversion which came only just in time. She swept into the room on a wave of faint perfume, her pastel silk striking a conventional note.

Lynne was charming, graceful and glaringly insincere. Beside Salley Perney's twinkling contentment her very flesh appeared synthetic. She nodded to them all in a correct, distant way, touched Jan's hand for a moment, and was smilingly infuriating to Gina.

Her coming brought the whole gathering to heel. The question of changing for the meal became a problem. Lynne was both gracious and amused, yet managed to convey that the omission was entirely due to Gina's incompetence as a hostess though of course Gina was notoriously incompetent and was to be forgiven.

Jan glanced at his wife reproachfully, and for a giddy moment Gina even felt incompetent. Perney grinned.

'I can't change, anyway,' he said. 'I didn't bring any clothes. I'm also starving.'

Mrs Agnew regarded him with interest for the first time. Her polite astonishment was devastating and he coloured.

Five minutes later they went in to the meal, a chastened company.

Mrs Agnew did her earnest best to put everyone at their ease, undeterred by the single vital objection that she was not the hostess. In spite of Jan's determined efforts to ward off the Perneys she insisted on bringing them into the brittle clatter of malicious gossip about her own acquaintances by pumping them tentatively about their own home and circle.

The Perneys were only too anxious to talk about themselves. After the discomfiture of the first ten minutes they had evidently decided on Mrs Agnew's place in their universe and were anxious to dispose of her quietly and get back to Jan and Gina. Mrs Agnew, therefore, got a little more than that for which she had bargained.

Sally Perney's domestic problems proved to be of that sensational nature which sometimes characterises the lives of the employers of the cheaper London help. Her amusements were simple not to say plebeian.

A well-directed snub, horrid in its cruelty, brought a blush to her cheek and Victor Perney to her defence. He regarded Mrs Agnew with lazy, friendly eyes and began to scoff at her with that misleadingly ingenuous questioning which is the savagest weapon in the world.

Lynne did not perceive the attack for a long time, and Gina sat helpless, her heart bleeding for Jan and her sense of humour titillated, while Mrs Agnew was led gently to convey that she thought herself the most beautiful woman in the district, that in her opinion one did not mix socially with people whose income was less than five thousand a year, and that good taste was largely a matter of patronising the most expensive shops.

Perney was delighted with his success and glanced at Jan for approbation. Gina saw the look and writhed in sympathetic discomfort.

After dinner they sat round in the sitting-room. The Perneys did not play bridge and said so cheerfully. They were anxious to do their best to make the enforced hour or so with the difficult guest as bearable as possible, however, and set themselves out to be entertaining.

They were, indeed, extremely amusing. Their chatter about their recent wedding, their parties, the picturesque characters they met, all helped to bring the old familiar gaiety of the early days of their own marriage back to the Barings with a vividness which Gina found stifling.

Lynne Agnew kept her head and stuck to her own rigid code of behaviour with a determination which was at times a little grim. She was a slow-witted woman, but not entirely without perception. She had become aware of her treatment at Perney's merciless hands quite within half an hour of the moment when he finished with her, and she was wary of him now. But he had grown used to her amused and tolerant expression and was no longer subdued by it.

Gina watched her husband with covert anxiety. She thought only of him. Her tragic part in the comedy was too poignant to be savoured, but she could appreciate his acute embarrassment and sympathise with it.

Jan did his best, but the cards were against him. The Perneys amused and stimulated him in spite of himself. Inevitably the talk turned to old times. Victor Perney lay back in a great armchair and with a few deft brush strokes sketched in a picture of the

Barings' Soho studio. He did this for Mrs Agnew's sole benefit, in a spirit of pure forgiveness. He was preparing to talk and wanted her to enjoy the performance, and his word-picture was in the nature of a stage set.

'They were the first of the gang to marry,' he said, his bright round eyes fixed earnestly on the fair, painted face in front of him. 'We were all more or less starving, you know. Not a bean between us. One decent suit between a dozen of us, and a good meal for everybody as soon as someone sold a drawing or a relation took pity. You know the sort of thing.'

'I'm afraid I don't,' said Mrs Agnew.

'Oh, well, you must imagine it, then,' said Perney kindly. 'Jan and Gina were the first to risk marriage. There was a howl from relations and elders generally, prophecies of death and disaster, and so on, and even we were a bit apprehensive.

'We let them alone for at least a week and then crept back, one by one, to see if the rot had set in. They looked much the same, but Gina had cleaned the place up and there was some decent food in the kitchen cupboard. After that, of course, we practically moved in.

'Gina looked after us all. She got Jan going, saw he had a clean space to work in, fixed up for him to sleep occasionally and fed us all at least once a week. It was a revelation to us.

'Our generation had the wind-up about marriage. We were all brought up to believe that for the thinking man marriage is death. Jan and Gina risked it and proved it to be a damn fine idea. We were convinced. We saw it work. Marriage is all right. Marriage is good.'

Lynne Agnew laughed. The little tinkling sound jarred in the breathless room.

'How terribly amusing!' she said, and turned to Jan. 'I didn't know you'd had such a difficult beginning, my dear.'

'Difficult?' roared Perney, suddenly infuriated. 'My dear girl, you don't understand. It wasn't difficult. It was glorious.'

Mrs Agnew flushed.

'You must forgive me,' she said, 'but I can't bear sordid stories. They're too Russian, too depressing.'

Gina caught a glimpse of Perney's wrathful face and Jan's pallid, tight-lipped mouth, and struggled with the nightmare.

'It was a long time ago,' she said feebly. 'We've almost forgotten it.'

'I haven't,' said Perney obstinately, 'and I'm never going to forget it.' He sat up. 'It was the most enlightening, stupendously comforting thing that ever happened to me, that discovery. I could thank you two on my knees for pointing it out to me. Marriage is all right. Given the right ingredients, it's the secret of happiness. It does exist. It can be done.'

Mrs Agnew rose. There was a set smile on her red lips, and her movements were studiously graceful.

'I have a long drive home,' she said. 'You'll be gone in the morning, won't you, Mr Perney? It's been so interesting meeting you. Good-bye. Good-bye, Gina. Good-bye, Mrs Perney. Jan, I shall see you tomorrow.'

She gathered up her bag and made her exit. Jan hurried after her.

Perney rose.

'I suppose I'd better go, too,' he said. 'I didn't mean to annoy the wretched woman, but she got me down.'

He went out to obtrude his friendly personality upon the departing guest. Gina dared not stop him. She was panic-stricken. She was dimly aware that a matter which a few hours before had seemed so very personal had now become a broader problem.

Sally Perney's sharp whisper cut through her thoughts.

'It's definitely female, isn't it?' she said. 'It's got its eye on your old man. I do admire you, Gina. You didn't murmur. I'd have scratched and disgraced myself.'

She plumped herself down on the rug and sat clasping her knees, her small, bright face raised to the other woman's.

'It's just instinctive with me. Vic says I behave like a bantam hen, but I can't help it. Even if I *know* it's quite safe and the silly little girls haven't got an earthly, yet I go for them with my claws out. Of course, it's different for you, in a way. You and Jan must be so absolutely one person after all this time. Still, I'd have snapped at her. She was so disgustingly possessive.'

Gina looked at the girl and smiled at the hopelessness of it all. Mrs Perney misunderstood her.

'I know I'm silly,' she said. 'I always remember you and Jan getting rid of the White Crow. In times of stress that recollection heartens me. It can be done. You do remember the Crow, Gina? She was a model or something, a great white face and a predatory leer. Doesn't that bring her back to you?'

Gina Baring's mind was jolted back to a scene in the studio in the third year of their marriage. She saw herself trembling, angry and excruciatingly jealous, with Jan, cold and uncomfortable, at her side.

'My dear, you're being damned silly,' she had said to the languid, vacant face before her. 'A little disgusting, too. Do go away.'

The *naïveté* of the words brought a blush to her cheeks as she remembered, and she wondered why. Was it that they were then all young, all so idealistically sure of the sanctity of the new love they had discovered?

'The White Crow,' she said aloud. 'Poor girl, we didn't like her, did we?'

'Jan hated her,' said Sally Perney complacently. 'Vic says Jan was shocked by her.'

Gina stared at her and her heart contracted as her early success was so lightly explained. She was saved from betraying herself by the return of the men. Perney came in grinning.

'She's gone, silly old trumpet,' he said, rubbing his bony hands together. 'Let's go along to the studio and look at Jan's stuff. Can I have some beer? Put the brandy away, Gina, now the guest has gone.'

Mrs Baring glanced at her husband and was startled to see that the expression in his eyes was as helpless as her own.

At three in the morning they were sitting before a fire still talking, with the room a chaos of canvases and pencil studies around them. Perney and Gina had raided the kitchen at midnight and the remains of a scratch meal lay on trays on the model's throne behind them.

For two hours Mrs Baring had not thought of Fergus Cappet. Jan sat on the hearthrug, his face alive and young with anger. He and Perney had been wrangling over the old argument of inspiration versus technique for the best part of the dawn and they had enjoyed themselves. Now, exhausted and satisfied, they were preparing to make the effort to go to bed.

Perney put an arm round his wife and presented her to his hosts. 'There she is,' he said. 'All my own work. Jan's recipe. Do you remember, Jan? You said to me, "Catch one young and train it, and then keep it down." It's taken me a long time, but I've done it'.

His lean, ugly face was bright with satisfaction, and his next remark startled them.

'We're following your footsteps. We're close on your heels,' he observed affably. 'You showed us the way and we're coming after you. What I said to that abysmally silly woman was quite true. You two put us all on to the right track when we were kids. You proved to us that it is possible to be free, egotistical, sophisticated, unconventional and at the same time perfectly happy. You two are both artists in the best sense of the word, both individualists and both experimenters in life. By all the rules you ought to be lonely, unsatisfied and discontented. But you've solved the whole problem by teaming up early and working as one man. Sally and I are coming after you. You people put on such a show. You were so happy, so gloriously successful, that you influenced a lot of us, you know.'

His voice died away and the studio was silent. Gina Baring laughed unnaturally.

'Oh, my dears,' she said unsteadily, 'don't go by us. I mean, it's not—not so easy.'

Jan leant forward and touched her arm warningly, and again she sympathised with his desire to avoid the unbearableness of an explanation. All the same, her conscience pricked her. She tried to compromise.

'Things get difficult,' she said, 'As one gets more money and more conventional in one's ordinary routine, conventional people get in. Then the trouble is that the word "conventional" doesn't mean what it used to any more. I mean, people aren't necessarily honest or pleasant or kind just because they happen to be conventional. You get them in the house and they play the devil with you because you're unprepared and unarmed. You're simple, unsuspecting, natural people. Everyone can see what *you* are at a glance. *Their* conventionality cloaks *them*. It's their disguise. They beat you when it comes to it.'

Sally Perney grinned. She looked very young and confident, clinging to her husband's arm.

'You can always chuck them out,' she said. 'I mean, they never get right in, do they? They never come between you and your old man. They can't.'

'Why not?' Jan spoke slowly and with genuine inquiry in his tone.

Mrs Perney stared at him; her eyes were round and shocked and a wave of scarlet colour swept over her face.

'Well, I mean, you—well, you love each other, don't you?' she said. 'That's the king-pin. You can't go and forget you're in love.'

Perney raised his eyes and groaned.

'Indecency!' he said, shaking her gently. 'Horrible little beast. Go to bed. Go on. Gina will take you up, then we'll come. Beat it.'

Ten minutes later Gina Baring stood on the landing with her back to her own bedroom door and said good night for the fifteenth time to Sally Perney, who had followed her along the passage from the guest room.

'It's a darling house,' the girl was saying. 'A peach of a house. It's made for you. Have you still got the brass barouche?'

'Our Italian bed from the flat?'

The old nickname for that monstrous couch sounded strange in the painted splendour of the new house and Gina Baring lied gallantly.

'Yes, it's still alive.'

Sally kissed her.

'I'm so glad. Vic and I are going to have a genuine four-poster when we get a room to hold it. Bless you, pet. It's grand to see you both again and to know that it really is all right and it can work out, whatever people say. You've proved it. Good-night.'

She bobbed off down the passage, looking like a child, and Gina Baring waited until the door of the guest room closed before she opened her own and switched on the light.

The photograph of Fergus Cappet met her as she went in. It regarded her with pallid intensity from the ledge above her narrow convent bed and for a moment she stood staring at it, her arms hanging limply at her sides.

'Oh, dear God,' whispered Mrs Baring.

In the early dawn she was aroused from her dazed apathy by hearty whispering outside her door. It went on for a long time. She did not understand it immediately, and it was not until the door opened and someone stepped just inside and closed it after him, to stand motionless, listening, that she realised what had happened.

Jan had found Vic even more difficult to shake off than Sally had been, and had been forced into subterfuge, after allowing it to be presumed that his wife's room was still also his own. There was something horribly amusing in the farce, and she began to laugh quietly, unaware that there were tears in her eyes.

'Shut up, Gina,' Jan's whisper was agonized. 'God, what a chap! He *wouldn't* go to bed. He wanted to see the brass barouche. Where is it?'

'In the attic,' she whispered breathlessly.

He came blundering softly towards her across the unfamiliar room and sat down on the end of the bed.

'We'll have to get it down. He'll find out. I know him. He's a most tenacious ass—always was.'

Gina Baring covered her eyes with the back of her hand, as though she were afraid the very darkness would betray her.

'We'll have to tell them, Jan.'

He was silent for a long time. Presently he leant over and found her among the pillows.

'Gina.'

'Yes?'

'How are we going to get out of this? What are we going to say?'

'Who to? The Perneys?'

'Oh, Heavens, no! Fergus and Lynne. What are we going to tell them? Temporary insanity?'

He was still whispering, and the quiet and the darkness gave the conversation a strange urgency.

Gina Baring lay still. She was crying and her breath trembled. 'I don't know,' she mumbled. 'Oh, Jan, I don't know.'

He laughed. The sound was gay, spontaneous and entirely young.

'We'll bunk,' he said. 'It's cowardly, childish and utterly disgusting, but it'll save a lot of trouble in the end. We'll go to France and lie low till it blows over. After all, it's the only thing we can do. We've got to go on, Gina. We haven't finished. We've got work to do. We've both been hysterical, darling. You do see that, don't you?'

She did not answer, and he repeated the question with a falter in his voice which demoralised her.

'Don't you?'

Gina Baring opened her arms to him and, after a while, they lay laughing at themselves in the darkness.

The Sexton's Wife

'THEY say it's unlucky to marry for love,' said the old woman, peering across the rag hearthrug to where I sat in the shadow. 'But I don't know. I often wonder how it would have been.'

'If you hadn't married for love?' I said.

Old Mrs Hartlebury shook her head and the firelight played over the wrinkles on her brown face.

'No,' she said. 'If I had.'

We were sitting in the downstairs room of her cottage, which stands midway between the church and the turning which leads through the Street to the Hard and the sea.

It was pouring, and I had dropped in to see her as I went back to the house after an expedition to the landing stage to get some fresh fish off the boats.

We had sat talking for some time while the room grew gradually darker. Now it was so dark that I could only catch a glimpse of the gold-spotted spaniels on the mantelshelf high above my head when an extra big flame spurted from the wood fire and lit up the small warm room for a second.

But it was still raining and I did not want to move. There was plenty of time to get back when it stopped, and I was drowsy and comfortable sitting there in the warm.

Mrs Hartlebury did not mind. She went on talking and sighing, hardly noticing me as I sat on the far side of the hearth, on a hassock borrowed from the church and with my back against the log heap which filled that corner of the room.

There was a long pause after her last remark. I did not speak. If she wanted to talk I was ready to listen; if she did not want to her business was not of any account to me. Like herself I had been bred on the Essex coast and we understood one another.

After a while I heard her stirring in her chair and I saw her eyes for a moment as they reflected the glow of the fire when she turned her head.

'Have you heard about Hartlebury, the way he died, or any-thing?' she asked suddenly.

'No,' I said not very truthfully.

I had heard something, of course, but then you hear something about the way everyone dies and I did not know if the gossip were true.

'He died the way he deserved to die,' she remarked, and although I could not see her face I knew it was unforgiving.

I made some non-committal sound and drowsed again.

'When I was a girl I was wonderful pretty,' she went on after a bit.

I could believe that, for she is a very fine looking old woman now and she is eighty-two years old.

'I had black hair,' she said proudly, 'and a skin you'll never see these days when girls get as many victuals as their fathers and brothers. That time there weren't much food about and men can't go fishin' hungry, so the women weren't overfed and I count that done 'un good. I had a sweetheart long before I was sixteen,' she added, and she spoke comfortably as though she was glad to think of it even after all this time.

'A fine boy he was,' she went on quickly. 'Seventeen or eighteen, with yellow hair and a soft sort of smile when he saw me coming down to the Hard to meet 'um.'

She paused and I saw her as she bent down to lift a stick on to the fire. For a moment she startled me. The shadows had crept into the hollows of her face and filled them, so that I suppose I saw her as she must have been when she stood on the Hard wait-ing for her sweetheart all that time ago.

When the flame died down she went on talking.

'We went about together, Will and me. Did I tell you his name? Will Lintle. His father, Joe, had a smack, and they two went out together almost every day. We couldn't get married. Neither on us had enough to live on. So we went on sweet-hearting, years it was, until I was turned nineteen.

'He was true to me,' she said. 'All that time he was true. I wasn't very old and I crossed him time and again, and I'd say

things to hurt, the way girls do. Yet he'd never walk out with
another girl, but would look at me puzzled and sort of wondering
why I'd hurt him, so that I'd be ready to tear my tongue out
rather than speak so again.'

She paused and I suppose I sighed, for she laughed and I could
feel her grinning at me in the darkness.

'Ah, you're young,' she said. 'I'm old, and, though I ain't
forgot, I'm different.'

I did not say anything and presently she went on in a sing-song
which was addressed more to herself than to me:

'I reckon I loved Will just as he loved me, and when it's like
that you can't be much less than happy. We counted we should
get married some day and we were content.'

She paused a moment and when she spoke again her voice was
sharper.

'But when I was nineteen Hartlebury stepped across to see my
father one day and told him and my mother that he was after
me.'

She broke off and mumbled rather irritatingly, as very old
people do, and I was sorry that I could not see her clearly as she
sat huddled up in her chair.

Presently, when I had almost forgotten what she had been
talking about, she went on with the story again.

'James Hartlebury was the carrier at that time, and he was
sexton too, so he lived right over against the church where the
Reading Room is now. Pretty little house he had, with a long
path up to the door which had rosemary bushes all down the
sides of it. I can't bear the smell of rosemary even now,' she put in
suddenly, 'though many's the time I've washed my hair with it
when I was a girl. It's a wonderful fine thing for black hair, is
rosemary.'

She stopped talking and I kicked the fire to make it blaze.

Outside the rain was lashing against the house and I was glad
to be indoors.

There was another long silence and I thought that perhaps she
had gone to sleep, so I did not move lest I should wake her. But

she was just thinking, for suddenly she went on again as though there had been no lull.

'No one knew much about James,' she said. 'There were one or two who called him Jim, but not many. I never did, not even after I married him. It wouldn't have been right somehow.

'He was a queer man. No one knew much about him. He kept himself alone among them all, yet he wasn't surly or proud. He'd take his drink at The Starlings with anyone. He went to church twice a Sunday, and people said he was rich. Yet he wasn't liked. He might almost have been one of the gentry, the way that no one spoke or stopped him when he came down the Street.

'My father was pleased right through when he came to our house that day. He didn't like him much, but he thought like everyone else did what a fine thing it was for me to get a husband who was carrier and sexton too.'

Once again she stopped, and then talked on much more briskly, as though she were coming to a part of the story which she did not enjoy remembering.

'Well, I married 'um,' she said. 'I don't know why, save that I counted it was time that I got married and I couldn't see that Will would ever be able to keep us both. And besides—' she hesitated, '—besides, I was taken by James at that time.'

She hurried on; she felt no doubt she ought to excuse herself.

'He hadn't never been after a girl before. There was a kind of mystery about him. It wasn't his money—for all anybody said, it wasn't his money. It was the honour of it. I was the only girl he ever went for. He was nearing forty, too, mind you. He wasn't a lad, and that pleased me.

'Besides,' she added, half laughing, as though she were remembering something after a long time, 'he had a sad, quiet way with him, as though he had some secret. I was sorry for him, all alone in the little house.'

It was eerie sitting there in the dark, listening to her droning voice talking of things that had happened so long ago. I made myself more comfortable against the logs.

'Life seems as though it's going on for ever when you're young, and almost any change looks good,' she remarked. 'I had a fine wedding. James being the sexton and to do with the church knew how a wedding should be.

'I had a fine wedding.' She repeated it softly. 'There were as many people outside the church as if it had been a gentry wedding. You see, everyone knew James and nobody liked him; and, too, they guessed the boy'd be there and they came to watch us.'

I nodded. People did not seem to have changed very much.

'James was always kind to me,' she remarked suddenly. 'That day in the church and before I couldn't have wished him better. But I was scared of him.

'No,' she corrected herself abruptly, 'I wasn't scared of him then. That came later. At the wedding I was shy of him, shy and a bit proud.'

'You would be,' I said feeling that it was about time I made some remark.

She sniffed. 'Ah,' she agreed. 'It was natural. Will did come to the church,' she continued, 'and at first I was afraid to look at him. But when we came out, and everyone was shouting and laughing and cheering us, I heard him louder than the others and I looked round and saw him staring straight at me and waving and shouting with the rest. I knew he meant to be laughing at me, so I looked at his eyes and he laughed louder and cheered louder. But I'd seen, and he knew I'd seen.'

She paused.

'I reckon I loved him,' she said and sighed, but she laughed afterwards and I remembered how terribly old she was.

'James took me down between the rosemary bushes to his house,' she went on, 'and I lived there after that. I didn't see Will, for I was never a bad girl, but I thought on him. I had plenty o' time for thinking,' she added dryly. 'James wouldn't let me out of the house, and I didn't see my mother more than five or six times all that winter.'

Her voice died away, and when she spoke again there was something about her tone which gave me my first feeling of uneasiness. She was certainly not trying to frighten me, but some of her remembered terror crept into her voice and I could hardly help but recognise it.

'It was then,' she said, 'that I began to notice James. He was so quiet. He'd sit whole evenings puzzling over figures and writing letters and never saying a word. And sometimes he'd get up in the night and go out, leaving me asleep. Just the same as he was to everyone in the village, so he was to me his wife; quiet and telling nothing. I was young,' she said, nodding at me, 'and I was used to being with people, but he wouldn't let me out of his sight a minute if he could help it. And when on Tuesdays and Saturday he went off in his cart, carrying, he'd give me so much to do that I couldn't leave the house. And when he came back he'd make me go through everything I'd done. If I'd seen anyone I had to tell him everything they'd said to me and everything I'd said back to them.

'And when I'd told him he'd put his hands on my shoulders and look at me with those dull eyes of his and say "Is that true?" And I'd say "Of course. Why should I lie to you?"

'Then he'd kiss me again and again, but he'd never tell me anything.'

A great squall of wind rattled the shutters and one or two raindrops fell down the chimney and the fire hissed.

'I soon found out I didn't love him,' she went on, glancing at me. 'But I made up my mind to that. I wasn't no fool. But, by and by, as the winter went on and I worked about the house, not seeing anyone but him from Sunday to Sunday, I began to watch him, and the more I watched him the more frightened I grew.

'He was queer,' she said, 'especially just after there'd been a burying. It was terrible cold that winter and there wasn't much food for them. There was several died.'

She lowered her voice and I, who am not very imaginative, began to feel uncomfortable.

'While James was at work on a grave he'd be more talkative and not so sad,' she went on, 'and then, after it was all done, he'd take to his going out at nights again. I'd lie awake wondering what had taken him out, and guessing and guessing aright, and yet not believing it.'

I moved closer to the old woman and I felt her small hard brown hand on my shoulder.

'At those times he wouldn't let me load the cart for him, as I usually did,' she whispered, 'but would keep me indoors while he did it himself. I grew more and more frightened, for I wasn't very old.'

I shivered. There was something gruesome in her suggestion and I was glad of the roaring fire.

'Soon after that,' she said, 'my mother came round to see me, and all the time she was with me he never left us alone. She was a cheerful body and she talked and told me what they were saying in the village: how the Playles–a wild lot, they were, who lived down by the Hard–had begun their smuggling tricks again, though one of 'em had got shot for it less than two years before.

'Then she told me that an old woman called Mrs Finch, who lived round the back of the church, was putting it about that she'd seen a ghost-light in the graveyard the night after young Nell Wooton was buried.

'I knew James had been out that night and as my mother was speaking I looked across at him, and I'll never forget his face.'

Mrs Hartlebury stopped and I realised suddenly that she was looking behind her. I stirred up the fire and moved closer to it, and she went on.

'When my mother had gone James sat indoors doing nothing, looking out of the window, and for a month after that he never went out at night.

'Then I began to think of Will again. I knew it wasn't right, but as the spring came round again and I could get out into the garden I used to find myself standing at the gate looking down the road and hoping maybe that I'd see him.

'I didn't want to talk to him. I only wanted just to see him again. I reckon James knew that, for he used to call me into the house and keep me busy there. Sometimes he used to make love to me, in his own way, and he'd bring me presents from the town. But I knew how he got his money, though I wouldn't think of it. I knew what he was and I was frightened out of my life.'

I had guessed what he was too, and I mentioned the ugly word to the old woman.

'Yes,' she said, 'that's what he was. Resurrection men they called them then. An awful thing for a young wife to find. He'd sell the bodies in the town to men who'd sell them to the doctors. But mind you, I didn't know that then as clear as I do now. If I had, I'd have run home and let the village say what it would. As it was, I was frightened enough although I'd only half guessed what he was. But I stayed with 'un.' She nodded her head. 'Yes, I stayed with 'un.

'And then one day,' she said in an entirely new voice, 'when I was cutting rosemary to put with the little linen I had, I heard someone going by in the road. I looked up and saw Will, as I had always known I should see him, swinging past with an eel fork and splashers on his shoulder. He didn't look at me and I couldn't help it, I called to him, and he turned and smiled at me and said "What cheer, Sis?"—they called me that then.

'I went down to the gate and we stood there talking. He stared in my face and of course I didn't look what I had been. How could I after a whole winter shut up in a little house?

'Presently he said "Are you all right, Sis?"

'I don't know what I said. Maybe I didn't speak. But anyway, he leaned over the gate and said, "Why, girl, I don't blame ye, I don't blame ye," kindly, just like that.

'When he had gone, and he didn't stay long, I turned round and saw James watching me through the window, and when I went in he stared at me angrily. He didn't say anything, but from that day he never left me alone if he could possibly help it, and Will didn't come again.'

The rain had stopped outside and the fire was dying, so I made it up. I moved quietly, though, and I did not disturb her thoughts and presently she went on with the story.

'Then for a long time no one died, so there were no buryings, and James used to come home from the town sullen, and drunk too sometimes. Then he began to talk in his sleep, saying terrible things, and I used to lie there trembling, staring up at the thatch, trying not to listen and wondering what I would do.

'Then one night–' her voice sank so low that I had to strain to hear her '–he came in quite different. He kissed me and started talking about the town and the folk he had seen, and making me laugh until I could hardly breathe.

'And the next morning this new way of his was still there. He seemed pleased about something, for I saw him smiling to himself when he thought I wasn't near.

'I thought perhaps I had been mistaken about him, but a week after that I woke in the night and I heard horses galloping past the house down the road to the Hard.

'I called to James, but he was awake already.

'"What would that be?"' I said.

'"Nothing," said he. "You go to sleep, girl." But I lay still, thinking for a while, and then I knew what it was.

'"God Almighty, the Excise Men!" I said. "Was there anything doing tonight at the Hard?"

'James didn't speak at first and then he said "How would I know?", but I heard him laughing to himself in the dark and I lay shivering beside him, wondering what he knew. I was more frightened of him than ever after that.'

Her voice died away again and I resettled myself against the log pile, after edging my way across the hearth.

'I heard all about it the next morning,' she said. 'My sister came up and told me soon after daylight. A fine morning it was, I remember; clear and hard, the sea a dull green and not very rough. Everywhere smelt fresh and clean. I'll never forget the rosemary. The whole house was sick and faint with it. It was quiet, too, like a Sunday.

'Cuddy came up the path as I was giving James his breakfast. She sat down with us, but she never ate, so busy was she telling us.

'I knew before she told us just how it had been: the Excise Men coming on the Playles and holding them up, and they–a wild lot they were–telling them to shoot and be damned to them, and the riders not shooting at first, but, when the boys took to their horses in the dark, letting loose and chasing after them all along the Winstree Road.

'Cuddy told it well and James listened to her every word, for she was talking more to him than to me. Women liked James for his very quietness and the way he never cared for them.

'Long before she had told all he said so carelessly that I knew he was play-acting, "Was there anyone killed?"

'"One," she said, and I caught her looking at me as though she was watching for something.

'"Did the others get away?" said James.

'"They did," she said. "But they think they've been seen, and they've gone out fishing for a bit till we see if anything more happens."

'"Did the Excise Men get the contraband?" said James.

'"Yes,' she said.

'"Then you'll not hear any more of them," said he, and he laughed.

'She smiled at him and then she said "It'll teach they Playles a lesson, but it's bad for 'un who's killed." And she peeked at me again.

'"Who's he?" said James, and he looked at me and not at her as an ordinary man would have been sure to do.

'"Haven't I told you?" said Cuddy, though she knew as well as anyone that she hadn't spoken his name "It was Will Lintle. He was out with the Playles and they got him first shot."

'She didn't say any more and they two just sat and peeked at me under their eyelashes, making believe they weren't looking. But I knew they were watching and so I didn't say anything, or look anything, for I was getting used to play-acting by that time, having lived with James so long.

'By and by Cuddy got up and said she was going back home, and I thought she looked at me angrily, as though I'd cheated her of something. I had cheated her, I expect.

'When she had gone I peeked at James the same as they two had peeked at me, and I saw he was laughing to himself.'

She leant forward as she spoke and I saw that even now she was angry with him for that.

'I could have killed 'um,' she said. 'I could have killed 'um, but I didn't say a word. I cleared away the breakfast and I washed the dishes, while he sat there laughing quietly to himself in the door-way. He just sat there mending a bit of harness and laughing to himself.

'For a time I thought about Will and I couldn't believe him dead. Several times I wondered if I would run down home to find out if it were true, but every time I turned to the door, there was James in the way, still laughing to himself.

'And then I went upstairs to make the bed and I began to think clearly for the first time in my life.'

Old Mrs Hartlebury's voice grew harder and her chair creaked as she leant forward.

'I knew he'd informed,' she said. 'I stood by the window thinking, and all in one minute it came to me that Will was dead and that James was downstairs laughing. I hated him, but I daren't do anything.

'By and by I saw Joe Lintle coming up the path, and I heard him speaking to James through the window. I didn't listen, but I knew what he was asking, and I knew then that it was true. That was a long time ago and I was only a girl,' she said slowly. 'So when I came from the window I lay on my face on the bed and I cried as if Will had still been my sweetheart and I had not been married to James.'

She paused and I wondered if she really remembered how she felt, or if it was like a ghost of an emotion after all that time.

'He came up and found me, James did,' she said suddenly. 'I didn't move. I lay there on the old bed sobbing and crying like a child would. He didn't say anything. He just stood there in the doorway looking at me, and laughed, and I hated him.

'By and by he grew tired of standing and staring, so he went off, stamping downstairs and out of the house, still laughing to himself. I heard him all the way.

'I didn't go to the burying,' she went on. 'I sat upstairs by the window. Hidden behind the curtain, I watched the people go by. They all looked up at the house and nudged each other as they passed. I knew they were wondering would I go to the church or not.'

She laughed.

'I hated them. I could have leant from the window and shouted to them that I loved Will and that I didn't care who knew it, but I didn't do anything. I only stood there watching the church gate.

'I could see it from the window, just the gate and no more. I waited till they brought the coffin up the Street and took it into the church, four of them carrying it and the others following.

'I remember it seemed an awful thing to me at that time that he should be dead.'

She sank lower in her chair and the firelight shone on her twisted, capable hands where they lay crossed and quiet in her lap.

'I don't want to die, even now,' she said. 'But the thought of it doesn't make me sick, as it did then. It's horrible when you're young.

'When I saw that they'd all gone into the church and the Street was empty I came away from the window and went down the stairs to get some victuals ready for James, for he was always wonderful hungry after a burying. And as I set the table and drew the ale for him, I hated him worse than ever, I did.

'By and by he came in, and that was the second and last time I saw him really happy and content with himself. He sat down at the table and I waited on him. He was smiling all the time he ate, and when he had done he pushed his chair back and pulled me down on to his knee, and he held me there whilst he told me every bit about the burying. And he watched me all the time he told me.

'I couldn't bear to listen to him,' she said, 'but I was too frightened to break away. So there he held me, laughing in my face and searching for something in it that would show the way I felt.

'I didn't show anything for a while, but he went on so long. It was a deep grave, he said, and a well-dug one. There were plenty worms in it.

'I felt right faint as I thought about it and I nearly fell off his lap. He saw I was beginning to give way and he held me tight to him.

'"He'll rot soon," he said, "and good riddance. He was a thief and he died like a thief".'

Old Mrs Hartlebury stirred.

'Then I could stand no more,' she said. 'I was sick and wild with his tale of the burying. "You're an evil devil," I said, "and as a devil, so you'll die." I don't know why I said it, but I knew it was true as soon as I heard my own words. James wouldn't die in any usual way.

'I pulled away from him and began to clear away the dirty crocks. All the time I daren't look at him. I knew he was staring at me, but I was frightened to look behind.

'Then suddenly he banged his shut hand down upon the table, so that the ale jug toppled over and spilt. I stood where I was, holding a plate just off the table, looking down at it, too frightened to move.

'I heard him get up slowly and come round towards me. I knew he was angry, but still I didn't stir. He put his hand on me and it was shaking and so strong that it bruised my shoulder.

'Then he jerked me round before him and I had to look up at his face. He was terrible. His great dull eyes were dead, like a fish's. His lip was drawn up and I saw his gums, red above his yellow teeth. Then he shook me and called me terrible things, and spoke of Will in a way that made me sure of all I thought.'

Mrs Hartlebury laughed a little bitterly and I felt uncomfortable. She was a strange old woman.

'I did nothing,' she said. 'I was so frightened of him I couldn't even speak. Presently he beat me. I'd not been thrashed before, so I wasn't used to it. He half killed me.

'When he had done he went out and left me on the floor. I couldn't move for a while. I just lay there crying and I called out to Will like a mad woman. But that wasn't much good with him lying dead in the churchyard.

'At last it grew dark and cold, and the smell of rosemary hung about the place, making me sick with it. I got up and cooked the supper as well as I could. Then I set it, and sat down shivering, waiting for James to come in. I hated him as I sat there, but when he came in I did what he told me and served him his food.

'He saw I was frightened and that pleased him, but he was still angry and we said nothing all that evening.

'After supper I cleared off the things and sat down sewing, and he sat in his chair looking up at the clock.

'When it was ten o'clock he spoke to me for the first time since he came in.

'"Go up to bed and sleep sound, Sis," he said.

'I stared at him, for it was that he always said before he went out at night, and I knew what that meant. I opened my mouth to speak to him, but I saw that dull look in his face and I daren't say anything, so I went upstairs without speaking a word and got into bed, but I did not sleep.

'Outside the window I could see everything, quiet and cold in the moonlight, and over by the churchyard the trees were black like lace against the sky. I thought of Will lying in there and I could have screamed with terror. I was young, and half mad with pain from James' beating, you see,' she put in apologetically, as though I might not understand.

'And when I thought of that man below stairs, creeping out at night to steal the boy's body and take it up out of its shroud to sell to a lot of doctors to cut about all sense went from me, and I lay panting and crying on the bed, praying to God one minute and screaming silently into my pillow the next.

'It was all so dark and so quiet, and even then the smell of rosemary seemed to be choking the breath out of me.

'After a while I grew quieter and I listened, holding my breath as I lay up there all alone under the thatch. There was no sound downstairs and I began to hope that James wasn't going out after all. I was always trying to fool myself that he wasn't what he was, you see.

'It grew later and later, and by and by the moon came full up over the garden and shone in upon my bed. It was quiet and I was tired and full of pain. James had beaten me well.

'I lay quite still and shut my eyes, hardly thinking at all. And then,' she said suddenly, leaning forward towards me, 'I heard the latch go. It sounded so loud that I thought it would have wakened half the village. I was sitting up in a moment, straining to hear everything.

'I heard him go out of the door, take his pick and shovel from the corner in the porch where they were always kept, and go out down the path.

'I crept out of bed and hid behind the window curtain to peek out. I'd never dared do that before, but tonight, as it was Will he was going for, it was different somehow.

'I saw him going softly down the road and I stood there by the window, praying and hoping he wasn't going for that. I could just see the church gate, as I told you, and I saw him getting nearer and nearer to it. I knew that he was going in.'

Mrs Hartlebury shuddered as though she still saw him.

'He went in,' she said quietly. 'He went in, and I watched him from the window. Then everything was lonely again. I wondered what I should do. One moment I was half a mind to rush out and wake the village and let them find him at his work, but we were some way from another house and to get to the Street I should have to go by the church gate, and I daren't do that.

'I was so frightened,' she whispered. 'Oh, I was so frightened. Presently I went downstairs and found the old horse-pistol James took against footpads. It hung on a nail by the chimney and I took it down and charged it, and then I went upstairs and got into bed again, and I lay there waiting with one arm out on the quilt and the pistol in that hand.

'I didn't think. I was past thinking. I knew when he came in I should kill him and I lay there waiting for him to come.'

The old voice died away and there was no sound in the little room. It seemed to have grown colder, but I did not move. I was trying to make out her face in the darkness.

Still she did not speak.

'But I thought . . .' I began at last.

'Ah,' she said quickly, 'there's been many tales, but this is the truth. That night I waited close on two hours with the pistol in my hand.

'And then at last,' she said, her voice dropping, 'at last, after hours and hours it seemed, I heard footsteps coming down the path. An awful fear of him came over me. I held the pistol as though it was the only hope I had.

'I heard him put the pick and shovel back in its place in the porch and I lay waiting for the latch to click.

'But I didn't hear it. Everything was still, quite still, like an empty church.

'Then I heard the steps going off again down the path. I jumped from the bed and ran to the window and pushed up the sash. I didn't care if he saw me or not that time. The moon was very bright and I could see almost as clear as if it was day.

'There was someone going down the path and when I leant out I saw it was not James. He had his back to me, but I saw it wasn't James. It was too tall and he wore a jersey like a fisherman and had no hat.

'I stood staring. I knew who it was. The pistol fell on to the floor, but I didn't notice it. I only thought about him who was going down the path. I thought I must be mad. He went slowly, as though he was loth to go, and when he reached the gate, which was swinging open, he turned and looked right up at me. I saw his face quite clearly in the moonlight. Then I was sure.

'It was Will.'

On the last words Mrs Hartlebury's tone had sunk to a whisper. Now it died completely. Outside the rain had stopped and the moon was coming up over the trees. I stirred up the fire and made it blaze, so I could see about me.

The old woman was sitting hunched up in her chair, her chin

on her breast, her hands still folded in her lap. The thick chenille hairnet she wore looked like bands of iron on her white hair, and her thin wrinkled face glowed like old yellow ivory.

'Then?' I said.

She looked down at me.

'He stood there a long time and if I could have found breath to speak to him he might have answered me. But I couldn't. I couldn't speak.

'I don't remember any more of that night. I reckon I must have fainted.

'In the morning they brought James in dead, with an awful story of how they had found him lying by Will's grave with the lad's body half out on top of him and the lad's arms round his neck.'

Once again she paused.

'That's all,' she said.

'But,' I said, 'wasn't there some sort of inquiry? I mean, even in those days . . .'

Mrs Hartlebury interrupted me. She was smiling contemptuously, her wide toothless mouth twisted at the corners.

'Ah, they had an inquest,' she said. 'I was there. But I didn't say any more than I was asked to. After a lot of talk they said James had been set on by Resurrection Men and had died defending the lad's grave. They proved it wasn't James himself who was body-snatching because his pick and shovel were back at home and never in the churchyard at all.'

'You didn't say anything?' I asked in surprise.

Old Mrs Hartlebury looked at me queerly.

'No,' she said. 'Who would have believed me?'

That was true and I had no answer.

'Still, I think I should have said something,' I said, rising to my feet.

The old woman shook her head.

'Say nothing or say all,' she said. 'Besides, what sort of a life should I have led afterwards, as a body-snatcher's wife? No, that was Will's way. He wanted it all left quiet. That's why he brought the pick and shovel back, I reckon.'

I looked at her sitting there by the fireside, quiet and smiling a little.

'Is . . . is it true?' I said suddenly.

Mrs Hartlebury shrugged.

'You needn't believe it if you don't want to,' she said in her placid Essex way. 'I know I saw him, and I know that's how James died. Anyone'll tell you James died by an open grave while his pick and shovel were at home, and they'll tell you too that he died of suffocation.'

I nodded. I knew that.

'But they'll not tell you one thing that I will,' she said. 'And that is that the pick and shovel were clogged with earth in the morning, that were clean and bright the night before.'

There was silence for a while. Then I said good-night and I thanked her for the story.

'Good-night,' she said. 'Don't believe it if you don't want to. But there's an old hurricane lamp in the corner if you like. You're going past the churchyard, aren't you?'

I hesitated.

'Good-night,' she said again. 'A good walk home to you.'

There was silence, save for the crackling of the fire. Then she looked round.

'What are you after now?' she demanded.

'I shan't be a minute,' said I. 'I'm just lighting the hurricane.'

The Wink

MR JUSTICE FORDRED sat nodding ever so slightly at the end of the polished dinner table still littered with lace and silver and the graceful glasses of wine. He looked, his guest reflected, much as he had done on the Bench the day he retired, his small face puckered and creased like a petulant baby's, his fine smooth hands folded, and only the little round blue eyes, surprisingly mild and ingenuous, flickering to show that he lived and did not sleep.

The guest stirred, and his heavy-lidded eyes rested unseeingly upon the plug of white ash forming on the end of his cigar.

He was a famous man.

As Mark Betterley he had made history in the courts. As a barrister he had been unsurpassed.

His practice had been general, and although the plums of the civil courts had fallen into his lap without coaxing he had not despised a few less lucrative but better publicised criminal cases. He had taken silk at an absurdly early age, and had finally retired to go into politics, with the result that he now sat in the Lords, a grateful party's honours at his feet.

The Earl of Coggeshall, then, was still a handsome man. The smothered fire of his personality, which had swept so many juries off their feet, and which in later days had carried so many Bills through perilous readings, still burned.

Mark Betterley had had many enemies, and the new earl was no more fortunate.

He had been blackballed from two famous clubs, it was true, but no one knew why, and if there were men of unswerving courage who had yet been known to turn in the street and hurriedly pursue some unlikely shopping excursion when his giant figure hove in sight, he yet appeared a contented man.

The comfortable silence continued for some time.

It was the judge who spoke first.

'When one is very old,' he observed in that thin quiet voice of his, 'sitting in the warm is perhaps the most delightful thing in life.'

His guest laughed.

'Warmth of body, warmth of mind, and the contemplation of great moments,' he said. 'I don't see how any man can ask for more. Ours was an interesting profession. I suppose we saw more of life than most men.'

'Yes,' said the old man without complacency. 'I suppose we did. So much looking on makes one impersonal. For comfort of mind I think I recommend the Bench. With you, Betterley, of course, it was different.

'I always felt that when you threw that amazing energy of yours into a defence, for the moment you actually identified yourself with your client. Was that so?'

Lord Coggeshall's heavy white lids were drawn down over his eyes. He looked, if anything, a trifle bored.

'Why, yes, I suppose I did,' he admitted at last. 'One's personal judgment is naturally biased on such occasions. The whole system of justice is absurd, of course; an imperfect formula for testing right and wrong.'

'Exactly. The set-piece battle between God and the devil,' said Mr Justice Fordred.

His guest looked up, and the heavy eyes, which were capable of so many changes of colour, flecked for a moment with interest.

'The old beliefs are breaking up,' he said. 'Who looks on good and evil as separate living entities nowadays?'

'I do,' said his host, without change of tone.

'In God, yes, perhaps, but not the devil.'

Lord Coggeshall seemed more surprised than amused and there was a flash of his old power behind his words.

'Evil itself, complete and unexplained, is surely not admitted now? Human excesses, accidents of heredity and the disasters of unintelligence cover everything, don't they?'

The judge spoke mildly and his little old-lady appearance was intensified by the blandness of his expression.

'I don't think so myself, but then perhaps I am unlucky. You see, I have seen the devil twice.'

Lord Coggeshall looked at him steadily. They were both men of intellect, equals, and in the circumstances it was natural that each should do the other the courtesy of a serious hearing.

'In the dock?'

'Yes.'

There was a pause, and the old judge's lips moved ruminatively for a moment as though they tried out words.

'Of course,' he said at last, 'you may wonder how I knew it was the devil, how I came to be sure on such an extraordinary point.

'The first time I was not sure. I was impressed, startled, even a little frightened, and although the explanation which I afterwards reached did then occur to me I was loath to admit it.

'It was soon after I was made a judge: my fifth murder trial. I was on circuit, and I reached the Wembourne Assize Court to find a *cause célèbre* awaiting me. It was difficult to know why this particular case had seized the public imagination. On the face of it the facts were very ordinary.'

Lord Coggeshall looked into the round blue eyes.

'I defended, didn't I?' he said.

'Yes, you defended. You know the man I'm talking about, so we needn't mention his name. I may as well go through the facts, though. The accused and his wife had a small grocery business in a prosperous country town. They were wealthy, as such people measure wealth, and they were tolerably happy.

'An old woman, a maiden lady, if I remember, took lodgings with them. She had very little money, barely enough to live on, but by practising economy she was just able to live in the respectability she loved.

'Yet from the moment she came into the house the evidence showed plainly that the husband began to make the plans which afterwards cost him his life. The old woman was persuaded to invest her entire savings in the business. She did this willingly, and never at any time, it seemed, did she complain or suggest that the very meagre profits the deal showed were in any way unfair.

'Now–and this, to my mind, was the horrible part of the case–the grocer murdered the old woman after obtaining her money. He already had her money. Presumably she could cost him nothing now, save her food, and she was not unpleasant, you understand. On the contrary, she was very useful. Yet he killed her deliberately after planning the method with care and a certain amount of intelligence. The jury convicted him and I sentenced him.

'Now, that's all there is to the story.'

He paused and regarded his guest thoughtfully.

'You remember him in court?' he inquired.

'Yes. Amazing, wasn't he? Rather proud of himself at first. In all my interviews with him, both before and during the trial, I found him incomprehensible. Some of these fellows, you know, never realise what they've done until they actually get into court, but he knew.'

'Yes, he knew,' said the judge. 'I remember the case revolted me and I spoke the sentence with less distaste than ever before. I can see his face now, white but perfectly controlled, rather stupid, I thought, callous, greedy perhaps, but not more marked than on a dozen or so of other faces in the court around me. What puzzled me was why. Why had he done it? It was not until I had actually given sentence and sat with the black cap on my head, looking across the flowers on my desk, that I suddenly knew.

'Actually as. the last words of the sentence left my mouth he looked at me and winked.'

'Winked?'

'Yes,' said Mr Justice Fordred solemnly. 'He winked. It's no good, Betterley, I can't explain it to you, but it was like no other sign I have ever seen on a man's face. First there was a kind of smirking, secret smile, and then came the wink.

'I've never told this to anyone before. It takes a person in one's own profession to whom to make such an extraordinary confession. Forgive me if I tell you that it was a desire to make this confession which prompted me to ask you here tonight.

'Of course I explained it to myself at the time as a nervous affliction, something physical, and yet I knew that I was deceiving myself, for I assure you, Betterley, that no words of mine can describe quite that smirk, quite that incongruous, utterly incomprehensible wink. That was the first time I saw the devil.

'The second time,' continued the judge, 'was very different. It was many years later. You were in court again, I remember.

'The second time, I say, was more curious, because the whole thing was even more incomprehensible than the first.'

Lord Coggeshall looked up.

'You mean the Stanton wife murder?'

'Yes. How did you know?'

The other man shrugged his shoulders.

'Intuition. Go on.'

'The defence, which you conducted so ably, was one of insanity, if I remember rightly,' said Mr Justice Fordred. 'Stanton was a gentleman. He had a big country house, a wife who adored him. They had two young children and there was no record of any quarrel they had ever had.

'And yet he killed his wife. Strangled her, if you remember, slowly and systematically.

'You had a fine array of expert witnesses, I remember. But so had the prosecution, and the court spent several days listening to doctors arguing.

'In the end, in spite of your oratory, and, if I may say so, the most brilliant defence a man ever had, the jury retired, and after only some twenty minutes or so Stanton was brought back into the dock to receive sentence of death.'

Mr Justice Fordred unfolded his smooth hands and leant forward a little in his high-backed chair.

'I was much perturbed in my own mind about the verdict. The facts of the case and the man who stood before me did not seem to tally. The facts told the story of a maniac. The man was sane.

'I have always tried to guard myself from the most dangerous of all emotions, that blinding, unreasoning pity which dulls the working of the brain like a drug, and yet I was sorry for the man. He looked so young, so obviously shaken by the ordeal through which he was passing. But my duty was clearly indicated, and I began those terrible words, the thought of which even now makes me feel physically sick.

'It was not until I had reached the final sentence, the brutal and disgusting truth stated so baldly that the meanest intelligence may grasp it, that the thing I never expected to see again happened.

'Across the face of the boy—for he was a good thirty years younger than myself, and I have always in my mind considered him that—there passed an incredible change. At first I thought my eyes were deceiving me and that my age was playing me tricks. But across that white, agonised face there passed that sneering, smirking smile which I had seen only once before, and then he winked.

'I remember very little that happened in the next two or three minutes. The Press, I know, reported that the judge seemed much overcome. It was a horrible experience—horrible, and yet enlightening.

'That was the second time I saw the devil.'

The quiet voice stopped, and the silence in the little room was no longer comfortable. The light of the candles seemed less mellow, less friendly, the silver seemed to have lost its gleam, and the cigar on the judge's plate had burned down to the butt and smelt acrid and unpleasant.

It had also turned a little cold.

Lord Coggeshall moved his head, so that his great handsome face, with its deep lines and heavily lidded eyes, was directly towards the older man.

'Yes,' he said, 'very interesting. You had found him out, you see.'

And then across the handsome face, so well known to the whole populace of the proudest race in the world, there formed the beginnings of a faint, secretive smile.

It grew and vanished. Then one of the thick white lids descended slowly over a dark eye.

The little judge sat very still. In his austerity he seemed to have grown in magnitude and importance. His fine hands quivered, but they were not clenched. He sighed, sharply, decisively.

'Yes,' he said. 'Yes, Betterley, that's what I wanted to know.'